Don·Quixote

STARRING
GOOFY and MICKEY MOUSE

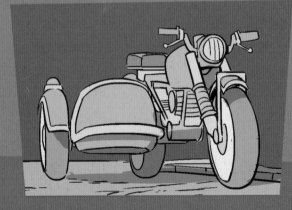

Disney
Don·Quixote

STARRING
GOOFY and MICKEY MOUSE

Script by . . . . **FAUSTO VITALIANO**

Art by . . . . **CLAUDIO SCIARRONE**

English Translation by . . . . **ERIN BRADY**

Lettering by . . . . **RICHARD STARKINGS**
and **COMICRAFT'S JIMMY BETANCOURT**

Based on the classic novel by
MIGUEL DE CERVANTES

DARK HORSE BOOKS

DARK HORSE BOOKS

President and Publisher . . . . MIKE RICHARDSON

Collection Editor . . . . FREDDYE MILLER

Collection Assistant Editor . . . . JUDY KHUU

Designer . . . . CINDY CACEREZ-SPRAGUE

Digital Art Technician . . . . SAMANTHA HUMMER

Special thanks to Annie Gullion.

NEIL HANKERSON Executive Vice President • TOM WEDDLE Chief Financial Officer • RANDY STRADLEY Vice President of Publishing • NICK McWHORTER Chief Business Development Officer • DALE LAFOUNTAIN Chief Information Officer • MATT PARKINSON Vice President of Marketing • CARA NIECE Vice President of Production and Scheduling • MARK BERNARDI Vice President of Book Trade and Digital Sales • KEN LIZZI General Counsel • DAVE MARSHALL Editor in Chief • DAVEY ESTRADA Editorial Director • CHRIS WARNER Senior Books Editor • CARY GRAZZINI Director of Specialty Projects • LIA RIBACCHI Art Director • VANESSA TODD-HOLMES Director of Print Purchasing • MATT DRYER Director of Digital Art and Prepress • MICHAEL GOMBOS Director of International Publishing and Licensing • KARI YADRO Director of Custom Programs • KARI TORSON Director of International Licensing

DISNEY PUBLISHING WORLDWIDE GLOBAL MAGAZINES, COMICS AND PARTWORKS

PUBLISHER Lynn Waggoner • EDITORIAL TEAM Bianca Coletti (Director, Magazines), Guido Frazzini (Director, Comics), Carlotta Quattrocolo (Executive Editor), Stefano Ambrosio (Executive Editor, New IP), Camilla Vedove (Senior Manager, Editorial Development), Behnoosh Khalili (Senior Editor), Julie Dorris (Senior Editor), Mina Riazi (Assistant Editor), Jonathan Manning (Assistant Editor) • DESIGN Enrico Soave (Senior Designer) • ART Ken Shue (VP, Global Art), Manny Mederos (Senior Illustration Manager, Comics and Magazines), Roberto Santillo (Creative Director), Marco Ghiglione (Creative Manager), Stefano Attardi (Computer Art Designer) • PORTFOLIO MANAGEMENT Olivia Ciancarelli (Director) • BUSINESS & MARKETING Mariantonietta Galla (Marketing Manager), Virpi Korhonen (Editorial Manager)

Published by Dark Horse Books
A division of Dark Horse Comics, LLC.
10956 SE Main Street
Milwaukie, OR 97222

DarkHorse.com
To find a comics shop in your area,
visit comicshoplocator.com

First edition: March 2019
ISBN 978-1-50671-216-1
Digital ISBN 978-1-50671-211-6

1 3 5 7 9 10 8 6 4 2
Printed in China

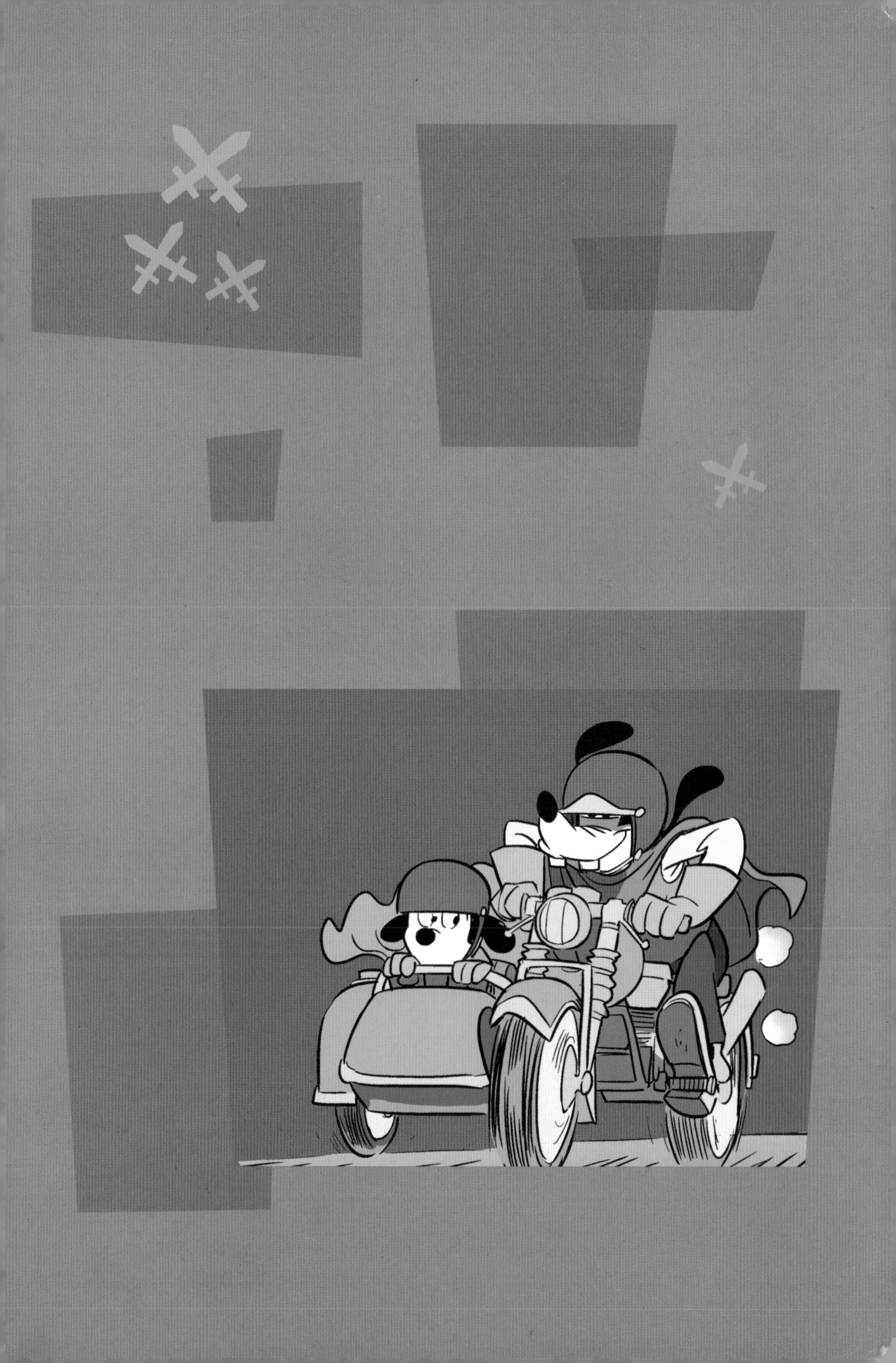

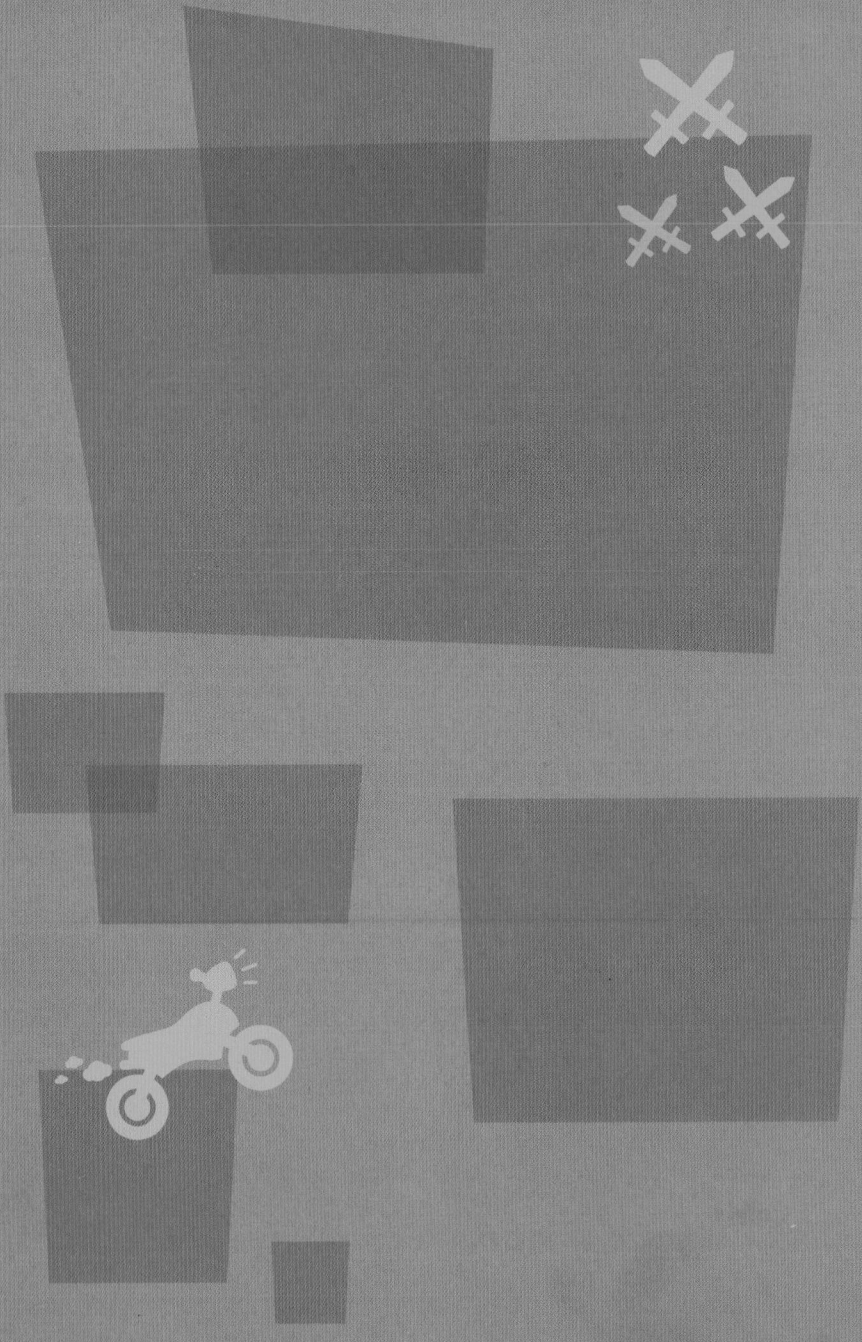

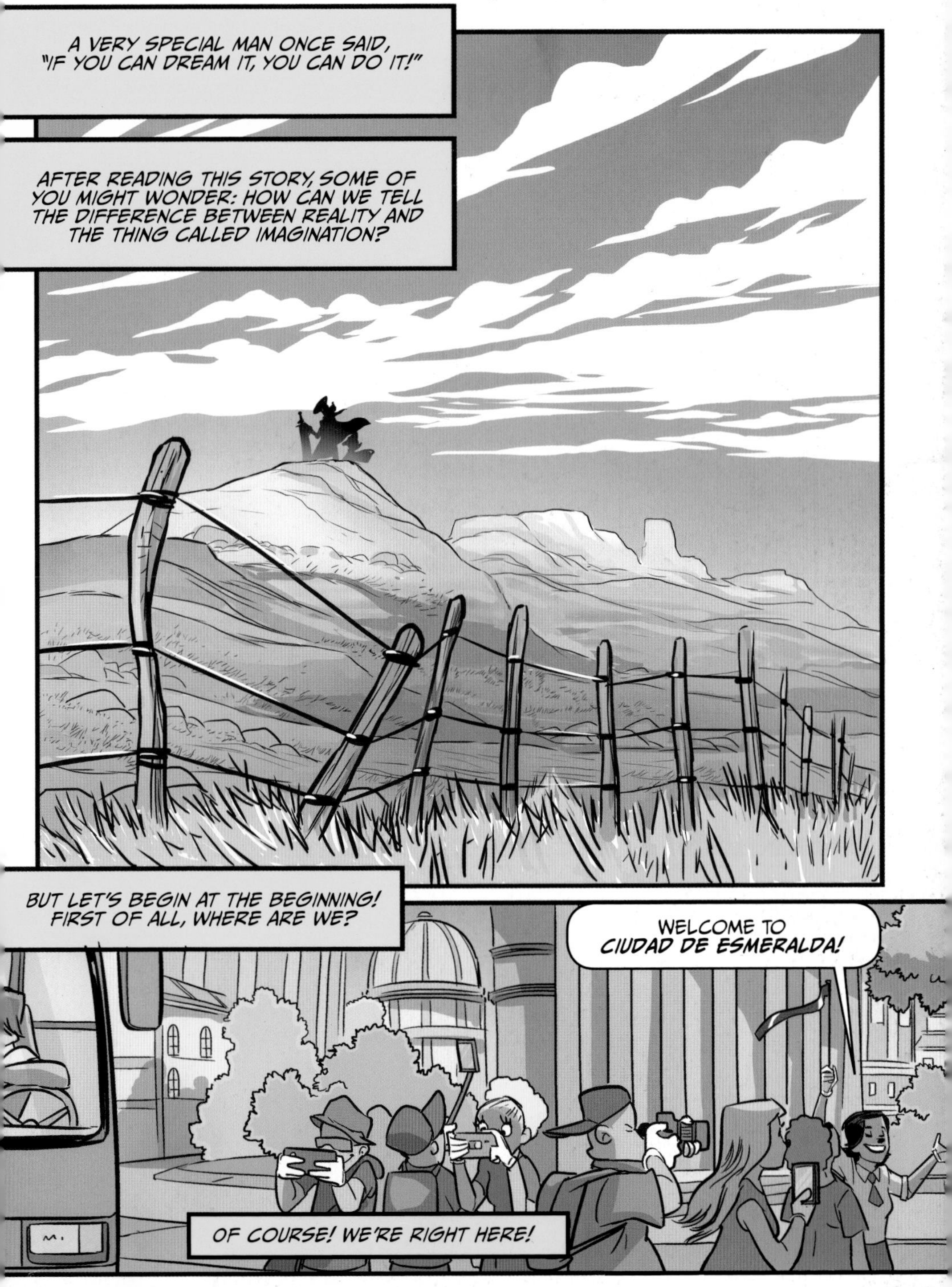
A VERY SPECIAL MAN ONCE SAID, "IF YOU CAN DREAM IT, YOU CAN DO IT!"
AFTER READING THIS STORY, SOME OF YOU MIGHT WONDER: HOW CAN WE TELL THE DIFFERENCE BETWEEN REALITY AND THE THING CALLED IMAGINATION?
BUT LET'S BEGIN AT THE BEGINNING! FIRST OF ALL, WHERE ARE WE?
WELCOME TO CIUDAD DE ESMERALDA!
OF COURSE! WE'RE RIGHT HERE!

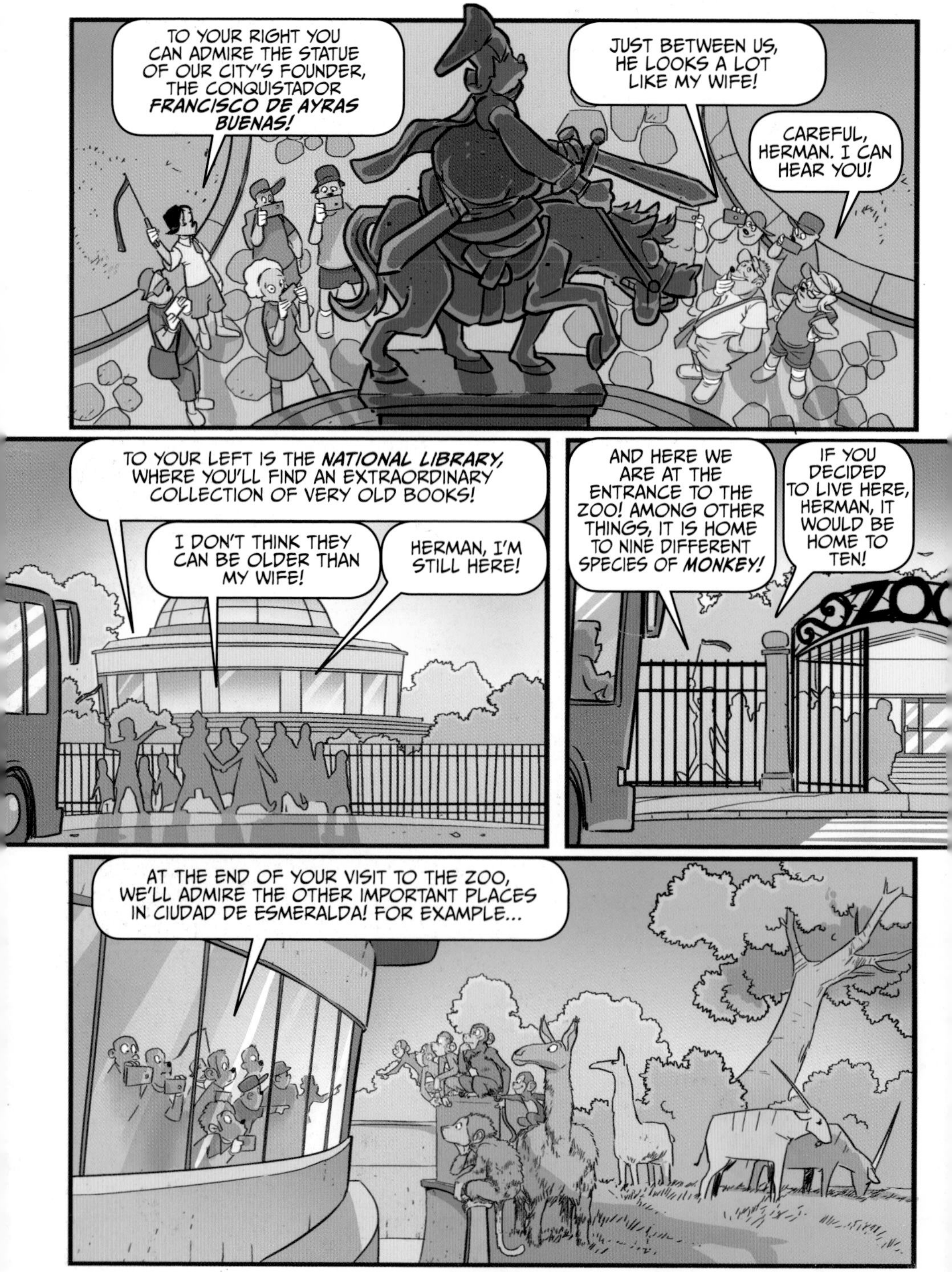
TO YOUR RIGHT YOU CAN ADMIRE THE STATUE OF OUR CITY'S FOUNDER, THE CONQUISTADOR *FRANCISCO DE AYRAS BUENAS!*
JUST BETWEEN US, HE LOOKS A LOT LIKE MY WIFE!
CAREFUL, HERMAN. I CAN HEAR YOU!
TO YOUR LEFT IS THE *NATIONAL LIBRARY,* WHERE YOU'LL FIND AN EXTRAORDINARY COLLECTION OF VERY OLD BOOKS!
I DON'T THINK THEY CAN BE OLDER THAN MY WIFE!
HERMAN, I'M STILL HERE!
AND HERE WE ARE AT THE ENTRANCE TO THE ZOO! AMONG OTHER THINGS, IT IS HOME TO NINE DIFFERENT SPECIES OF *MONKEY!*
IF YOU DECIDED TO LIVE HERE, HERMAN, IT WOULD BE HOME TO TEN!
ZOO
AT THE END OF YOUR VISIT TO THE ZOO, WE'LL ADMIRE THE OTHER IMPORTANT PLACES IN CIUDAD DE ESMERALDA! FOR EXAMPLE...

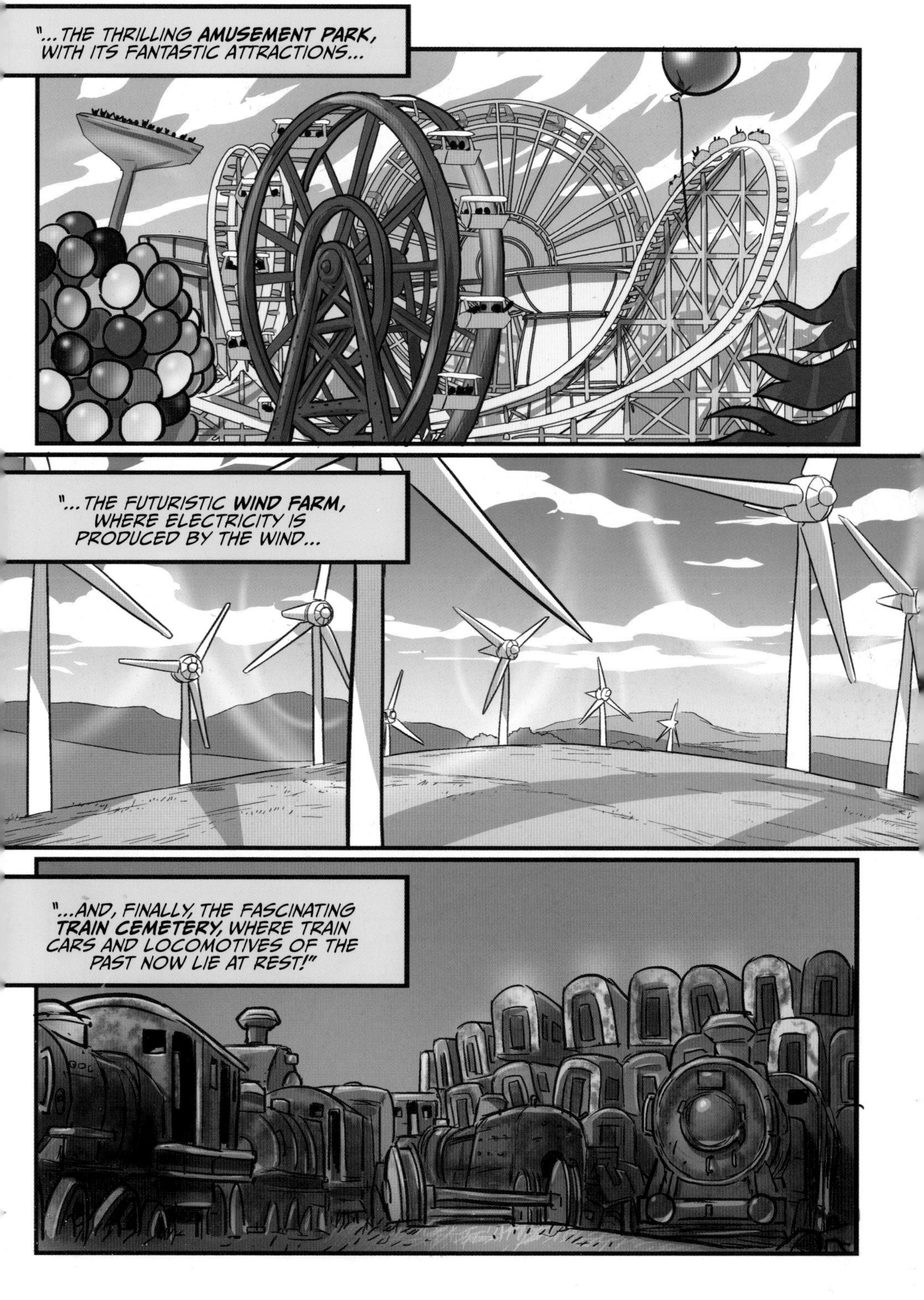
"...THE THRILLING AMUSEMENT PARK, WITH ITS FANTASTIC ATTRACTIONS...
"...THE FUTURISTIC WIND FARM, WHERE ELECTRICITY IS PRODUCED BY THE WIND...
"...AND, FINALLY, THE FASCINATING TRAIN CEMETERY, WHERE TRAIN CARS AND LOCOMOTIVES OF THE PAST NOW LIE AT REST!"

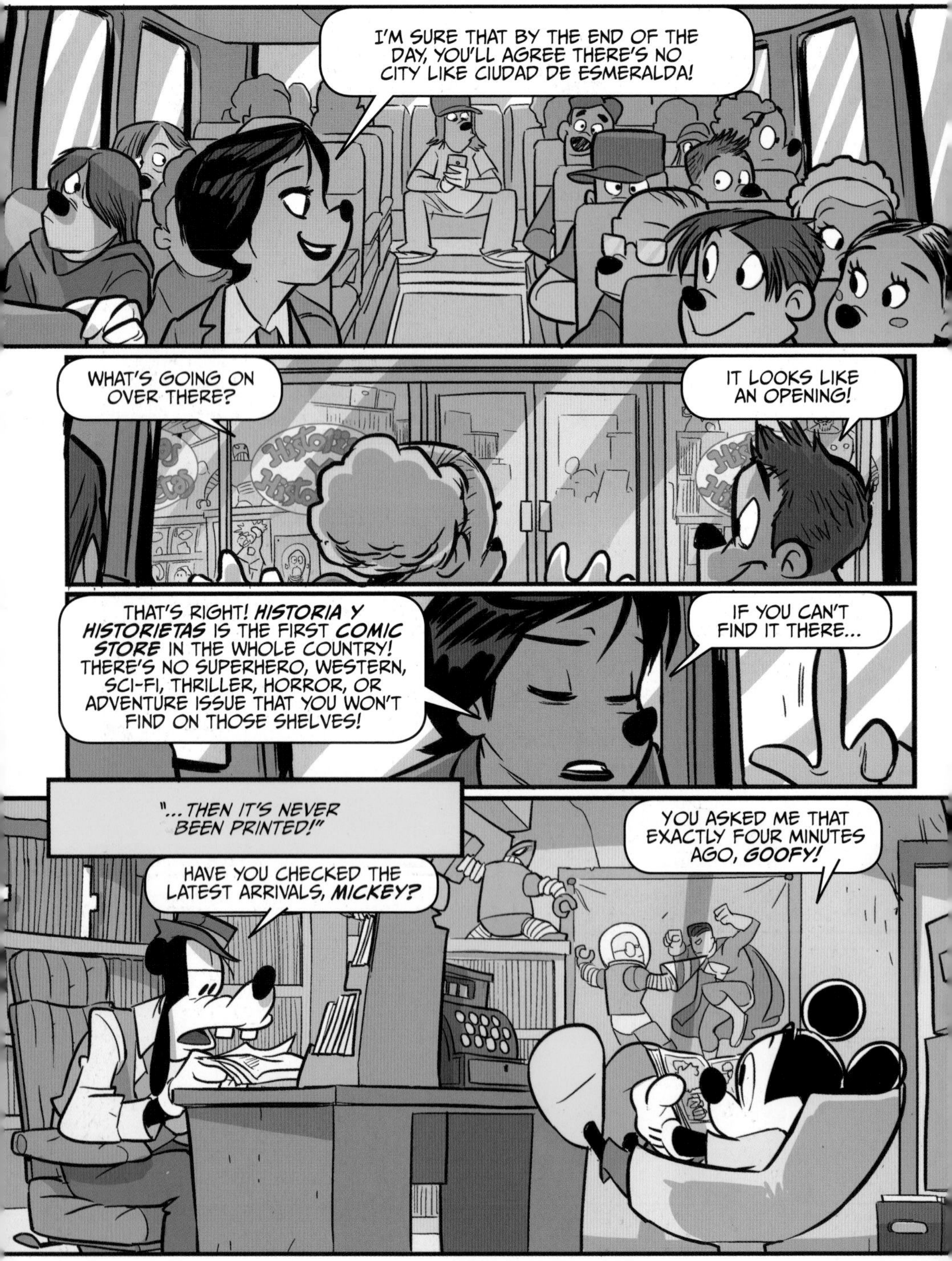

I'M SURE THAT BY THE END OF THE DAY, YOU'LL AGREE THERE'S NO CITY LIKE CIUDAD DE ESMERALDA!
WHAT'S GOING ON OVER THERE?
IT LOOKS LIKE AN OPENING!
THAT'S RIGHT! HISTORIA Y HISTORIETAS IS THE FIRST COMIC STORE IN THE WHOLE COUNTRY! THERE'S NO SUPERHERO, WESTERN, SCI-FI, THRILLER, HORROR, OR ADVENTURE ISSUE THAT YOU WON'T FIND ON THOSE SHELVES!
IF YOU CAN'T FIND IT THERE...
"...THEN IT'S NEVER BEEN PRINTED!"
HAVE YOU CHECKED THE LATEST ARRIVALS, MICKEY?
YOU ASKED ME THAT EXACTLY FOUR MINUTES AGO, GOOFY!

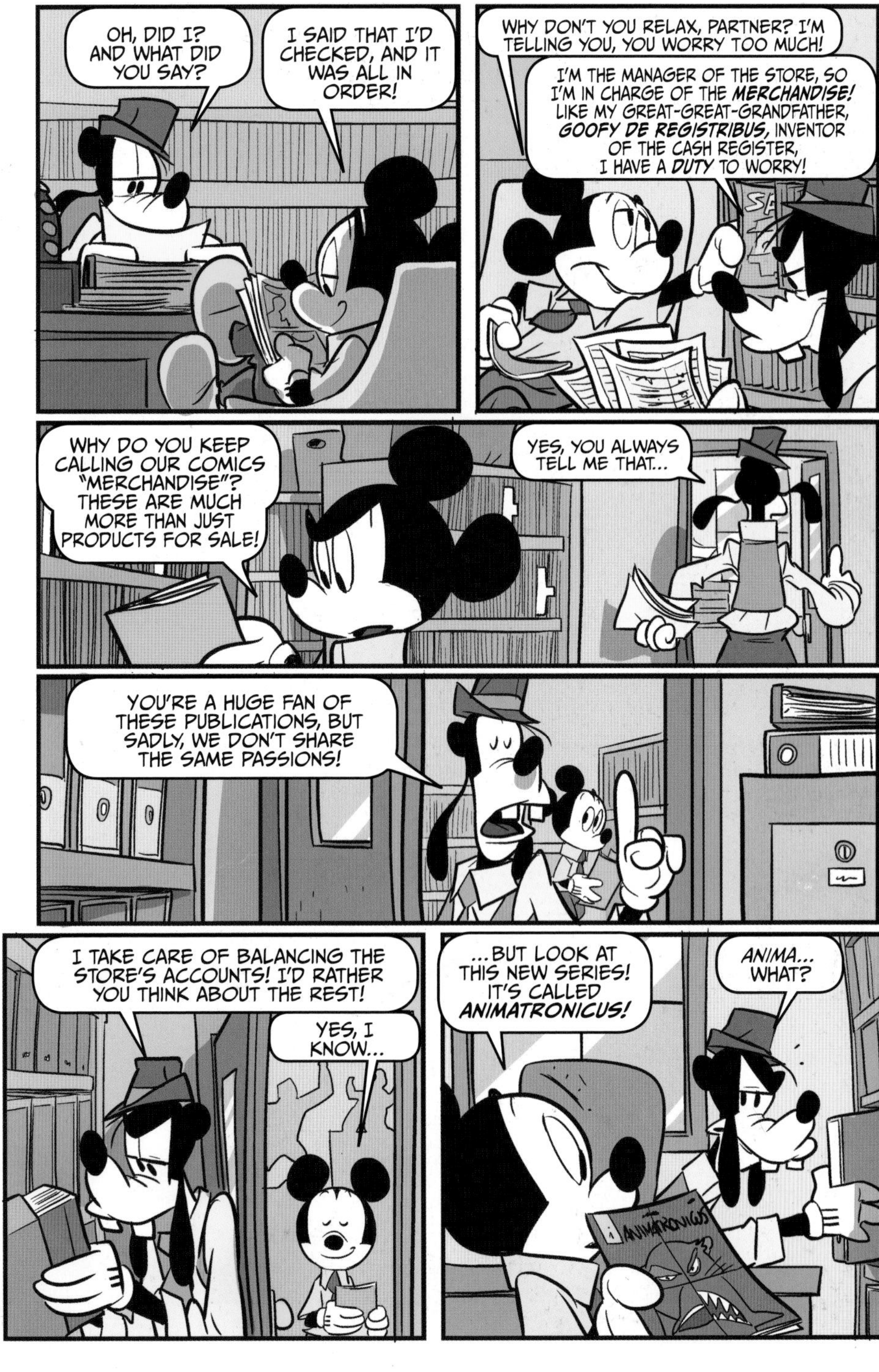
OH, DID I? AND WHAT DID YOU SAY?
I SAID THAT I'D CHECKED, AND IT WAS ALL IN ORDER!
WHY DON'T YOU RELAX, PARTNER? I'M TELLING YOU, YOU WORRY TOO MUCH!
I'M THE MANAGER OF THE STORE, SO I'M IN CHARGE OF THE **MERCHANDISE!** LIKE MY GREAT-GREAT-GRANDFATHER, ***GOOFY DE REGISTRIBUS,*** INVENTOR OF THE CASH REGISTER, I HAVE A ***DUTY*** TO WORRY!
WHY DO YOU KEEP CALLING OUR COMICS "MERCHANDISE"? THESE ARE MUCH MORE THAN JUST PRODUCTS FOR SALE!
YES, YOU ALWAYS TELL ME THAT...
YOU'RE A HUGE FAN OF THESE PUBLICATIONS, BUT SADLY, WE DON'T SHARE THE SAME PASSIONS!
I TAKE CARE OF BALANCING THE STORE'S ACCOUNTS! I'D RATHER YOU THINK ABOUT THE REST!
YES, I KNOW...
...BUT LOOK AT THIS NEW SERIES! IT'S CALLED ***ANIMATRONICUS!***
ANIMA... WHAT?
ANIMATRONICUS

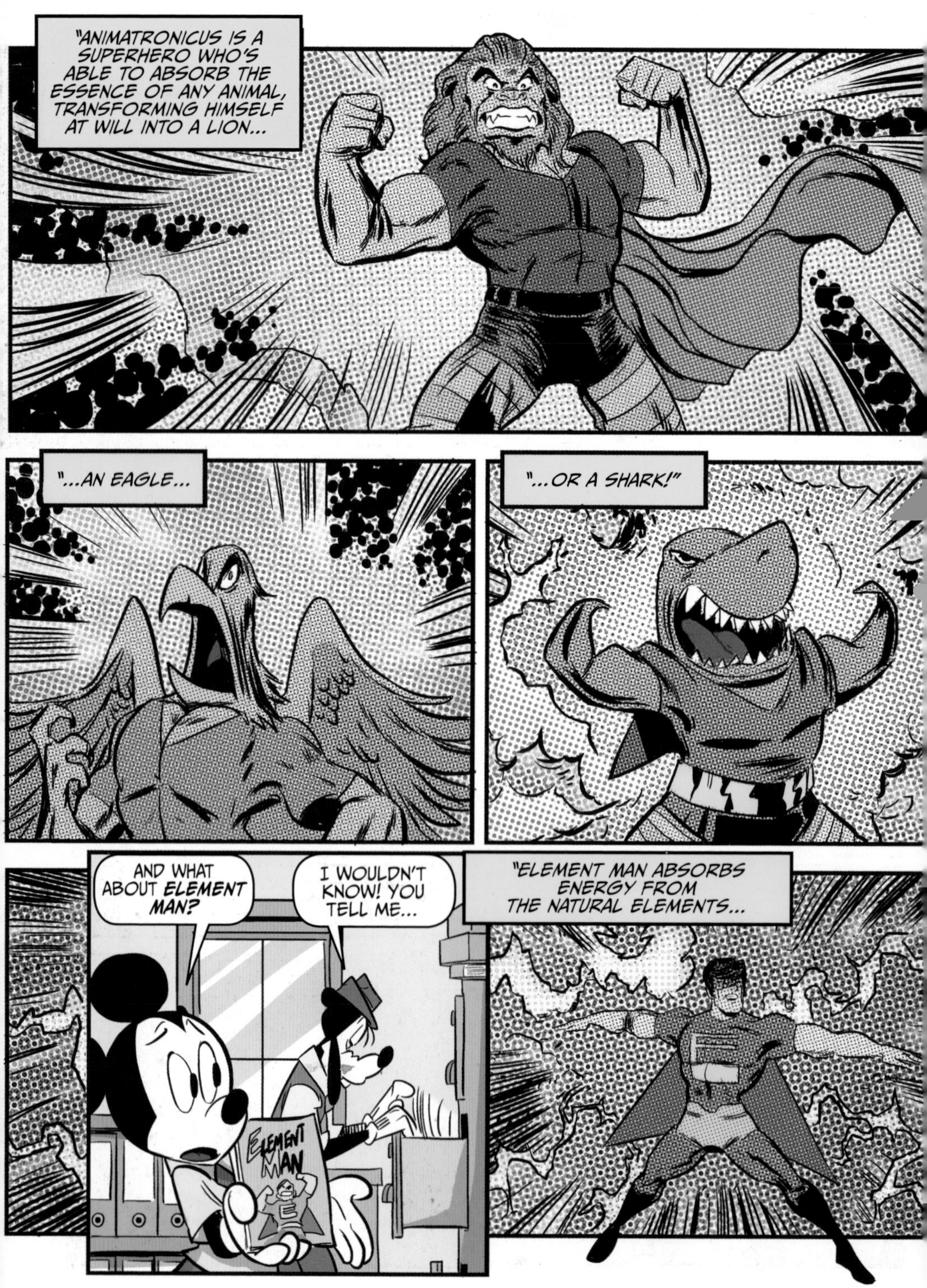
"ANIMATRONICUS IS A SUPERHERO WHO'S ABLE TO ABSORB THE ESSENCE OF ANY ANIMAL, TRANSFORMING HIMSELF AT WILL INTO A LION...
"...AN EAGLE...
"...OR A SHARK!"
AND WHAT ABOUT ELEMENT MAN?
I WOULDN'T KNOW! YOU TELL ME...
ELEMENT MAN
"ELEMENT MAN ABSORBS ENERGY FROM THE NATURAL ELEMENTS...

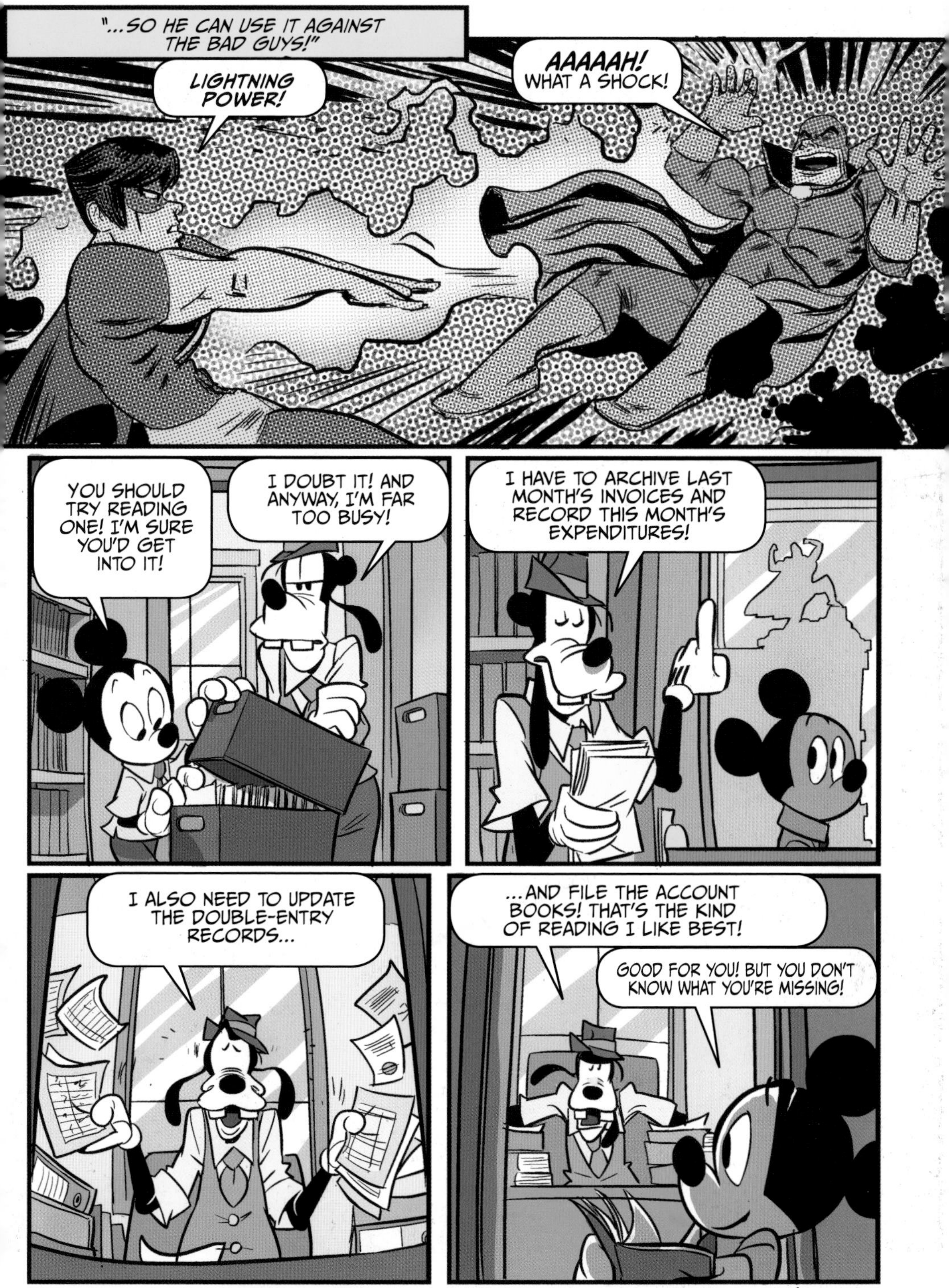
"...SO HE CAN USE IT AGAINST THE BAD GUYS!"
LIGHTNING POWER!
AAAAAH! WHAT A SHOCK!
YOU SHOULD TRY READING ONE! I'M SURE YOU'D GET INTO IT!
I DOUBT IT! AND ANYWAY, I'M FAR TOO BUSY!
I HAVE TO ARCHIVE LAST MONTH'S INVOICES AND RECORD THIS MONTH'S EXPENDITURES!
I ALSO NEED TO UPDATE THE DOUBLE-ENTRY RECORDS...
...AND FILE THE ACCOUNT BOOKS! THAT'S THE KIND OF READING I LIKE BEST!
GOOD FOR YOU! BUT YOU DON'T KNOW WHAT YOU'RE MISSING!

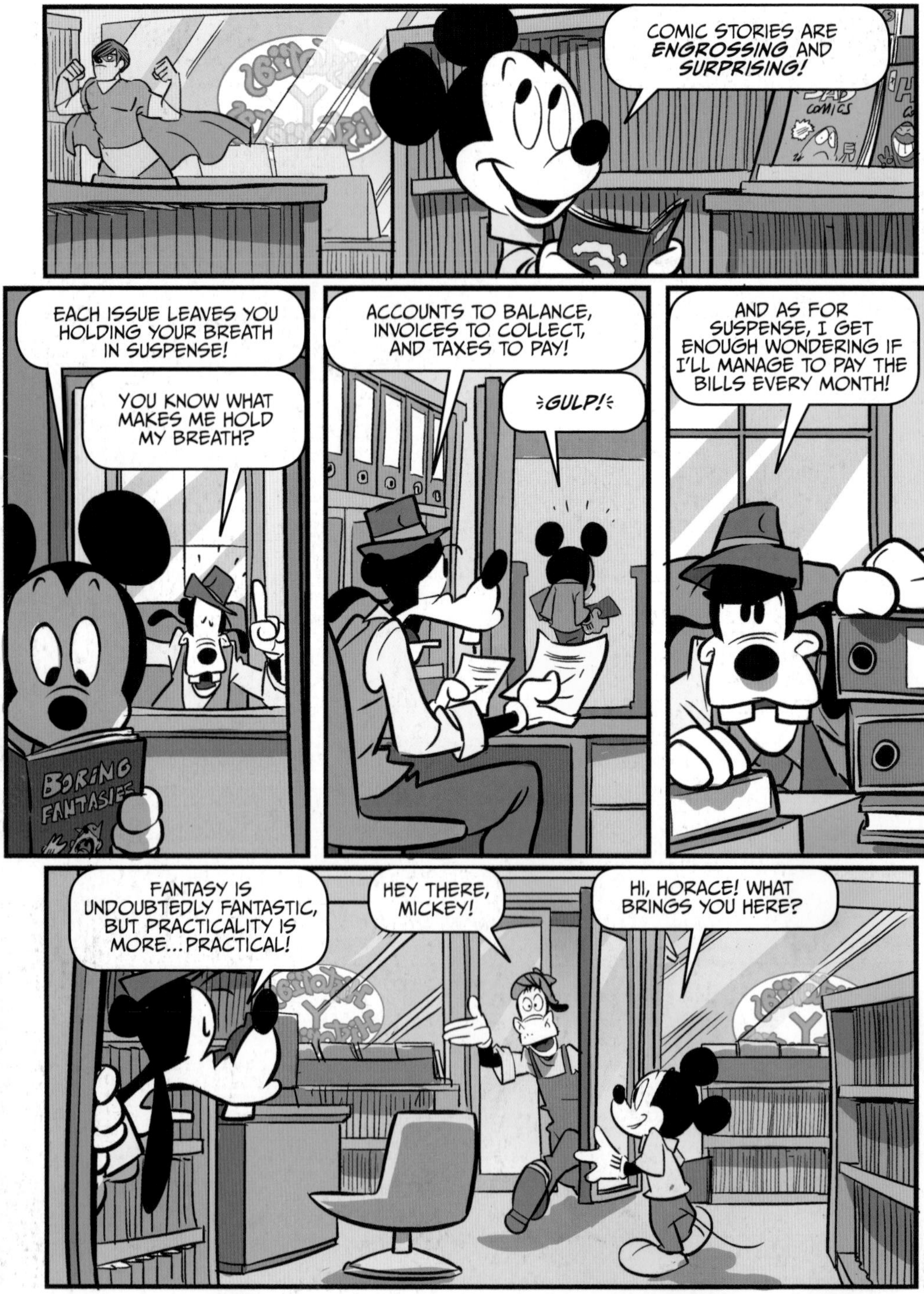

COMIC STORIES ARE ENGROSSING AND SURPRISING!
EACH ISSUE LEAVES YOU HOLDING YOUR BREATH IN SUSPENSE!
YOU KNOW WHAT MAKES ME HOLD MY BREATH?
BORING FANTASIES
ACCOUNTS TO BALANCE, INVOICES TO COLLECT, AND TAXES TO PAY!
GULP!
AND AS FOR SUSPENSE, I GET ENOUGH WONDERING IF I'LL MANAGE TO PAY THE BILLS EVERY MONTH!
FANTASY IS UNDOUBTEDLY FANTASTIC, BUT PRACTICALITY IS MORE...PRACTICAL!
HEY THERE, MICKEY!
HI, HORACE! WHAT BRINGS YOU HERE?

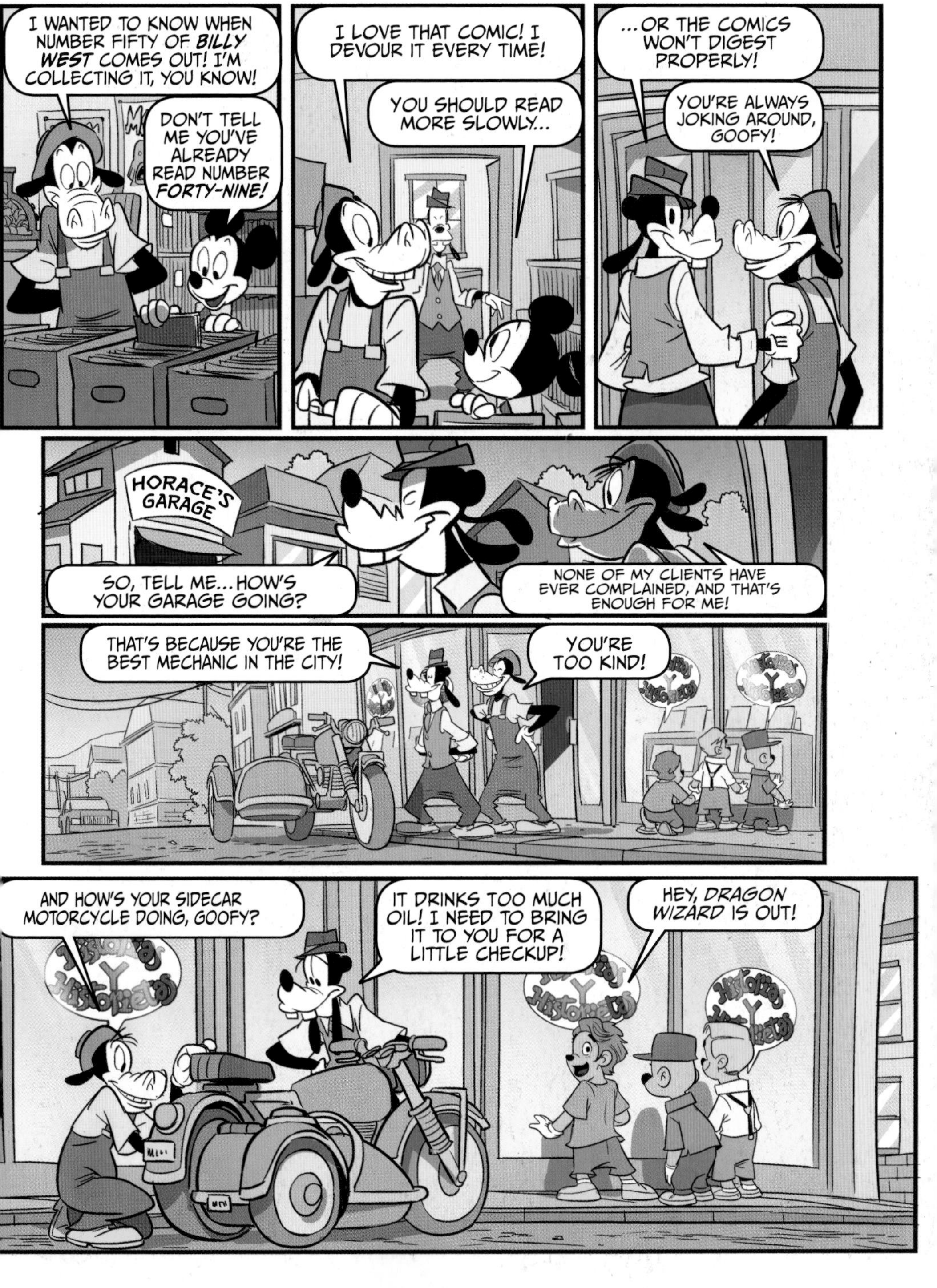
I WANTED TO KNOW WHEN NUMBER FIFTY OF *BILLY WEST* COMES OUT! I'M COLLECTING IT, YOU KNOW!
DON'T TELL ME YOU'VE ALREADY READ NUMBER *FORTY-NINE!*
I LOVE THAT COMIC! I DEVOUR IT EVERY TIME!
YOU SHOULD READ MORE SLOWLY...
...OR THE COMICS WON'T DIGEST PROPERLY!
YOU'RE ALWAYS JOKING AROUND, GOOFY!
HORACE'S GARAGE
SO, TELL ME... HOW'S YOUR GARAGE GOING?
NONE OF MY CLIENTS HAVE EVER COMPLAINED, AND THAT'S ENOUGH FOR ME!
THAT'S BECAUSE YOU'RE THE BEST MECHANIC IN THE CITY!
YOU'RE TOO KIND!
AND HOW'S YOUR SIDECAR MOTORCYCLE DOING, GOOFY?
IT DRINKS TOO MUCH OIL! I NEED TO BRING IT TO YOU FOR A LITTLE CHECKUP!
HEY, *DRAGON WIZARD* IS OUT!

YEAH, COME GET IT WHILE IT'S HOT!

I'LL FINALLY FIND OUT HOW THE BATTLE AGAINST *OKOTOMO* ENDS!

I WANT *ALIEN ATTACK!*

I'M LOOKING FOR *SATURN MISSION!*

CAPTAIN STONE FOR ME!

COMMANDER JACK FOR ME!

THE *MAGNIFICENT SIX!*

THE *INCREDIBLE SEVEN!*

CALM DOWN, CALM DOWN...THERE'S ENOUGH FOR EVERYONE!

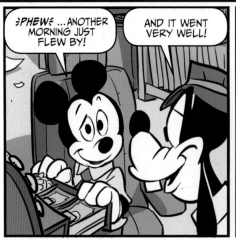

≶PHEW≶ ...ANOTHER MORNING JUST FLEW BY!

AND IT WENT VERY WELL!

EVEN YOU'RE HAPPY, HUH?

I MIGHT NOT BE A FAN OF COMICS, BUT I'M VERY HAPPY WHEN WE SELL SO MANY! NOW, LET'S GO HAVE LUNCH!

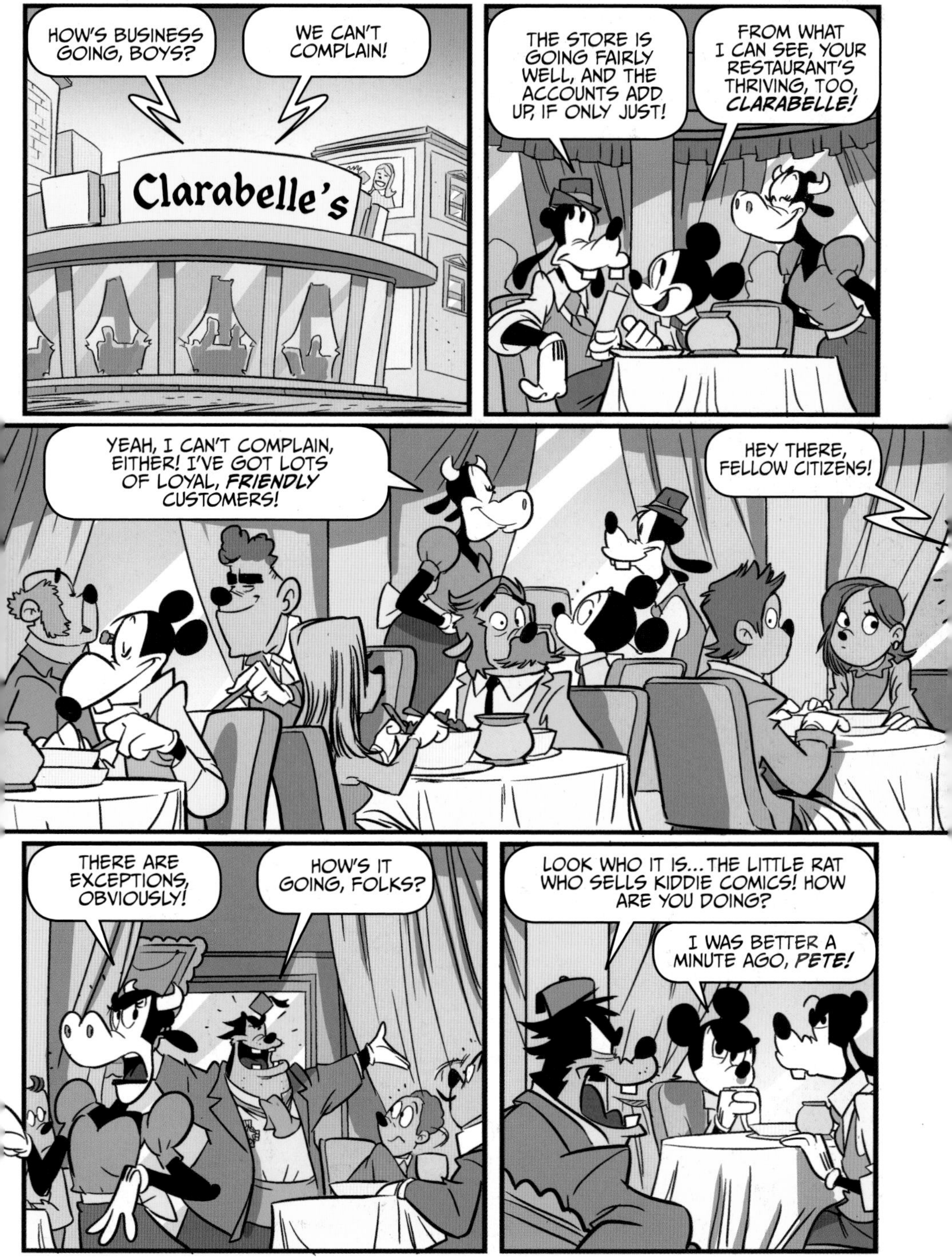
HOW'S BUSINESS GOING, BOYS?
WE CAN'T COMPLAIN!
Clarabelle's
THE STORE IS GOING FAIRLY WELL, AND THE ACCOUNTS ADD UP, IF ONLY JUST!
FROM WHAT I CAN SEE, YOUR RESTAURANT'S THRIVING, TOO, CLARABELLE!
YEAH, I CAN'T COMPLAIN, EITHER! I'VE GOT LOTS OF LOYAL, FRIENDLY CUSTOMERS!
HEY THERE, FELLOW CITIZENS!
THERE ARE EXCEPTIONS, OBVIOUSLY!
HOW'S IT GOING, FOLKS?
LOOK WHO IT IS...THE LITTLE RAT WHO SELLS KIDDIE COMICS! HOW ARE YOU DOING?
I WAS BETTER A MINUTE AGO, PETE!

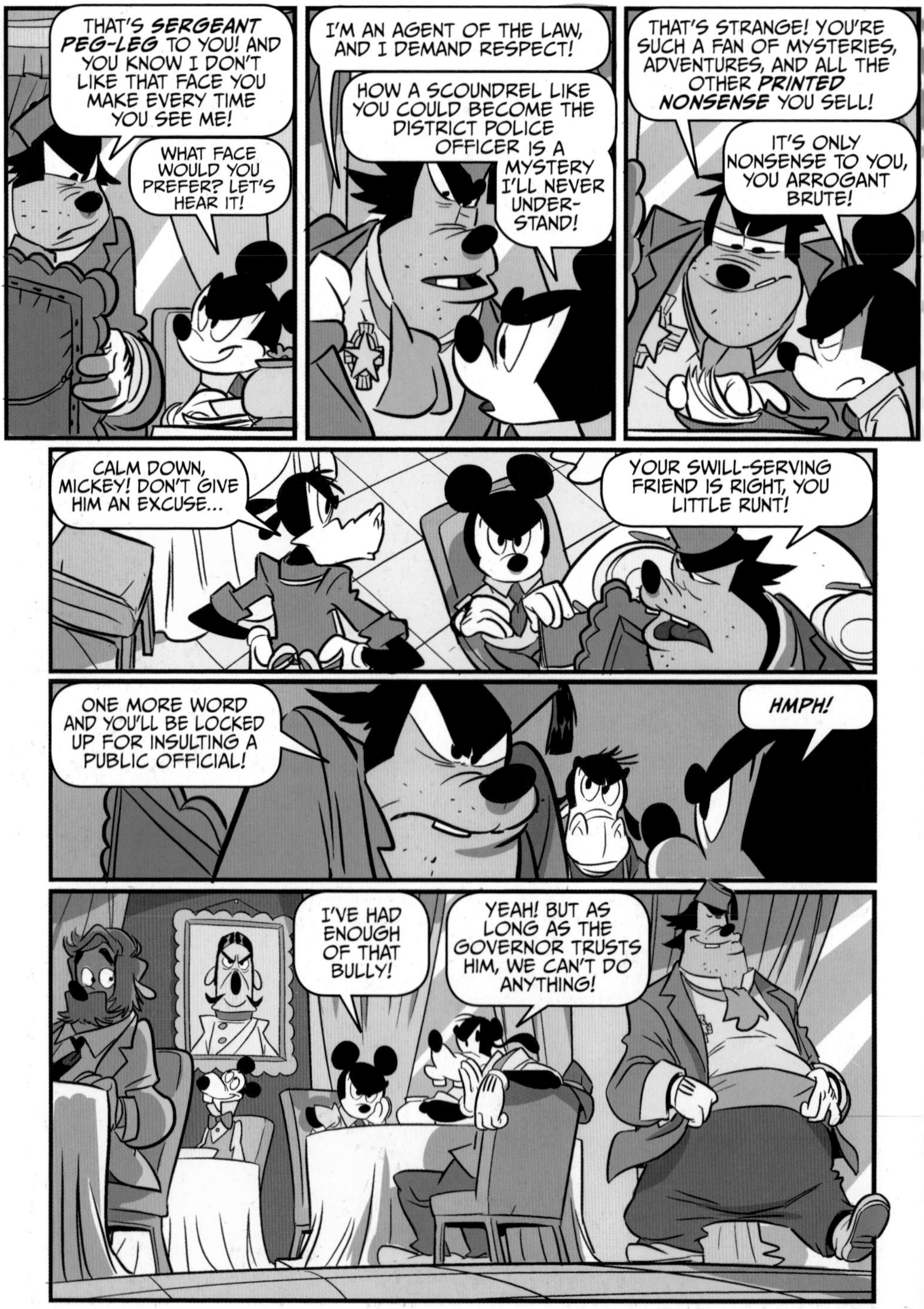
THAT'S SERGEANT PEG-LEG TO YOU! AND YOU KNOW I DON'T LIKE THAT FACE YOU MAKE EVERY TIME YOU SEE ME!
WHAT FACE WOULD YOU PREFER? LET'S HEAR IT!
I'M AN AGENT OF THE LAW, AND I DEMAND RESPECT!
HOW A SCOUNDREL LIKE YOU COULD BECOME THE DISTRICT POLICE OFFICER IS A MYSTERY I'LL NEVER UNDER-STAND!
THAT'S STRANGE! YOU'RE SUCH A FAN OF MYSTERIES, ADVENTURES, AND ALL THE OTHER PRINTED NONSENSE YOU SELL!
IT'S ONLY NONSENSE TO YOU, YOU ARROGANT BRUTE!
CALM DOWN, MICKEY! DON'T GIVE HIM AN EXCUSE...
YOUR SWILL-SERVING FRIEND IS RIGHT, YOU LITTLE RUNT!
ONE MORE WORD AND YOU'LL BE LOCKED UP FOR INSULTING A PUBLIC OFFICIAL!
HMPH!
I'VE HAD ENOUGH OF THAT BULLY!
YEAH! BUT AS LONG AS THE GOVERNOR TRUSTS HIM, WE CAN'T DO ANYTHING!

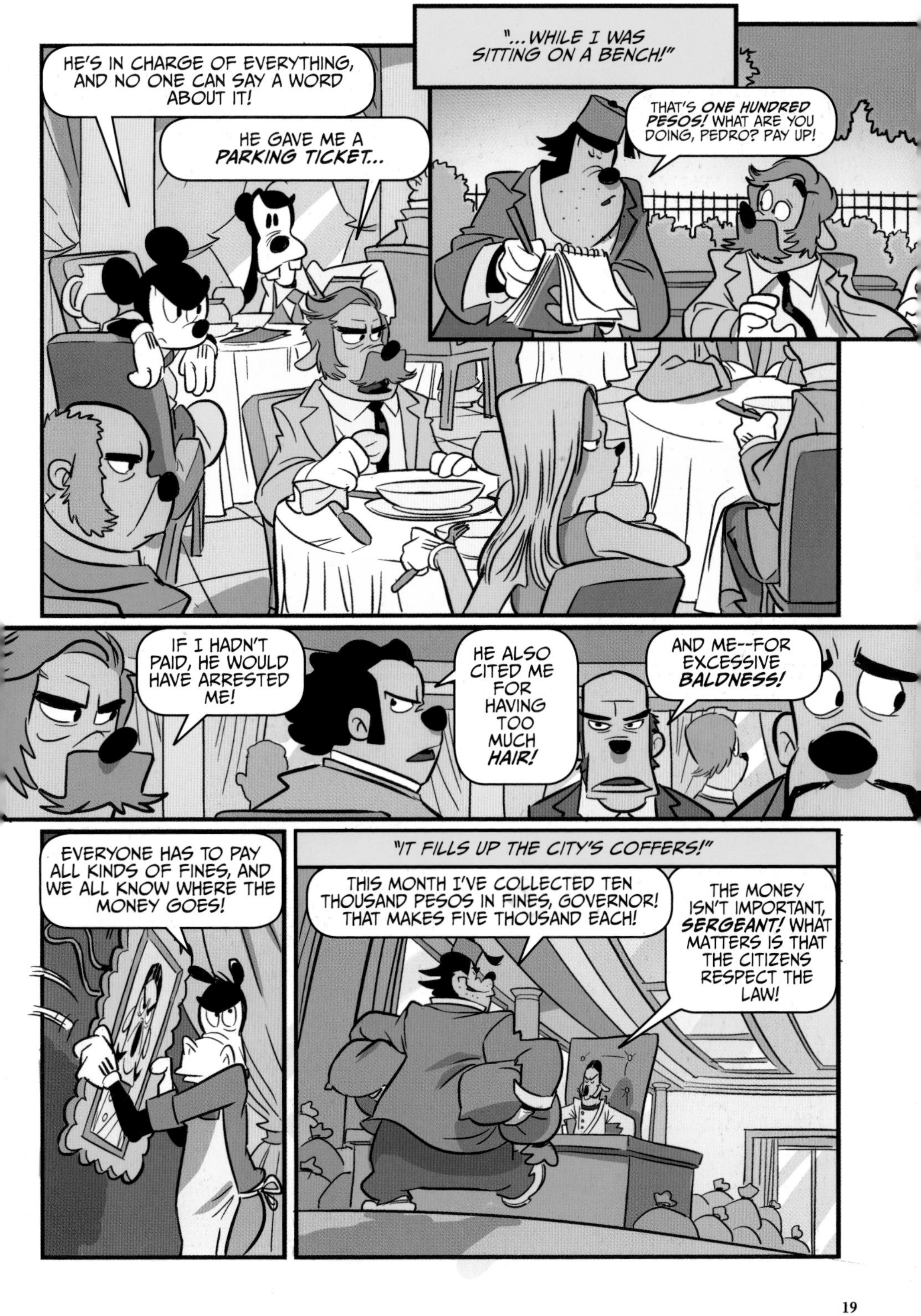

HE'S IN CHARGE OF EVERYTHING, AND NO ONE CAN SAY A WORD ABOUT IT!
HE GAVE ME A *PARKING TICKET*...
"...WHILE I WAS SITTING ON A BENCH!"
THAT'S **ONE HUNDRED PESOS!** WHAT ARE YOU DOING, PEDRO? PAY UP!
IF I HADN'T PAID, HE WOULD HAVE ARRESTED ME!
HE ALSO CITED ME FOR HAVING TOO MUCH **HAIR!**
AND ME--FOR EXCESSIVE **BALDNESS!**
EVERYONE HAS TO PAY ALL KINDS OF FINES, AND WE ALL KNOW WHERE THE MONEY GOES!
"IT FILLS UP THE CITY'S COFFERS!"
THIS MONTH I'VE COLLECTED TEN THOUSAND PESOS IN FINES, GOVERNOR! THAT MAKES FIVE THOUSAND EACH!
THE MONEY ISN'T IMPORTANT, **SERGEANT!** WHAT MATTERS IS THAT THE CITIZENS RESPECT THE LAW!

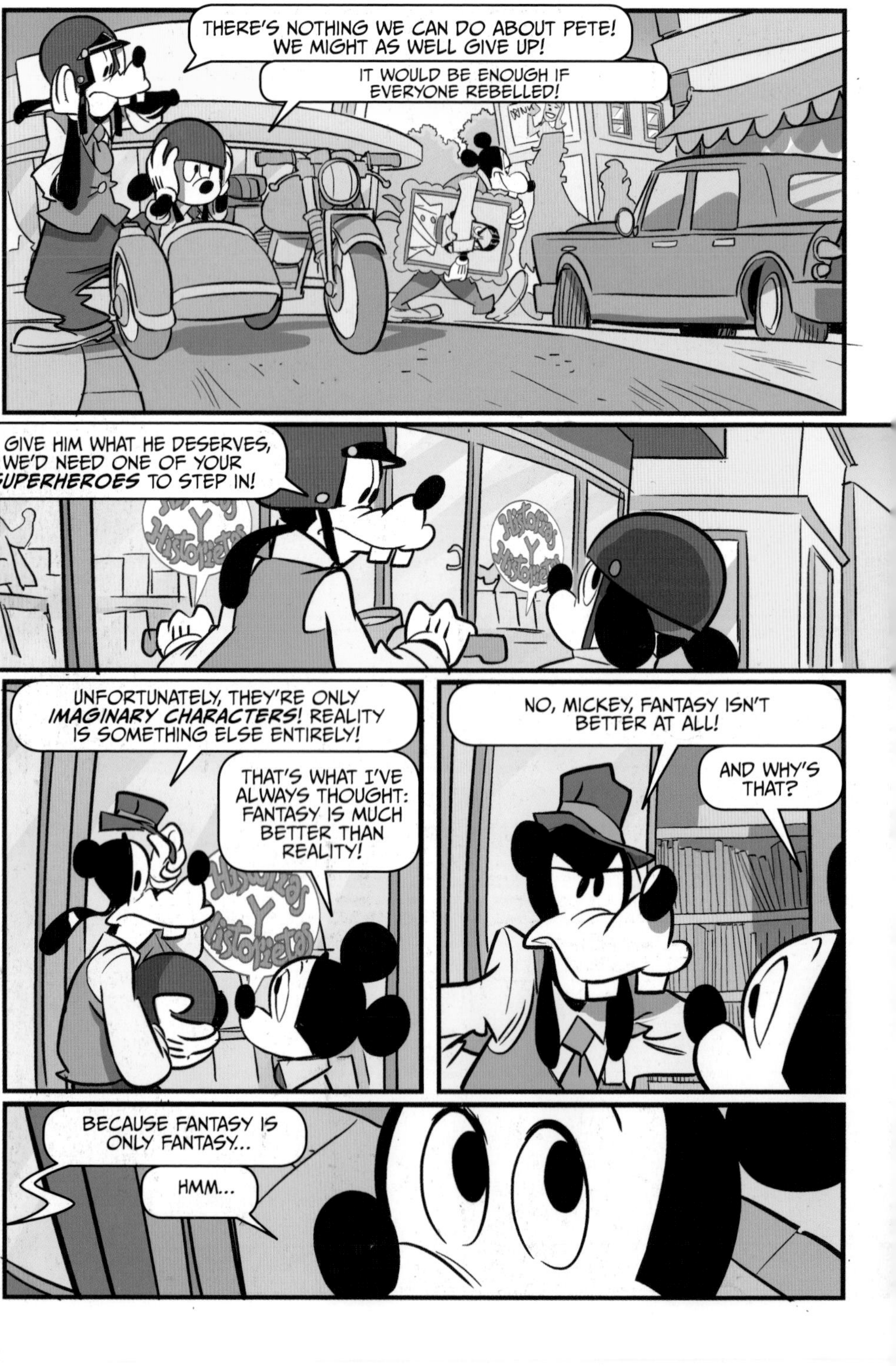
THERE'S NOTHING WE CAN DO ABOUT PETE! WE MIGHT AS WELL GIVE UP!
IT WOULD BE ENOUGH IF EVERYONE REBELLED!
TO GIVE HIM WHAT HE DESERVES, WE'D NEED ONE OF YOUR *SUPERHEROES* TO STEP IN!
Historietas Y Historietas
UNFORTUNATELY, THEY'RE ONLY *IMAGINARY CHARACTERS*! REALITY IS SOMETHING ELSE ENTIRELY!
THAT'S WHAT I'VE ALWAYS THOUGHT: FANTASY IS MUCH BETTER THAN REALITY!
NO, MICKEY, FANTASY ISN'T BETTER AT ALL!
AND WHY'S THAT?
BECAUSE FANTASY IS ONLY FANTASY...
HMM...

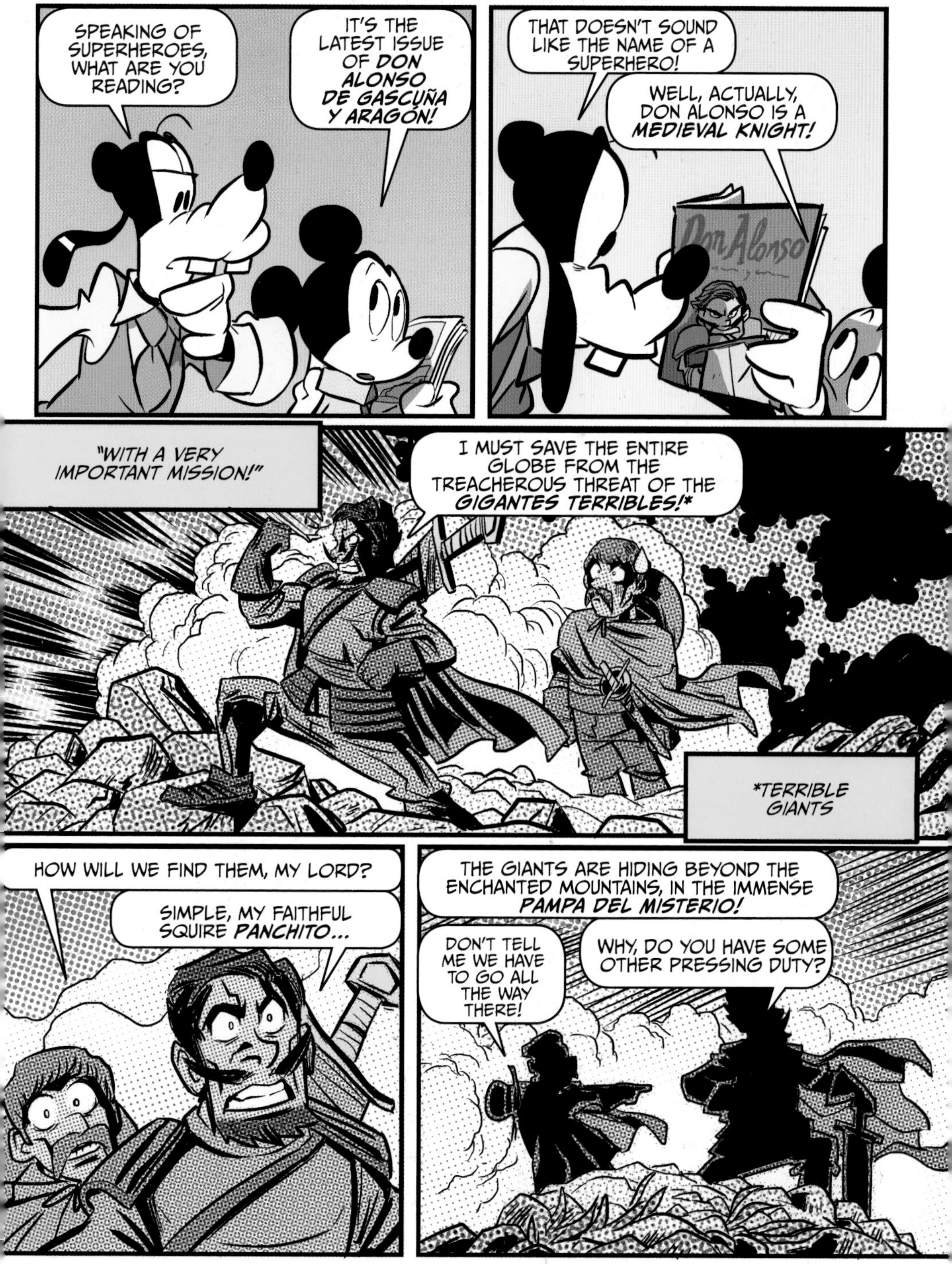
SPEAKING OF SUPERHEROES, WHAT ARE YOU READING?
IT'S THE LATEST ISSUE OF DON ALONSO DE GASCUÑA Y ARAGÓN!
THAT DOESN'T SOUND LIKE THE NAME OF A SUPERHERO!
WELL, ACTUALLY, DON ALONSO IS A MEDIEVAL KNIGHT!
Don Alonso
"WITH A VERY IMPORTANT MISSION!"
I MUST SAVE THE ENTIRE GLOBE FROM THE TREACHEROUS THREAT OF THE GIGANTES TERRIBLES!*
*TERRIBLE GIANTS
HOW WILL WE FIND THEM, MY LORD?
SIMPLE, MY FAITHFUL SQUIRE PANCHITO...
THE GIANTS ARE HIDING BEYOND THE ENCHANTED MOUNTAINS, IN THE IMMENSE PAMPA DEL MISTERIO!
DON'T TELL ME WE HAVE TO GO ALL THE WAY THERE!
WHY, DO YOU HAVE SOME OTHER PRESSING DUTY?

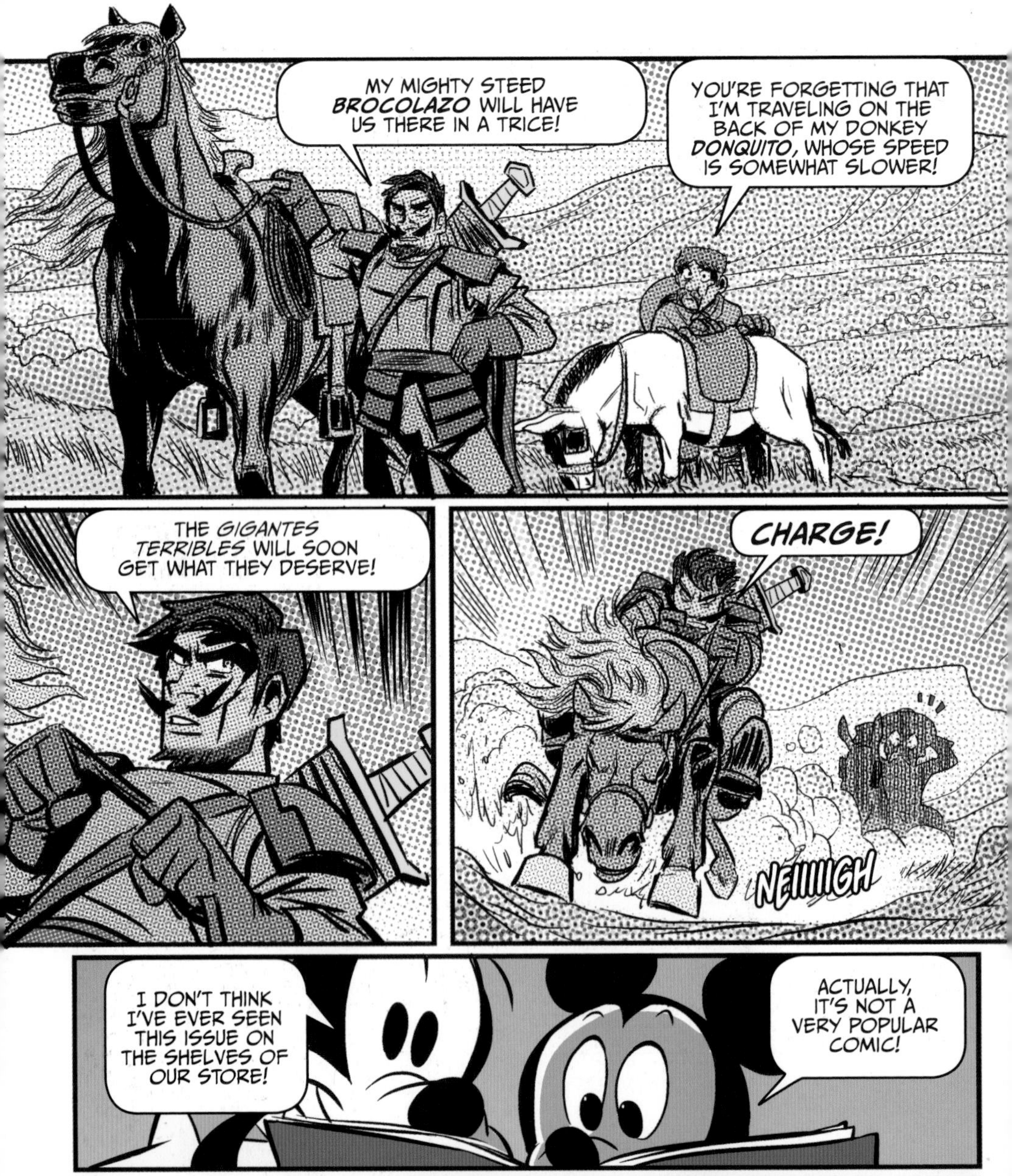

MY MIGHTY STEED *BROCOLAZO* WILL HAVE US THERE IN A TRICE!
YOU'RE FORGETTING THAT I'M TRAVELING ON THE BACK OF MY DONKEY *DONQUITO*, WHOSE SPEED IS SOMEWHAT SLOWER!
THE *GIGANTES TERRIBLES* WILL SOON GET WHAT THEY DESERVE!
CHARGE!
NEIIIIIGH
I DON'T THINK I'VE EVER SEEN THIS ISSUE ON THE SHELVES OF OUR STORE!
ACTUALLY, IT'S NOT A VERY POPULAR COMIC!
THAT'S THE CRATE OF UNSOLD COPIES!
THIS NEEDS TO BE STACKED BETTER. IT'S **WOBBLY!**

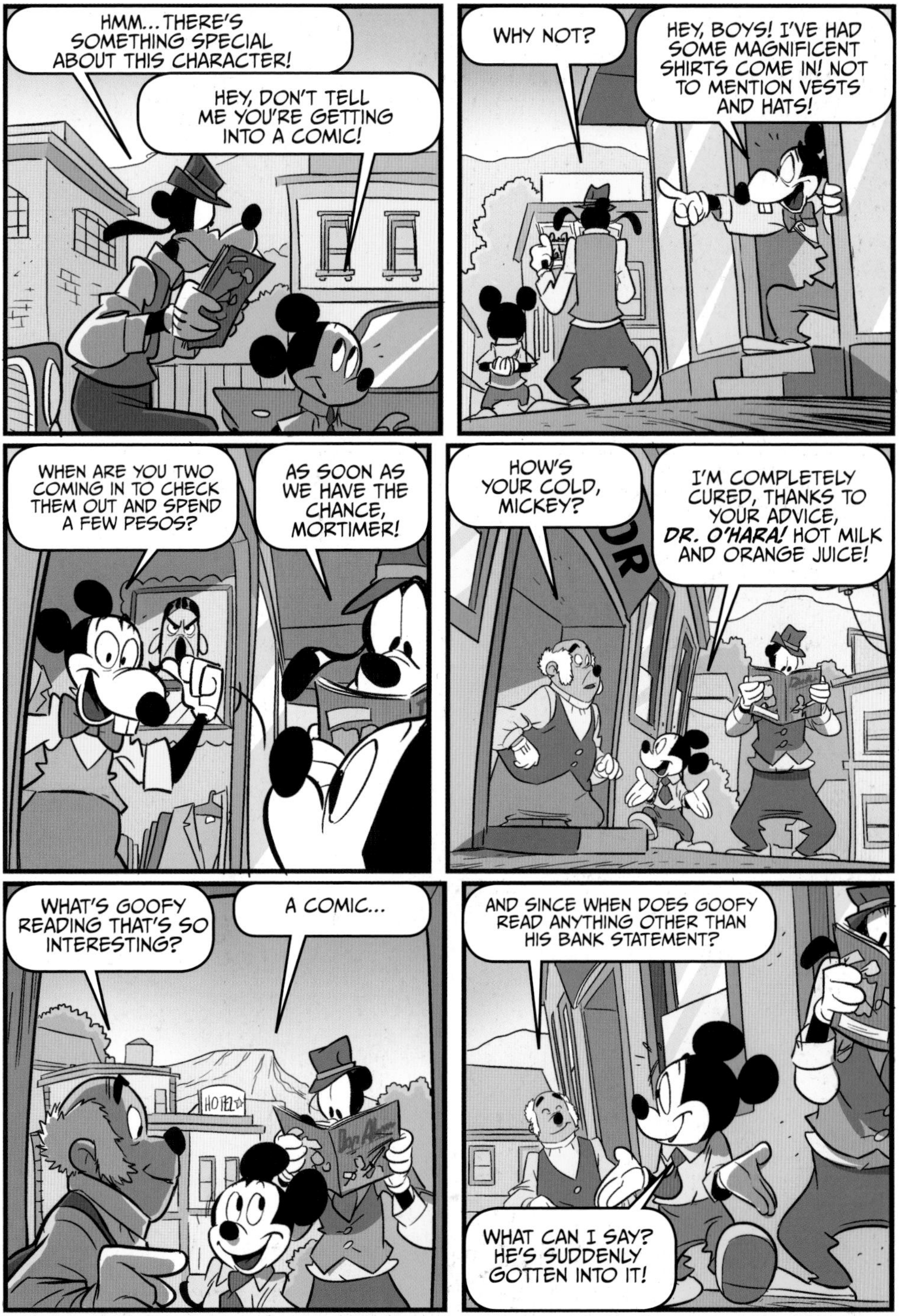
HMM... THERE'S SOMETHING SPECIAL ABOUT THIS CHARACTER!
HEY, DON'T TELL ME YOU'RE GETTING INTO A COMIC!
WHY NOT?
HEY, BOYS! I'VE HAD SOME MAGNIFICENT SHIRTS COME IN! NOT TO MENTION VESTS AND HATS!
WHEN ARE YOU TWO COMING IN TO CHECK THEM OUT AND SPEND A FEW PESOS?
AS SOON AS WE HAVE THE CHANCE, MORTIMER!
HOW'S YOUR COLD, MICKEY?
I'M COMPLETELY CURED, THANKS TO YOUR ADVICE, DR. O'HARA! HOT MILK AND ORANGE JUICE!
WHAT'S GOOFY READING THAT'S SO INTERESTING?
A COMIC...
HOTEL
AND SINCE WHEN DOES GOOFY READ ANYTHING OTHER THAN HIS BANK STATEMENT?
WHAT CAN I SAY? HE'S SUDDENLY GOTTEN INTO IT!

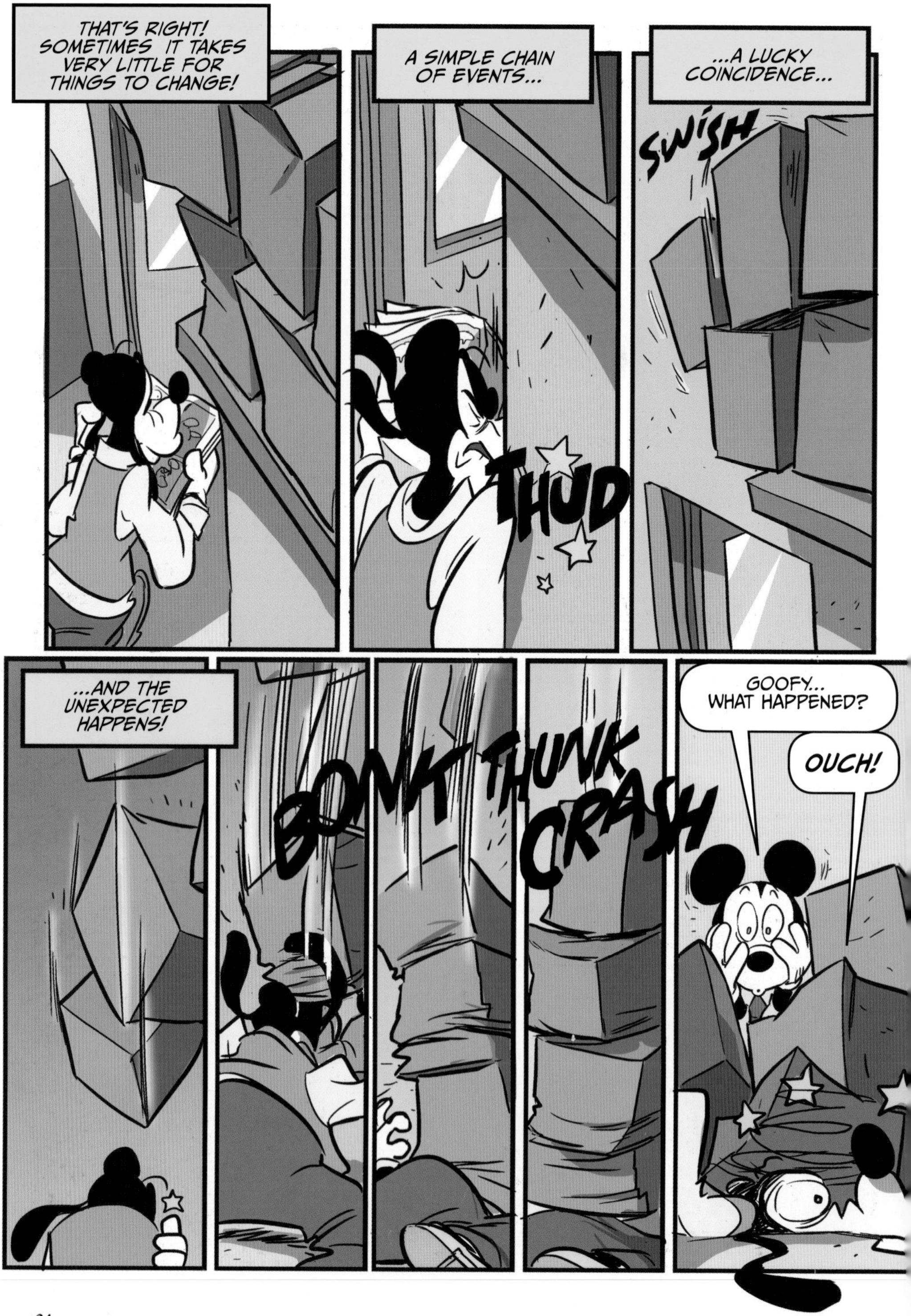
THAT'S RIGHT! SOMETIMES IT TAKES VERY LITTLE FOR THINGS TO CHANGE!
A SIMPLE CHAIN OF EVENTS...
THUD
...A LUCKY COINCIDENCE...
SWISH
...AND THE UNEXPECTED HAPPENS!
BONK
THUNK
CRASH
GOOFY... WHAT HAPPENED?
OUCH!

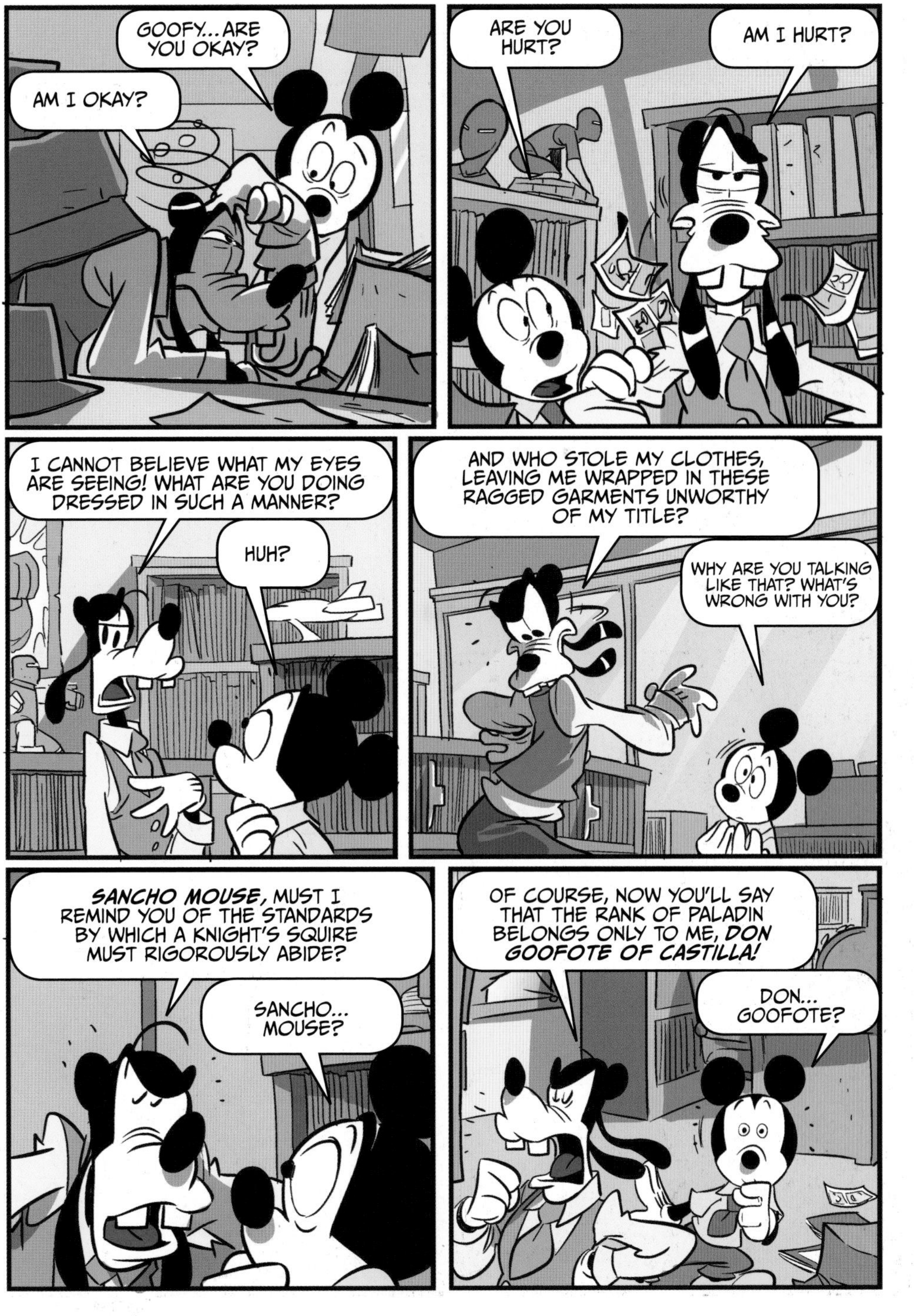
GOOFY... ARE YOU OKAY?
AM I OKAY?
ARE YOU HURT?
AM I HURT?
I CANNOT BELIEVE WHAT MY EYES ARE SEEING! WHAT ARE YOU DOING DRESSED IN SUCH A MANNER?
HUH?
AND WHO STOLE MY CLOTHES, LEAVING ME WRAPPED IN THESE RAGGED GARMENTS UNWORTHY OF MY TITLE?
WHY ARE YOU TALKING LIKE THAT? WHAT'S WRONG WITH YOU?
SANCHO MOUSE, MUST I REMIND YOU OF THE STANDARDS BY WHICH A KNIGHT'S SQUIRE MUST RIGOROUSLY ABIDE?
SANCHO... MOUSE?
OF COURSE, NOW YOU'LL SAY THAT THE RANK OF PALADIN BELONGS ONLY TO ME, DON GOOFOTE OF CASTILLA!
DON... GOOFOTE?

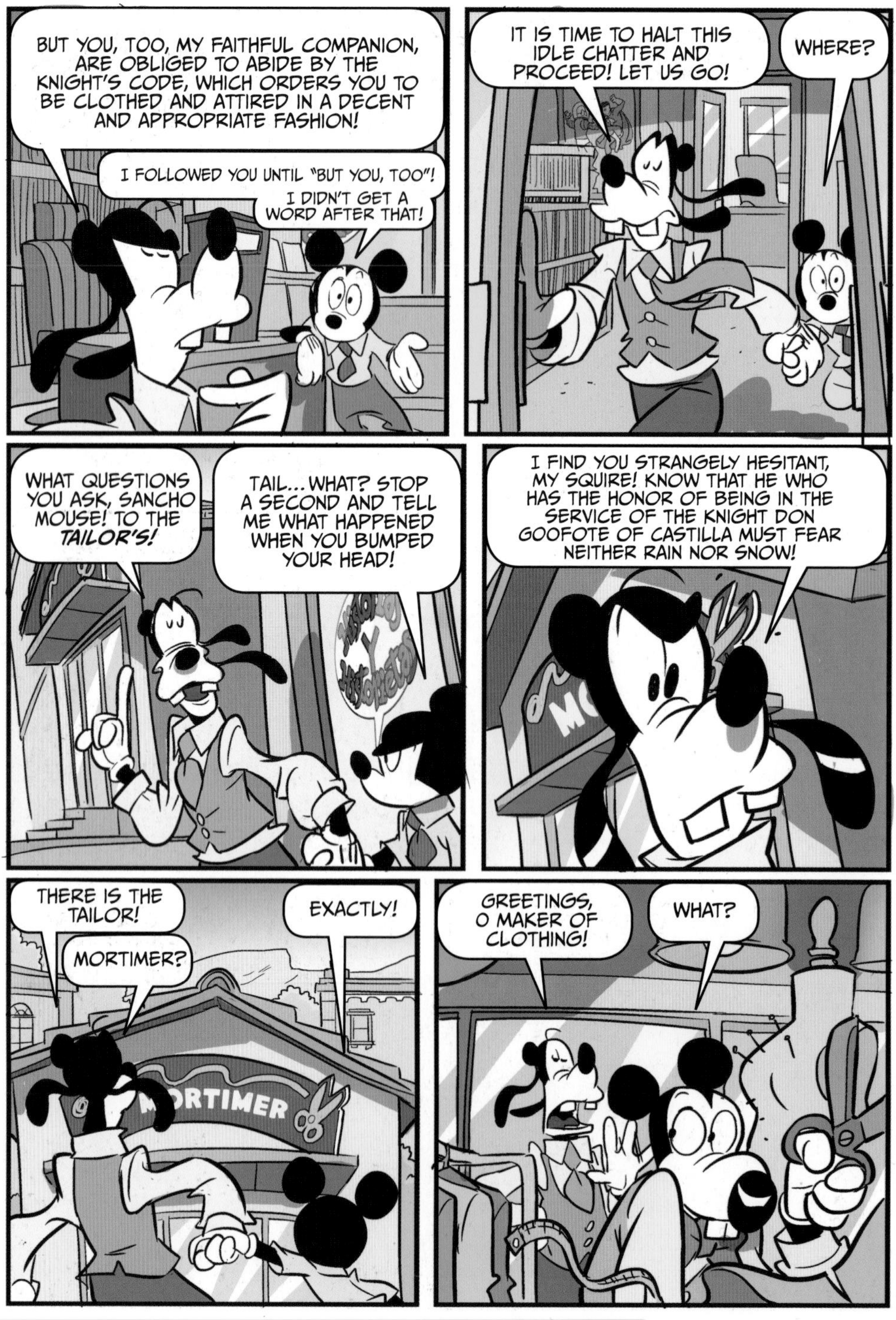
BUT YOU, TOO, MY FAITHFUL COMPANION, ARE OBLIGED TO ABIDE BY THE KNIGHT'S CODE, WHICH ORDERS YOU TO BE CLOTHED AND ATTIRED IN A DECENT AND APPROPRIATE FASHION!
I FOLLOWED YOU UNTIL "BUT YOU, TOO"!
I DIDN'T GET A WORD AFTER THAT!
IT IS TIME TO HALT THIS IDLE CHATTER AND PROCEED! LET US GO!
WHERE?
WHAT QUESTIONS YOU ASK, SANCHO MOUSE! TO THE *TAILOR'S!*
TAIL... WHAT? STOP A SECOND AND TELL ME WHAT HAPPENED WHEN YOU BUMPED YOUR HEAD!
I FIND YOU STRANGELY HESITANT, MY SQUIRE! KNOW THAT HE WHO HAS THE HONOR OF BEING IN THE SERVICE OF THE KNIGHT DON GOOFOTE OF CASTILLA MUST FEAR NEITHER RAIN NOR SNOW!
THERE IS THE TAILOR!
MORTIMER?
EXACTLY!
MORTIMER
GREETINGS, O MAKER OF CLOTHING!
WHAT?

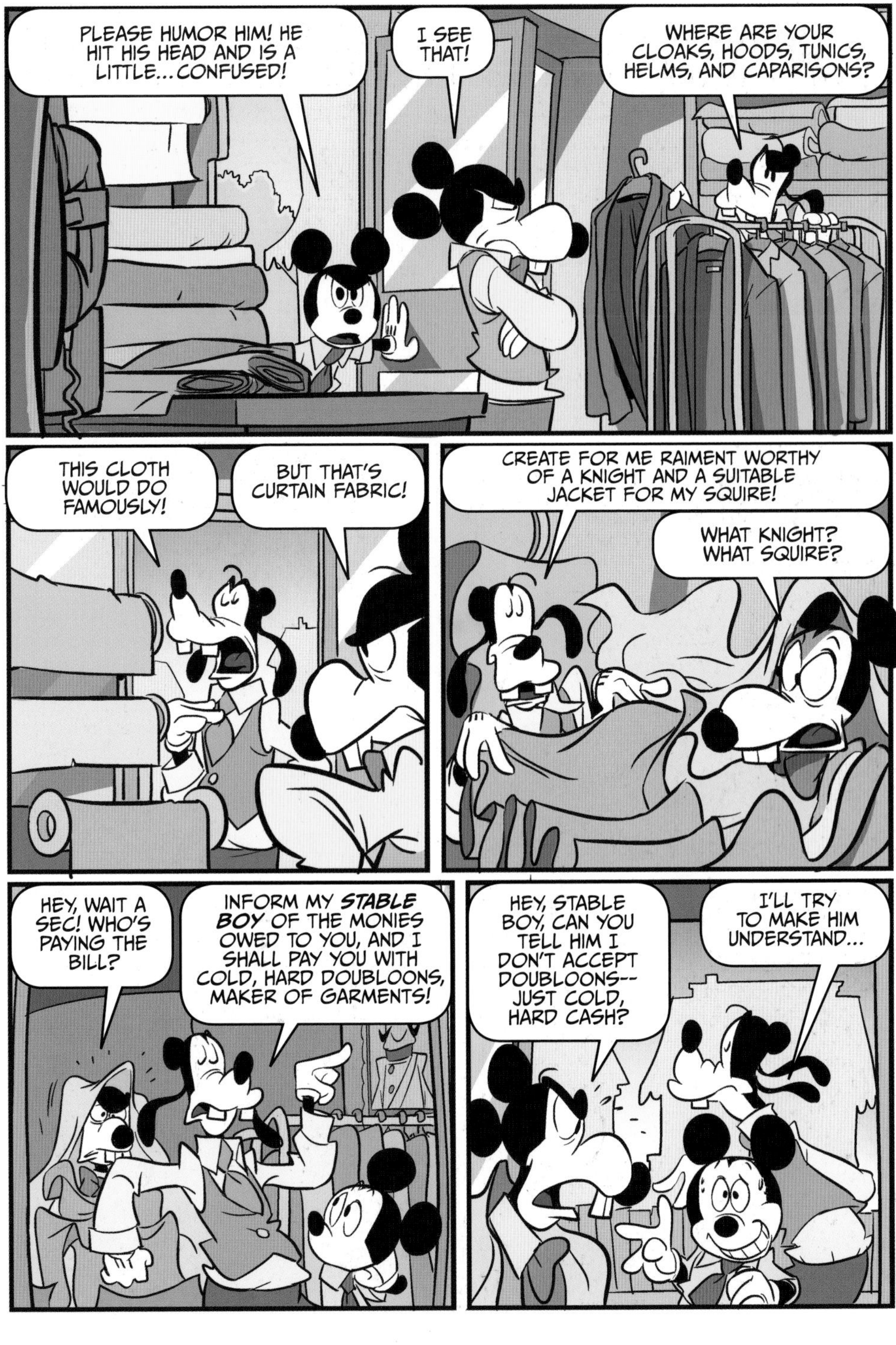
PLEASE HUMOR HIM! HE HIT HIS HEAD AND IS A LITTLE...CONFUSED!
I SEE THAT!
WHERE ARE YOUR CLOAKS, HOODS, TUNICS, HELMS, AND CAPARISONS?
THIS CLOTH WOULD DO FAMOUSLY!
BUT THAT'S CURTAIN FABRIC!
CREATE FOR ME RAIMENT WORTHY OF A KNIGHT AND A SUITABLE JACKET FOR MY SQUIRE!
WHAT KNIGHT? WHAT SQUIRE?
HEY, WAIT A SEC! WHO'S PAYING THE BILL?
INFORM MY ***STABLE BOY*** OF THE MONIES OWED TO YOU, AND I SHALL PAY YOU WITH COLD, HARD DOUBLOONS, MAKER OF GARMENTS!
HEY, STABLE BOY, CAN YOU TELL HIM I DON'T ACCEPT DOUBLOONS-- JUST COLD, HARD CASH?
I'LL TRY TO MAKE HIM UNDERSTAND...

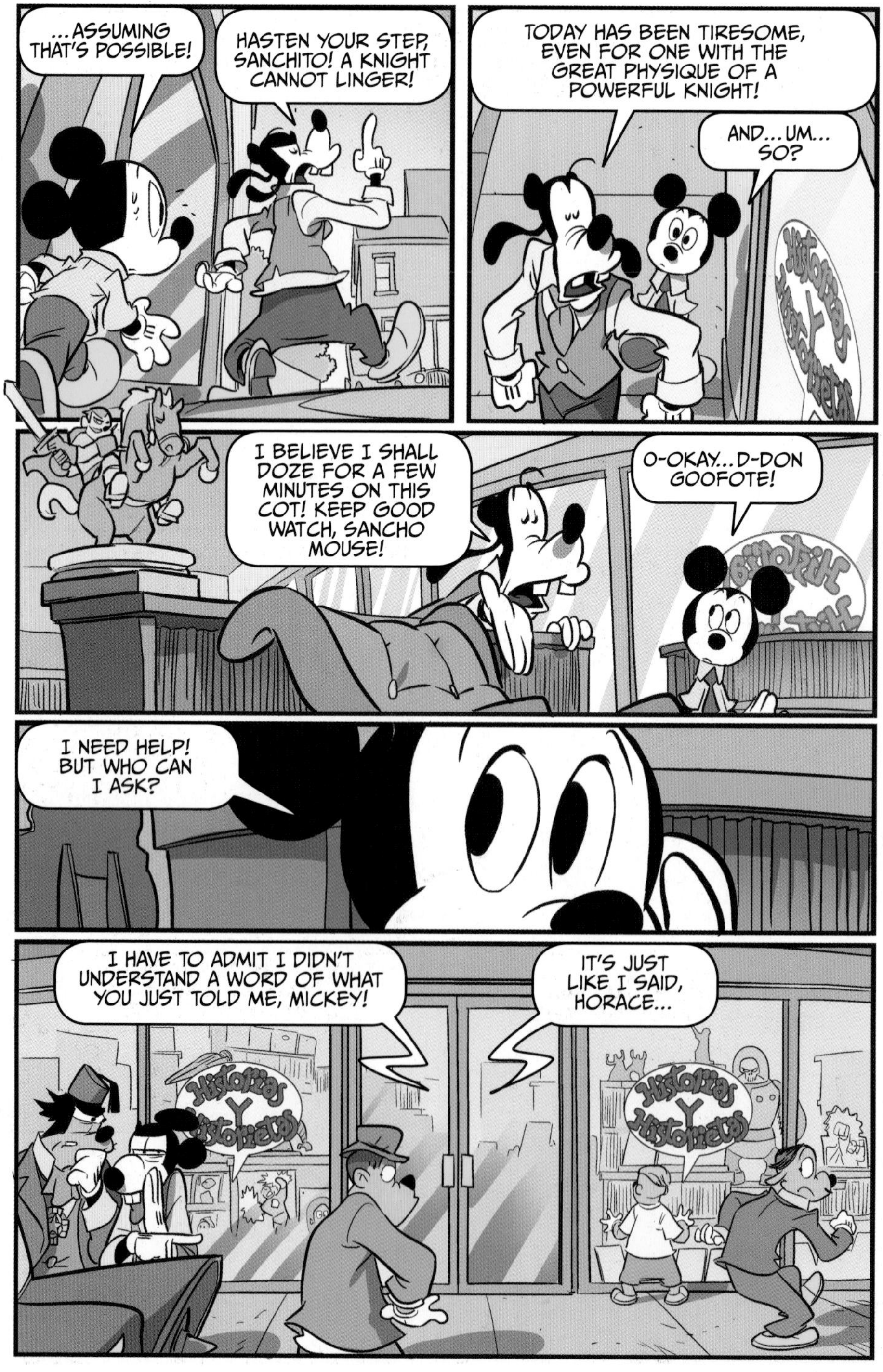
...ASSUMING THAT'S POSSIBLE!
HASTEN YOUR STEP, SANCHITO! A KNIGHT CANNOT LINGER!
TODAY HAS BEEN TIRESOME, EVEN FOR ONE WITH THE GREAT PHYSIQUE OF A POWERFUL KNIGHT!
AND... UM... SO?
I BELIEVE I SHALL DOZE FOR A FEW MINUTES ON THIS COT! KEEP GOOD WATCH, SANCHO MOUSE!
O-OKAY... D-DON GOOFOTE!
I NEED HELP! BUT WHO CAN I ASK?
I HAVE TO ADMIT I DIDN'T UNDERSTAND A WORD OF WHAT YOU JUST TOLD ME, MICKEY!
IT'S JUST LIKE I SAID, HORACE...
Historias Y Historietas
Historias Y Historietas

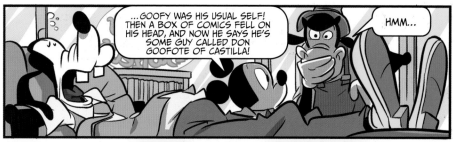

...GOOFY WAS HIS USUAL SELF! THEN A BOX OF COMICS FELL ON HIS HEAD, AND NOW HE SAYS HE'S SOME GUY CALLED DON GOOFOTE OF CASTILLA!

HMM...

AND I DON'T KNOW WHAT MIGHT HAPPEN WHEN HE WAKES UP!

I REALLY DON'T KNOW HOW TO HELP YOU!

YOU'RE A MECHANIC! YOU'RE GOOD AT REPAIRING THINGS!

IT'S ONE THING TO FIX A *CARBURETOR*. IT'S QUITE ANOTHER TO SORT OUT THE BRAIN OF SOMEONE WHO THINKS HE'S A *MEDIEVAL KNIGHT*!

DON'T WORRY! YOU'LL SEE-- WHEN HE WAKES UP, HE WON'T REMEMBER ANY OF THIS!

YOU THINK?

THE FACT IS, YOU READ TOO MANY COMICS! YOU ALWAYS THINK EXTRAORDINARY THINGS ARE HAPPENING, BUT MOST OF THE TIME, IN THE *REAL WORLD,* NOTHING IS GOING ON AT ALL!

I HAVE TO GO! I PROMISED CLARABELLE I'D TAKE HER TO THE *AMUSEMENT PARK*!

OKAY! SEE YOU LATER, THEN!

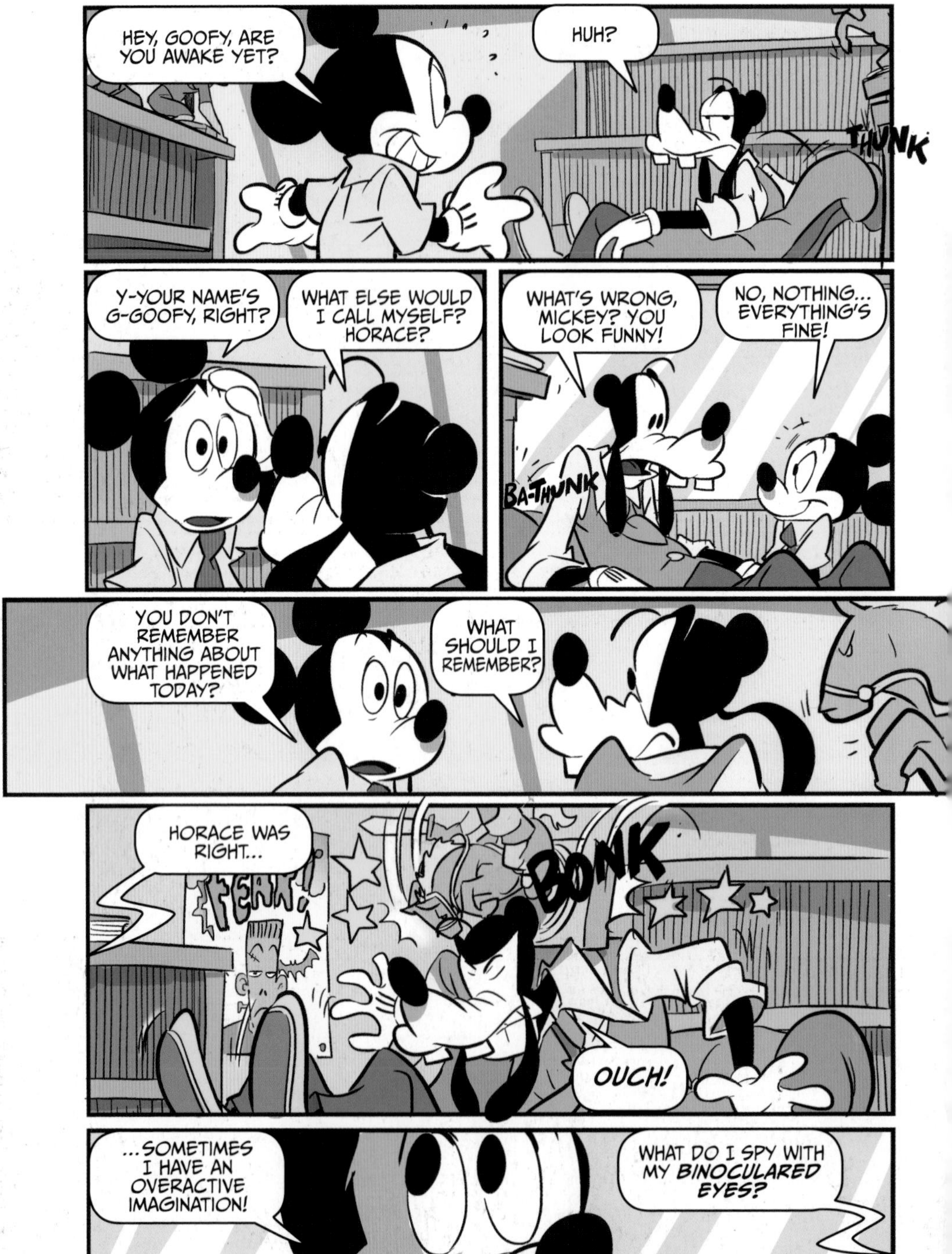

HEY, GOOFY, ARE YOU AWAKE YET?
HUH?
THUNK
Y-YOUR NAME'S G-GOOFY, RIGHT?
WHAT ELSE WOULD I CALL MYSELF? HORACE?
WHAT'S WRONG, MICKEY? YOU LOOK FUNNY!
NO, NOTHING... EVERYTHING'S FINE!
BA-THUNK
YOU DON'T REMEMBER ANYTHING ABOUT WHAT HAPPENED TODAY?
WHAT SHOULD I REMEMBER?
HORACE WAS RIGHT...
FEAR!
BONK
OUCH!
...SOMETIMES I HAVE AN OVERACTIVE IMAGINATION!
WHAT DO I SPY WITH MY *BINOCULARED EYES?*

A DAMSEL HELD PRISONER BY AN EQUINE EVILDOER WHO IS LEADING HER TO THE DUNGEONS OF A BEWITCHED CASTLE!

OH, NO...HERE WE GO AGAIN!

"GOOFY, CAN'T YOU SEE THAT IT'S HORACE TAKING CLARABELLE TO THE RIDES?"

GOOFY?! WHO IS THIS GOOFY OF WHOM YOU SPEAK? I AM DON GOOFOTE OF CASTILLA, OR HAVE YOU FORGOTTEN?

ACTUALLY, I WAS HOPING *YOU'D* FORGOTTEN!

FOLLOW ME, SANCHO MOUSE! OUR TASK IS TO FREE THE YOUNG MAIDEN, SAVING HER FROM THE PERIL INTO WHICH SHE SOON SHALL FALL!

I'M TAKING AN UMBRELLA. THEY SAY IT MIGHT RAIN!

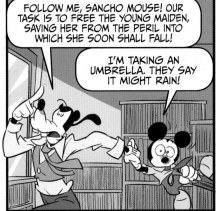

WE SHALL MOUNT THE FAITHFUL *THUNDERO*, THE MECHANICAL HORSE THAT SPITS FIRE!

NOT ONLY THAT, IT ALSO DRINKS OIL!

HORACE'S GARAGE

DON GOOFOTE FEARS NEITHER DRAGON NOR ANY OTHER TERRIFYING CREATURE!

NOR SHOULD YOU, SINCE THEY'RE MADE OF PAPIER-MÂCHÉ!

WE SHALL REACH THE MAIDEN IN A TRICE!

VROOOOOM

HERE WE ARE, IN THE REALM OF EVIL AND DECEIT! THERE IS THE CASTLE WHERE A CRUEL ALCHEMIST HOLDS HIS INNOCENT VICTIMS HOSTAGE!

TWO TICKETS, PLEASE!

TICKE

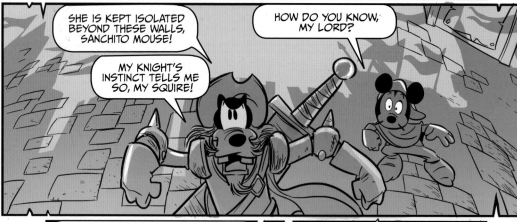

SHE IS KEPT ISOLATED BEYOND THESE WALLS, SANCHITO MOUSE!

HOW DO YOU KNOW, MY LORD?

MY KNIGHT'S INSTINCT TELLS ME SO, MY SQUIRE!

STAY BACK A FEW PACES! I SHALL TEAR DOWN THESE WALLS OF THICK ROCK WITH MY POWERFUL SWORD, WHOSE IRON COMES FROM THE HEAVENLY MINES OF THE *SIERRA DURENDAL!*

BE CAREFUL NOT TO HURT YOURSELF, KNIGHT!

KATAKRASH

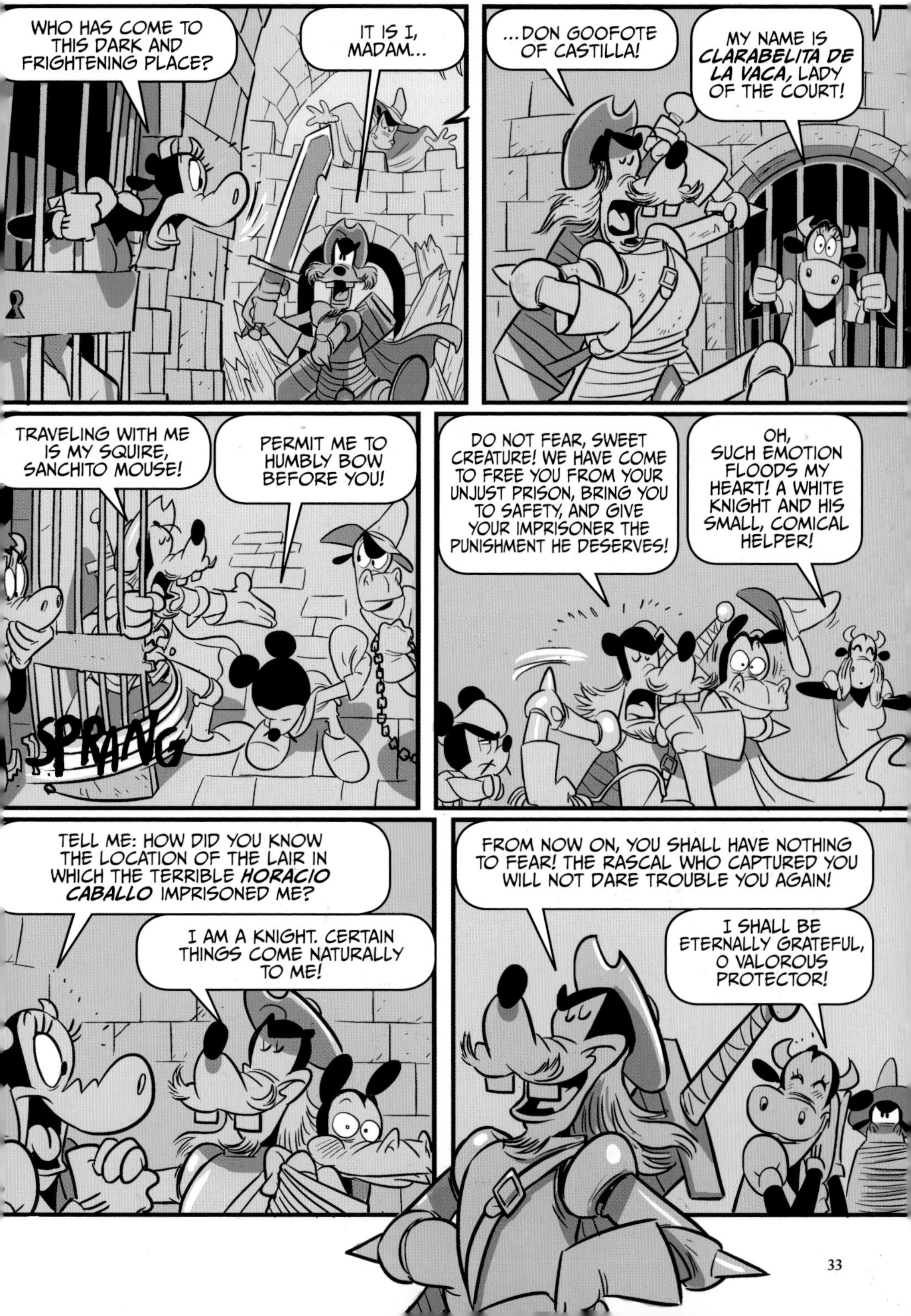
WHO HAS COME TO THIS DARK AND FRIGHTENING PLACE?
IT IS I, MADAM...
...DON GOOFOTE OF CASTILLA!
MY NAME IS *CLARABELITA DE LA VACA,* LADY OF THE COURT!
TRAVELING WITH ME IS MY SQUIRE, SANCHITO MOUSE!
PERMIT ME TO HUMBLY BOW BEFORE YOU!
SPRANG
DO NOT FEAR, SWEET CREATURE! WE HAVE COME TO FREE YOU FROM YOUR UNJUST PRISON, BRING YOU TO SAFETY, AND GIVE YOUR IMPRISONER THE PUNISHMENT HE DESERVES!
OH, SUCH EMOTION FLOODS MY HEART! A WHITE KNIGHT AND HIS SMALL, COMICAL HELPER!
TELL ME: HOW DID YOU KNOW THE LOCATION OF THE LAIR IN WHICH THE TERRIBLE *HORACIO CABALLO* IMPRISONED ME?
I AM A KNIGHT. CERTAIN THINGS COME NATURALLY TO ME!
FROM NOW ON, YOU SHALL HAVE NOTHING TO FEAR! THE RASCAL WHO CAPTURED YOU WILL NOT DARE TROUBLE YOU AGAIN!
I SHALL BE ETERNALLY GRATEFUL, O VALOROUS PROTECTOR!

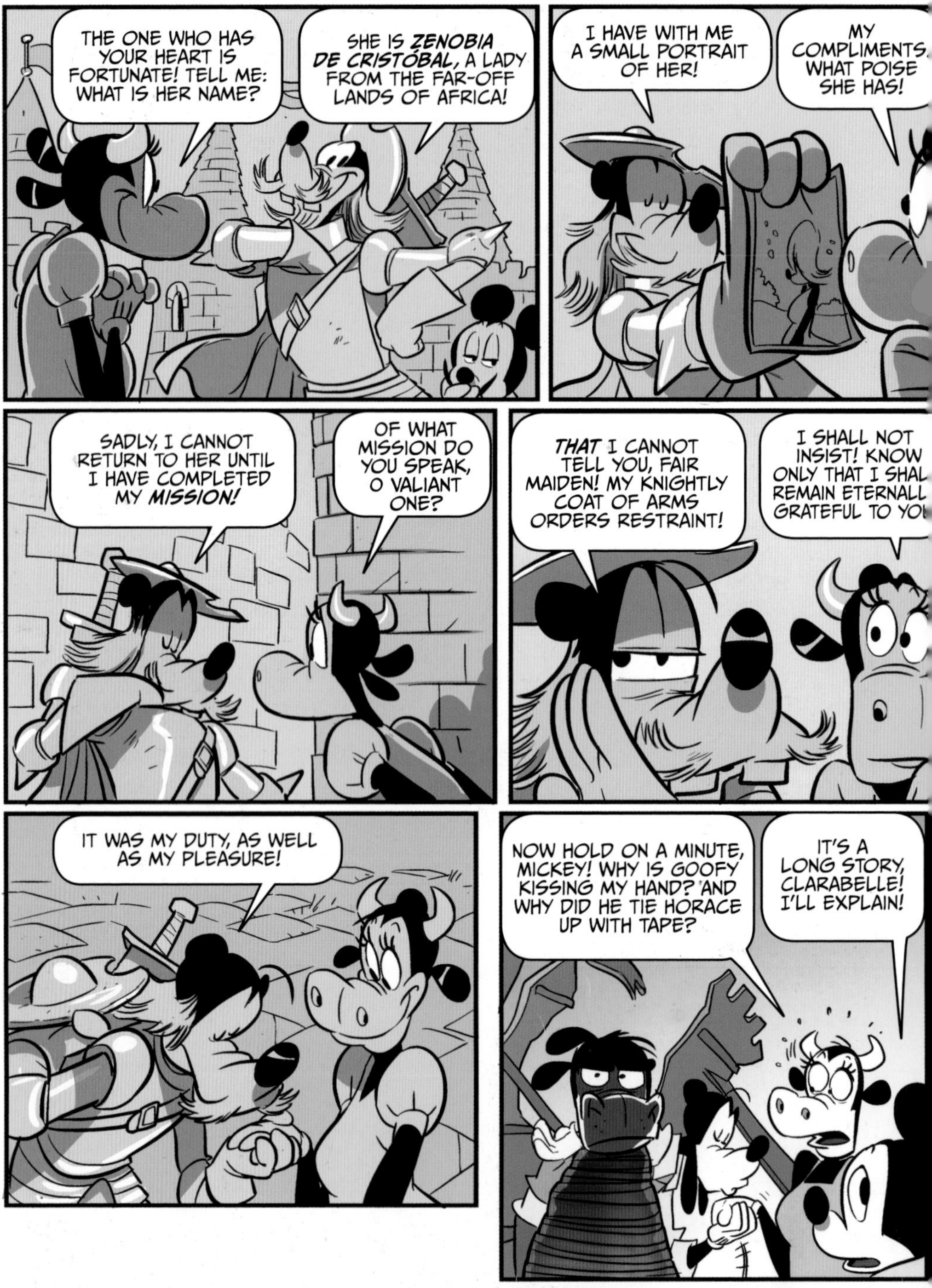
THE ONE WHO HAS YOUR HEART IS FORTUNATE! TELL ME: WHAT IS HER NAME?
SHE IS ZENOBIA DE CRISTÓBAL, A LADY FROM THE FAR-OFF LANDS OF AFRICA!
I HAVE WITH ME A SMALL PORTRAIT OF HER!
MY COMPLIMENTS. WHAT POISE SHE HAS!
SADLY, I CANNOT RETURN TO HER UNTIL I HAVE COMPLETED MY MISSION!
OF WHAT MISSION DO YOU SPEAK, O VALIANT ONE?
THAT I CANNOT TELL YOU, FAIR MAIDEN! MY KNIGHTLY COAT OF ARMS ORDERS RESTRAINT!
I SHALL NOT INSIST! KNOW ONLY THAT I SHAL REMAIN ETERNALL GRATEFUL TO YO
IT WAS MY DUTY, AS WELL AS MY PLEASURE!
NOW HOLD ON A MINUTE, MICKEY! WHY IS GOOFY KISSING MY HAND? AND WHY DID HE TIE HORACE UP WITH TAPE?
IT'S A LONG STORY, CLARABELLE! I'LL EXPLAIN!

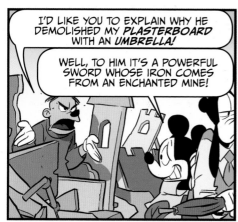

I'D LIKE YOU TO EXPLAIN WHY HE DEMOLISHED MY *PLASTERBOARD* WITH AN *UMBRELLA!*

WELL, TO HIM IT'S A POWERFUL SWORD WHOSE IRON COMES FROM AN ENCHANTED MINE!

LET US BE OFF, SANCHO MOUSE! SWEET REST AWAITS US!

SANCHO MOUSE?

THAT'S ALSO PART OF THE STORY!

TODAY HAS BEEN MOST FRUITFUL!

I'VE GOT TO ASK YOU SOMETHING, GOO...I MEAN, SIR DON GOOFOTE!

EARLIER YOU MENTIONED A CERTAIN...UM... *MISSION!* WHAT IS IT?

YOU ARE MOST FORGETFUL, SANCHITO MOUSE!

OUR TASK IS TO SAVE THE WORLD FROM THE *IRON GIANTS!* PERHAPS YOU HAVE FORGOTTEN, OR ARE YOU FEIGNING AMNESIA?

IRON... GIANTS?!

"THE MONSTERS COME FROM THE *MECHANICAL WORLD,* BEYOND THE GREAT RIVER, PAST THE FIELD OF WINDMILLS!

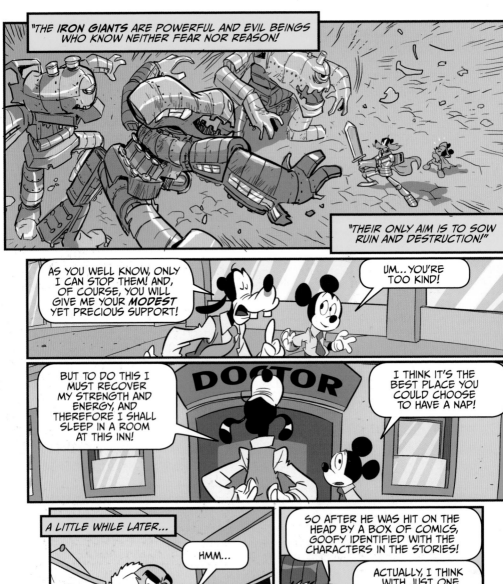

"THE *IRON GIANTS* ARE POWERFUL AND EVIL BEINGS WHO KNOW NEITHER FEAR NOR REASON!

"THEIR ONLY AIM IS TO SOW RUIN AND DESTRUCTION!"

AS YOU WELL KNOW, ONLY I CAN STOP THEM! AND, OF COURSE, YOU WILL GIVE ME YOUR *MODEST* YET PRECIOUS SUPPORT!

UM...YOU'RE TOO KIND!

BUT TO DO THIS I MUST RECOVER MY STRENGTH AND ENERGY, AND THEREFORE I SHALL SLEEP IN A ROOM AT THIS INN!

DOCTOR

I THINK IT'S THE BEST PLACE YOU COULD CHOOSE TO HAVE A NAP!

A LITTLE WHILE LATER...

HMM...

SO AFTER HE WAS HIT ON THE HEAD BY A BOX OF COMICS, GOOFY IDENTIFIED WITH THE CHARACTERS IN THE STORIES!

ACTUALLY, I THINK WITH JUST ONE CHARACTER...

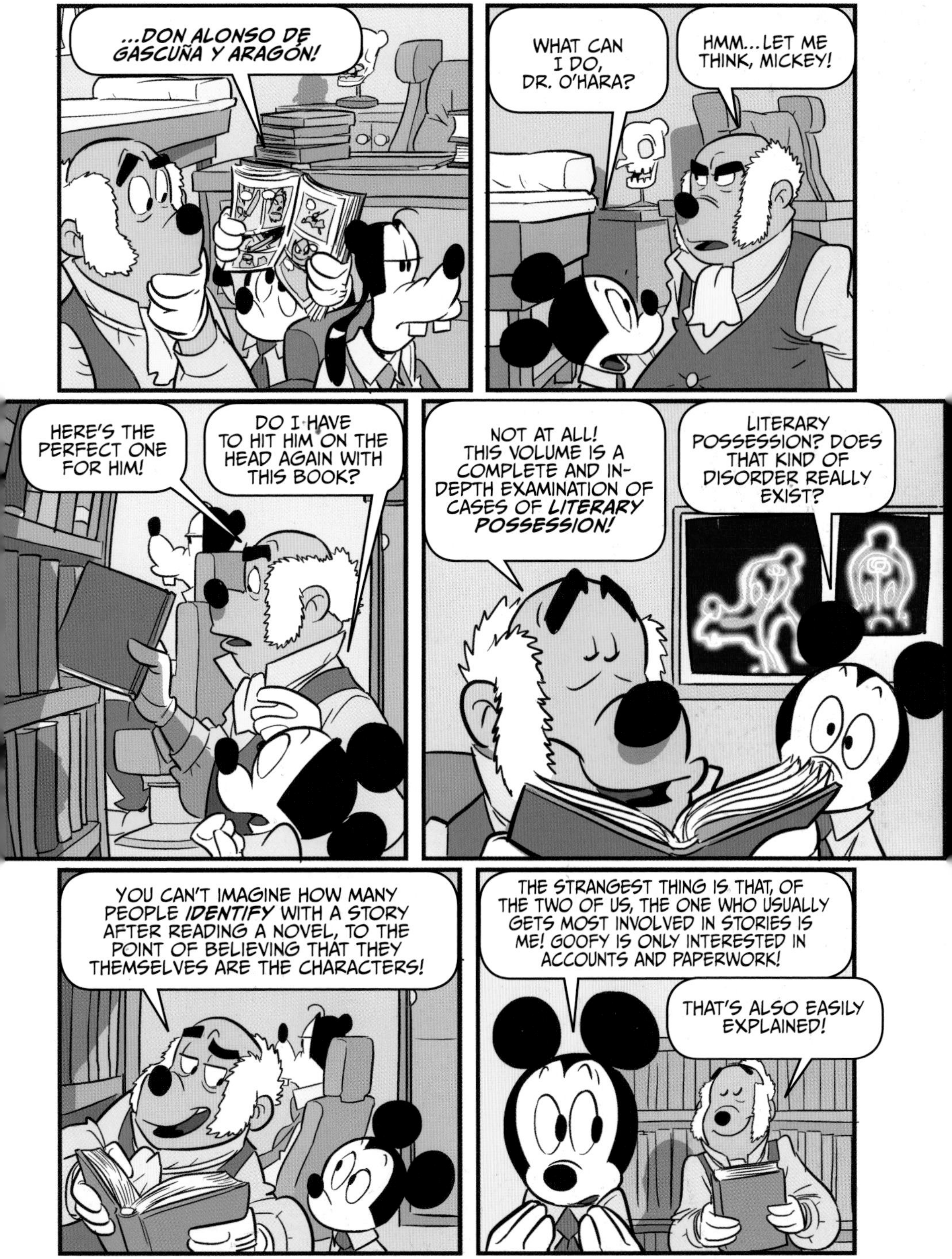
...DON ALONSO DE GASCUÑA Y ARAGÓN!
WHAT CAN I DO, DR. O'HARA?
HMM... LET ME THINK, MICKEY!
HERE'S THE PERFECT ONE FOR HIM!
DO I HAVE TO HIT HIM ON THE HEAD AGAIN WITH THIS BOOK?
NOT AT ALL! THIS VOLUME IS A COMPLETE AND IN-DEPTH EXAMINATION OF CASES OF LITERARY POSSESSION!
LITERARY POSSESSION? DOES THAT KIND OF DISORDER REALLY EXIST?
YOU CAN'T IMAGINE HOW MANY PEOPLE IDENTIFY WITH A STORY AFTER READING A NOVEL, TO THE POINT OF BELIEVING THAT THEY THEMSELVES ARE THE CHARACTERS!
THE STRANGEST THING IS THAT, OF THE TWO OF US, THE ONE WHO USUALLY GETS MOST INVOLVED IN STORIES IS ME! GOOFY IS ONLY INTERESTED IN ACCOUNTS AND PAPERWORK!
THAT'S ALSO EASILY EXPLAINED!

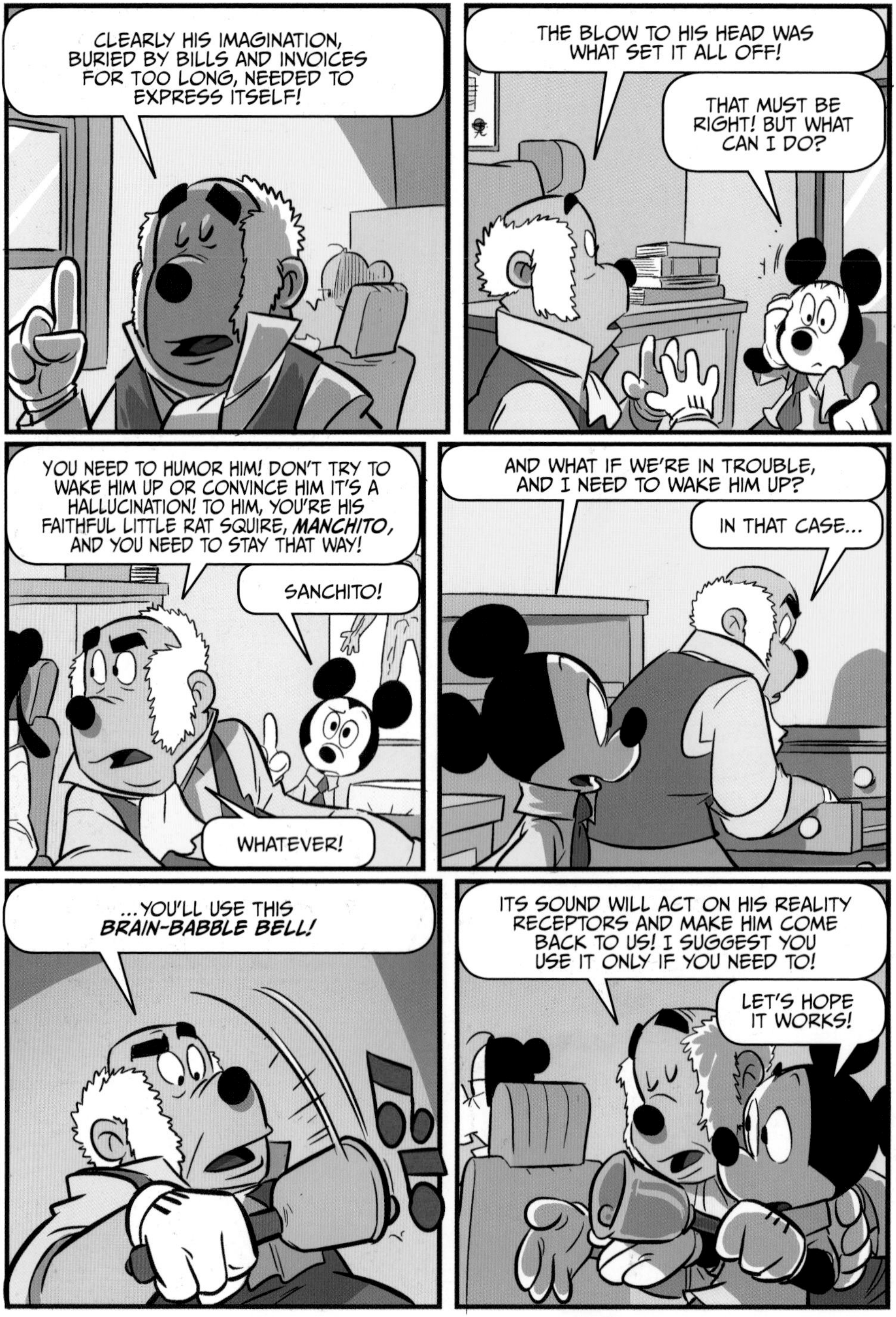

CLEARLY HIS IMAGINATION, BURIED BY BILLS AND INVOICES FOR TOO LONG, NEEDED TO EXPRESS ITSELF!
THE BLOW TO HIS HEAD WAS WHAT SET IT ALL OFF!
THAT MUST BE RIGHT! BUT WHAT CAN I DO?
YOU NEED TO HUMOR HIM! DON'T TRY TO WAKE HIM UP OR CONVINCE HIM IT'S A HALLUCINATION! TO HIM, YOU'RE HIS FAITHFUL LITTLE RAT SQUIRE, *MANCHITO,* AND YOU NEED TO STAY THAT WAY!
SANCHITO!
WHATEVER!
AND WHAT IF WE'RE IN TROUBLE, AND I NEED TO WAKE HIM UP?
IN THAT CASE...
...YOU'LL USE THIS **BRAIN-BABBLE BELL!**
ITS SOUND WILL ACT ON HIS REALITY RECEPTORS AND MAKE HIM COME BACK TO US! I SUGGEST YOU USE IT ONLY IF YOU NEED TO!
LET'S HOPE IT WORKS!

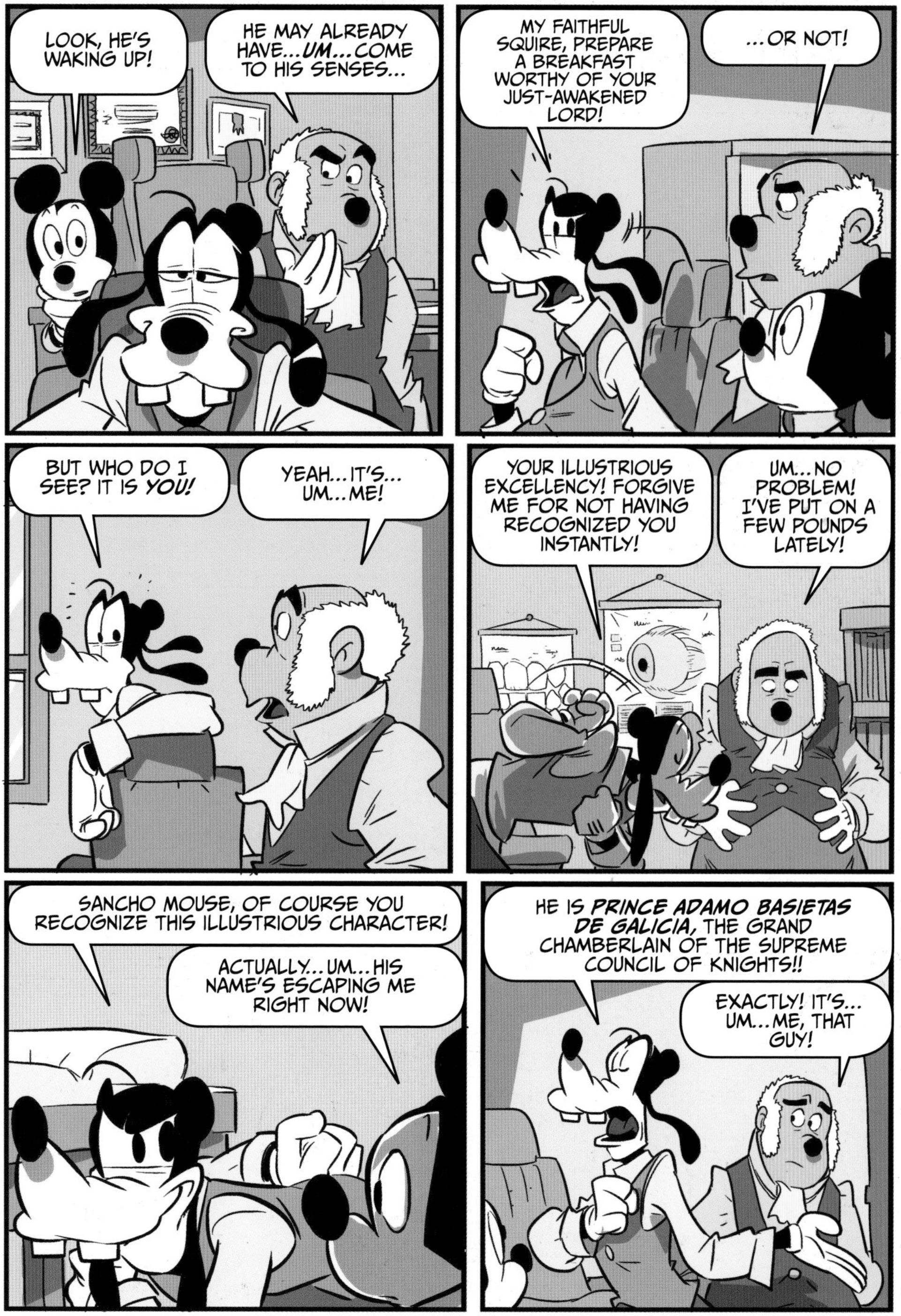
LOOK, HE'S WAKING UP!
HE MAY ALREADY HAVE... *UM...* COME TO HIS SENSES...
MY FAITHFUL SQUIRE, PREPARE A BREAKFAST WORTHY OF YOUR JUST-AWAKENED LORD!
...OR NOT!
BUT WHO DO I SEE? IT IS *YOU!*
YEAH... IT'S... UM... ME!
YOUR ILLUSTRIOUS EXCELLENCY! FORGIVE ME FOR NOT HAVING RECOGNIZED YOU INSTANTLY!
UM... NO PROBLEM! I'VE PUT ON A FEW POUNDS LATELY!
SANCHO MOUSE, OF COURSE YOU RECOGNIZE THIS ILLUSTRIOUS CHARACTER!
ACTUALLY... UM... HIS NAME'S ESCAPING ME RIGHT NOW!
HE IS *PRINCE ADAMO BASIETAS DE GALICIA,* THE GRAND CHAMBERLAIN OF THE SUPREME COUNCIL OF KNIGHTS!!
EXACTLY! IT'S... UM... ME, THAT GUY!

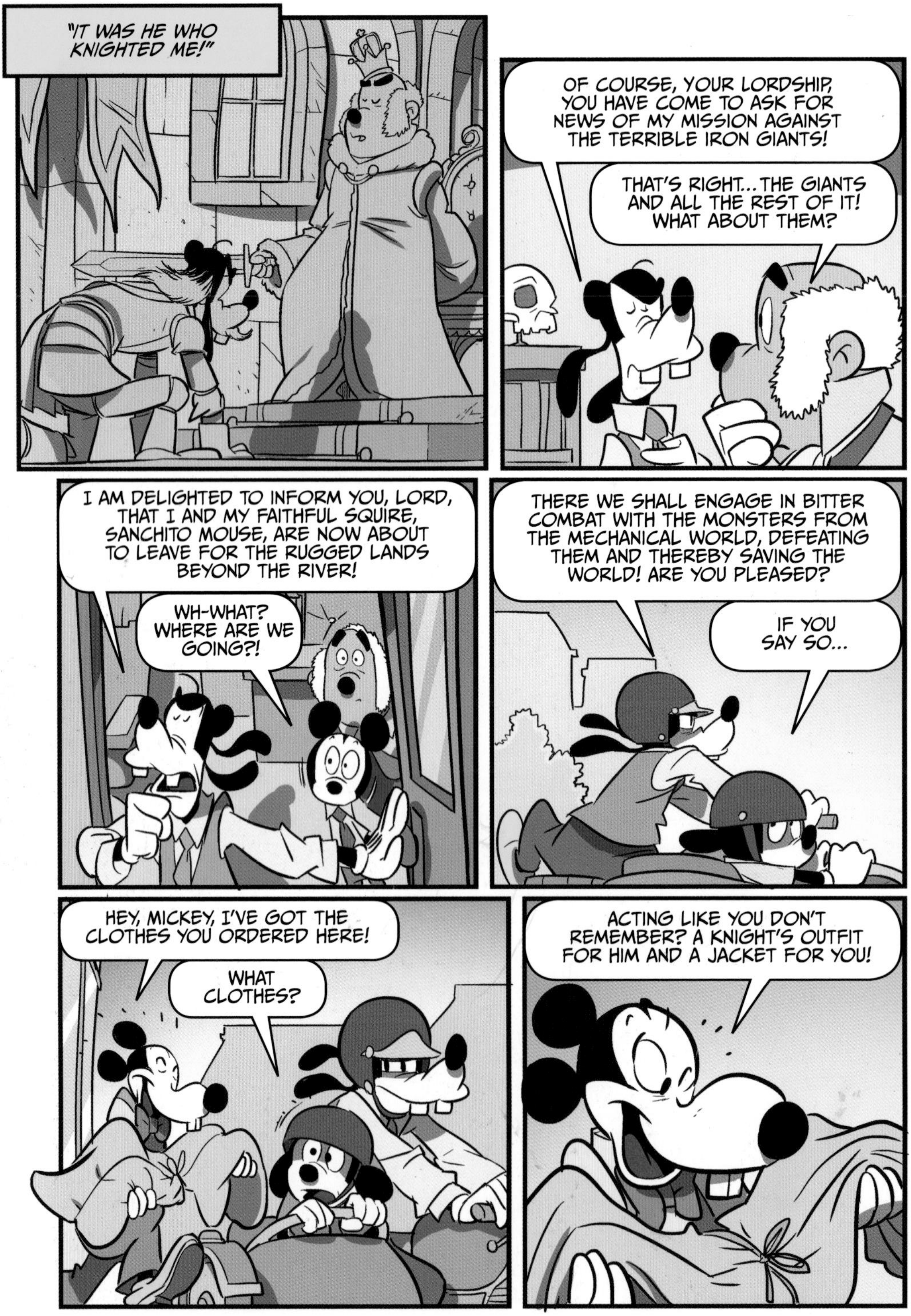
"IT WAS HE WHO KNIGHTED ME!"
OF COURSE, YOUR LORDSHIP, YOU HAVE COME TO ASK FOR NEWS OF MY MISSION AGAINST THE TERRIBLE IRON GIANTS!
THAT'S RIGHT... THE GIANTS AND ALL THE REST OF IT! WHAT ABOUT THEM?
I AM DELIGHTED TO INFORM YOU, LORD, THAT I AND MY FAITHFUL SQUIRE, SANCHITO MOUSE, ARE NOW ABOUT TO LEAVE FOR THE RUGGED LANDS BEYOND THE RIVER!
WH-WHAT? WHERE ARE WE GOING?!
THERE WE SHALL ENGAGE IN BITTER COMBAT WITH THE MONSTERS FROM THE MECHANICAL WORLD, DEFEATING THEM AND THEREBY SAVING THE WORLD! ARE YOU PLEASED?
IF YOU SAY SO...
HEY, MICKEY, I'VE GOT THE CLOTHES YOU ORDERED HERE!
WHAT CLOTHES?
ACTING LIKE YOU DON'T REMEMBER? A KNIGHT'S OUTFIT FOR HIM AND A JACKET FOR YOU!

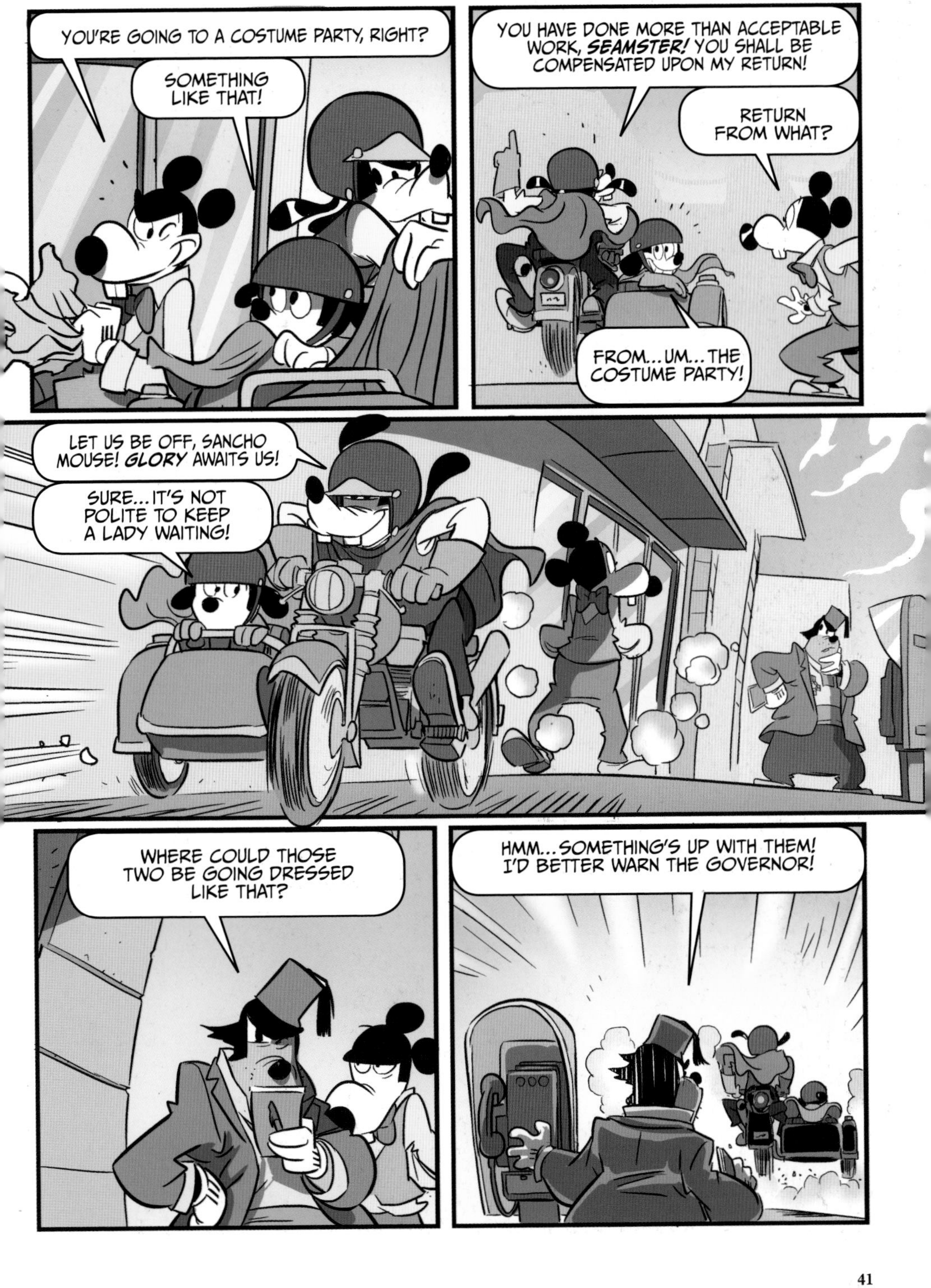
YOU'RE GOING TO A COSTUME PARTY, RIGHT?
SOMETHING LIKE THAT!
YOU HAVE DONE MORE THAN ACCEPTABLE WORK, SEAMSTER! YOU SHALL BE COMPENSATED UPON MY RETURN!
RETURN FROM WHAT?
FROM...UM...THE COSTUME PARTY!
LET US BE OFF, SANCHO MOUSE! GLORY AWAITS US!
SURE...IT'S NOT POLITE TO KEEP A LADY WAITING!
WHERE COULD THOSE TWO BE GOING DRESSED LIKE THAT?
HMM...SOMETHING'S UP WITH THEM! I'D BETTER WARN THE GOVERNOR!

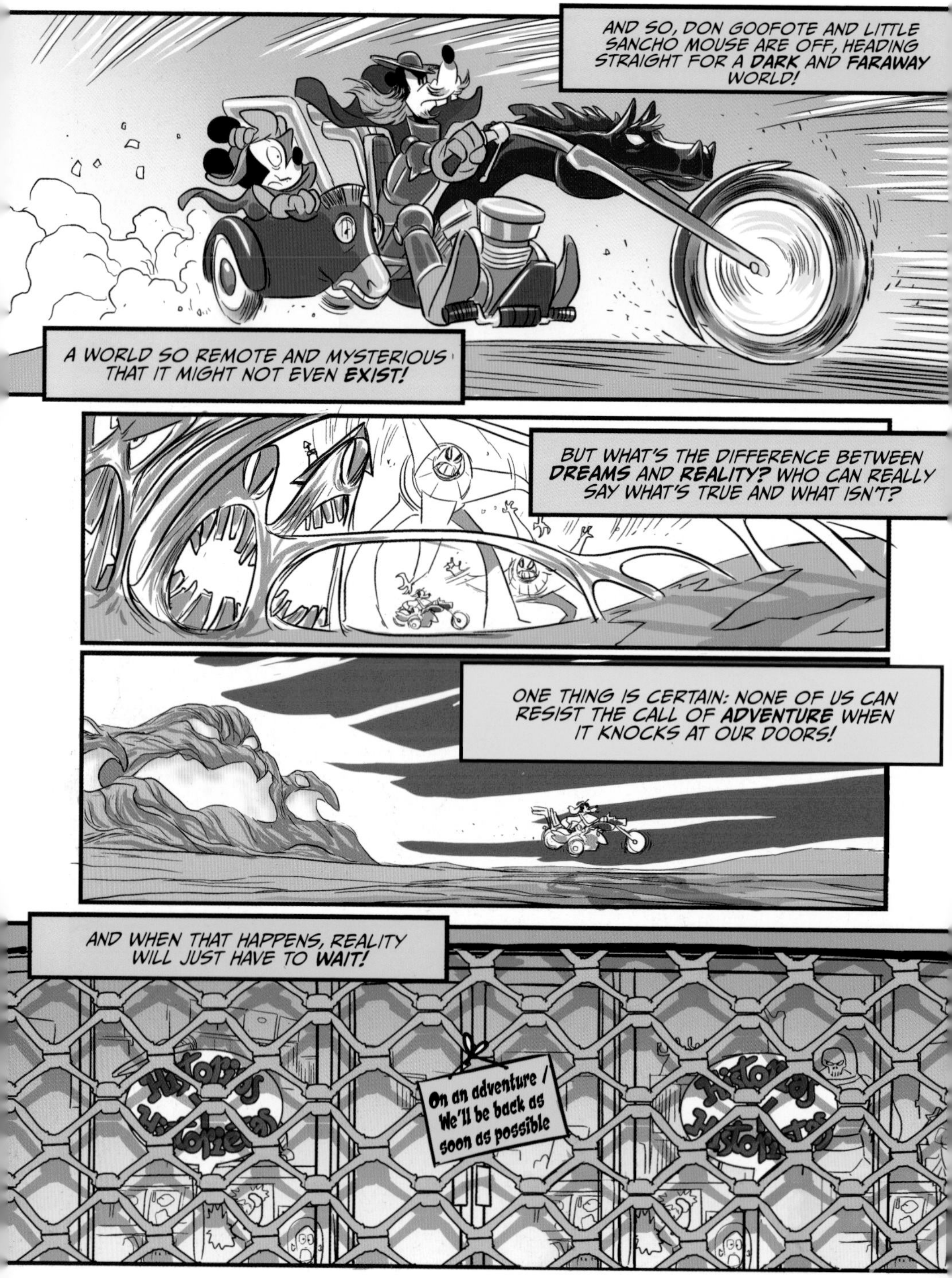
AND SO, DON GOOFOTE AND LITTLE SANCHO MOUSE ARE OFF, HEADING STRAIGHT FOR A DARK AND FARAWAY WORLD!
A WORLD SO REMOTE AND MYSTERIOUS THAT IT MIGHT NOT EVEN EXIST!
BUT WHAT'S THE DIFFERENCE BETWEEN DREAMS AND REALITY? WHO CAN REALLY SAY WHAT'S TRUE AND WHAT ISN'T?
ONE THING IS CERTAIN: NONE OF US CAN RESIST THE CALL OF ADVENTURE WHEN IT KNOCKS AT OUR DOORS!
AND WHEN THAT HAPPENS, REALITY WILL JUST HAVE TO WAIT!
On an adventure / We'll be back as soon as possible

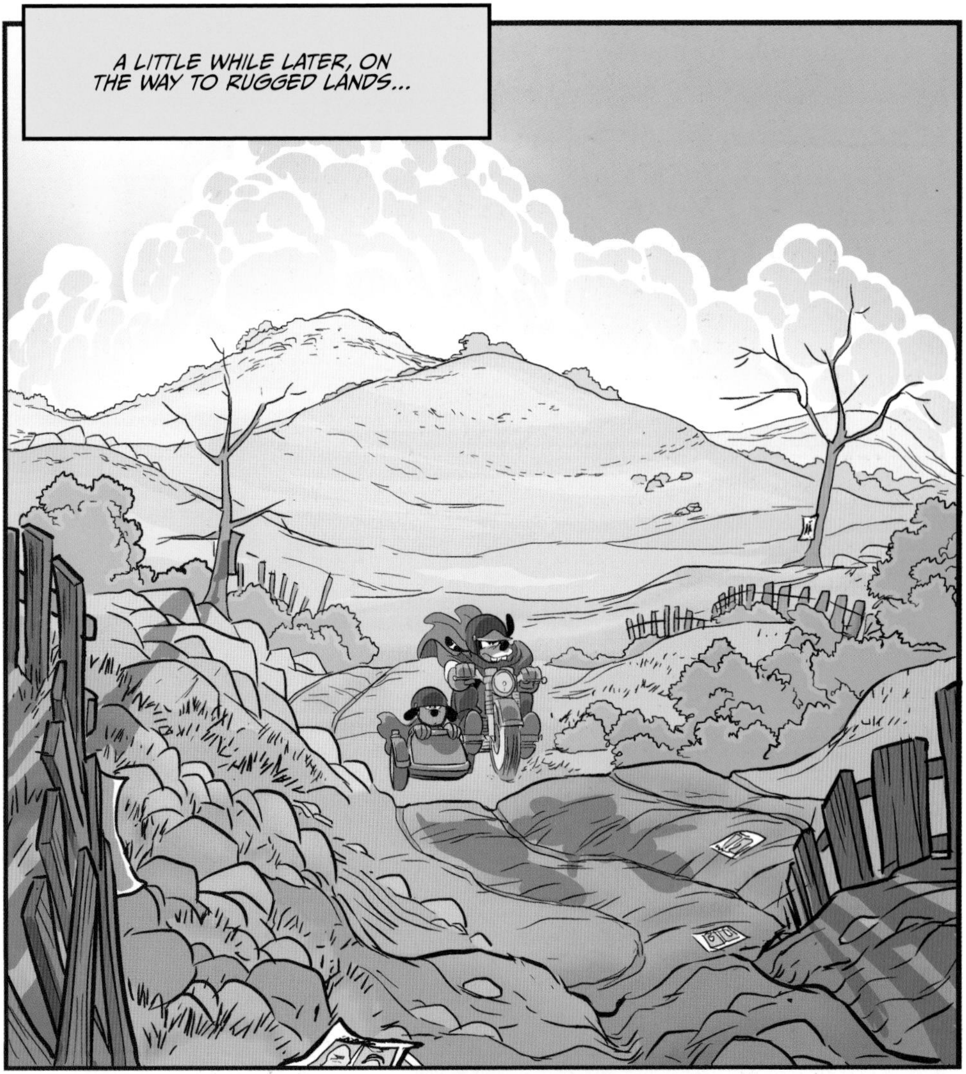
A LITTLE WHILE LATER, ON THE WAY TO RUGGED LANDS...

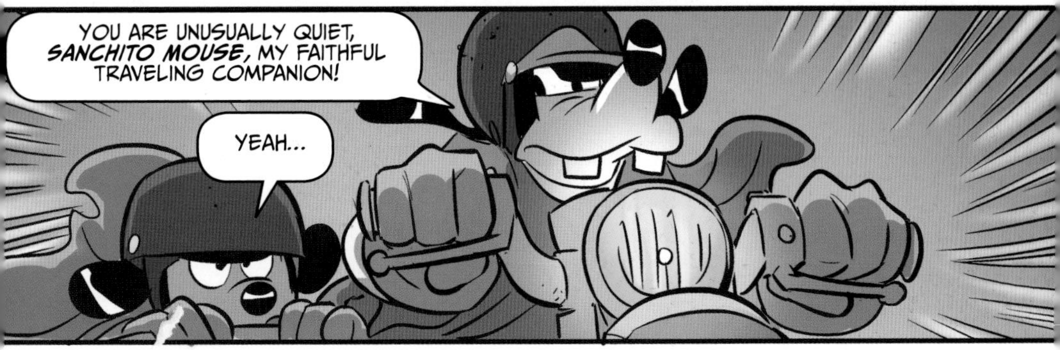
YOU ARE UNUSUALLY QUIET, *SANCHITO MOUSE*, MY FAITHFUL TRAVELING COMPANION!
YEAH...

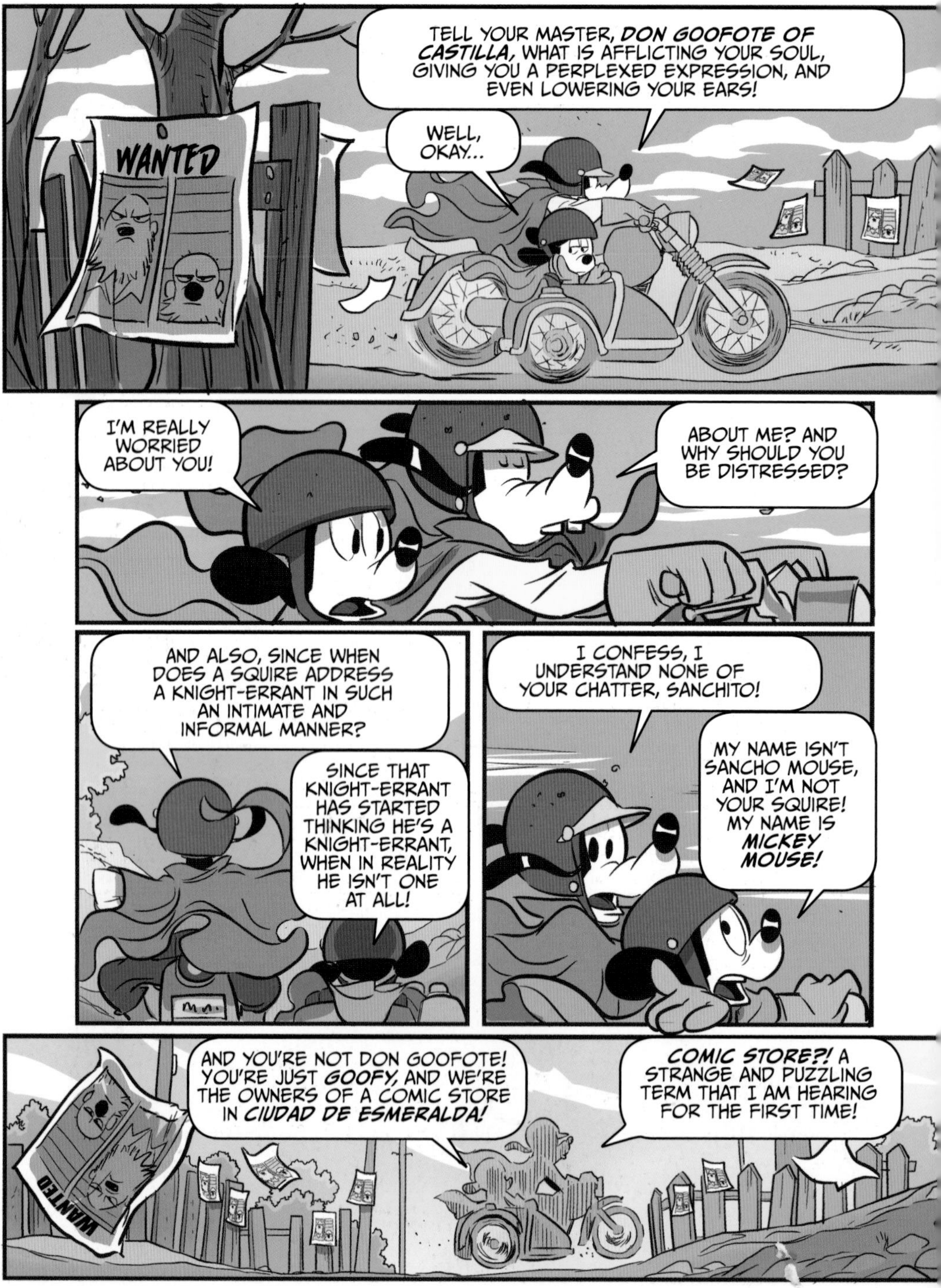
WANTED
TELL YOUR MASTER, DON GOOFOTE OF CASTILLA, WHAT IS AFFLICTING YOUR SOUL, GIVING YOU A PERPLEXED EXPRESSION, AND EVEN LOWERING YOUR EARS!
WELL, OKAY...
I'M REALLY WORRIED ABOUT YOU!
ABOUT ME? AND WHY SHOULD YOU BE DISTRESSED?
AND ALSO, SINCE WHEN DOES A SQUIRE ADDRESS A KNIGHT-ERRANT IN SUCH AN INTIMATE AND INFORMAL MANNER?
SINCE THAT KNIGHT-ERRANT HAS STARTED THINKING HE'S A KNIGHT-ERRANT, WHEN IN REALITY HE ISN'T ONE AT ALL!
I CONFESS, I UNDERSTAND NONE OF YOUR CHATTER, SANCHITO!
MY NAME ISN'T SANCHO MOUSE, AND I'M NOT YOUR SQUIRE! MY NAME IS MICKEY MOUSE!
AND YOU'RE NOT DON GOOFOTE! YOU'RE JUST GOOFY, AND WE'RE THE OWNERS OF A COMIC STORE IN CIUDAD DE ESMERALDA!
COMIC STORE?! A STRANGE AND PUZZLING TERM THAT I AM HEARING FOR THE FIRST TIME!
WANTED

TRY TO REMEMBER! THE OTHER DAY A BOX OF COMICS FELL ON YOUR HEAD, AND SINCE THEN YOU'VE THOUGHT YOU'RE A KNIGHT!

HMM...I BELIEVE I UNDERSTAND WHAT IS HAPPENING TO YOU!

YOU ARE UNDER A CURSE! THE POWERFUL WIZARD *KNUCKLEHEAD* HAS CLOUDED YOUR REASON WITH ONE OF HIS POWERFUL ENCHANTMENTS!

ON, NO...NOW THERE'S A WIZARD, TOO!

"THE WIZARD KNUCKLEHEAD, MY BITTER NEMESIS, PREVENTS OTHERS FROM SEEING REALITY, MAKING IT SEEM LIKE A DREAM OR, WORSE, A HALLUCINATION!"

THAT'S EXACTLY WHAT I'M TRYING TO TELL YOU! WHAT YOU THINK IS REAL ISN'T AT ALL!

WHAT SOLDIERS?

OH, ISN'T IT? AND WHAT ABOUT THOSE CAPTIVE SOLDIERS, THEN?

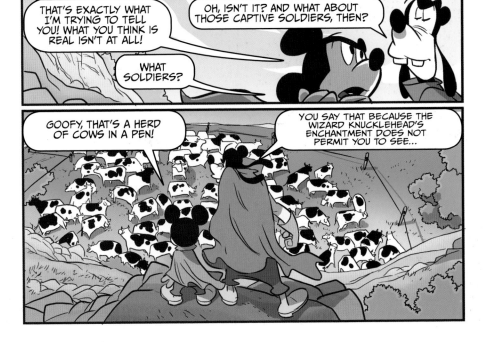

GOOFY, THAT'S A HERD OF COWS IN A PEN!

YOU SAY THAT BECAUSE THE WIZARD KNUCKLEHEAD'S ENCHANTMENT DOES NOT PERMIT YOU TO SEE...

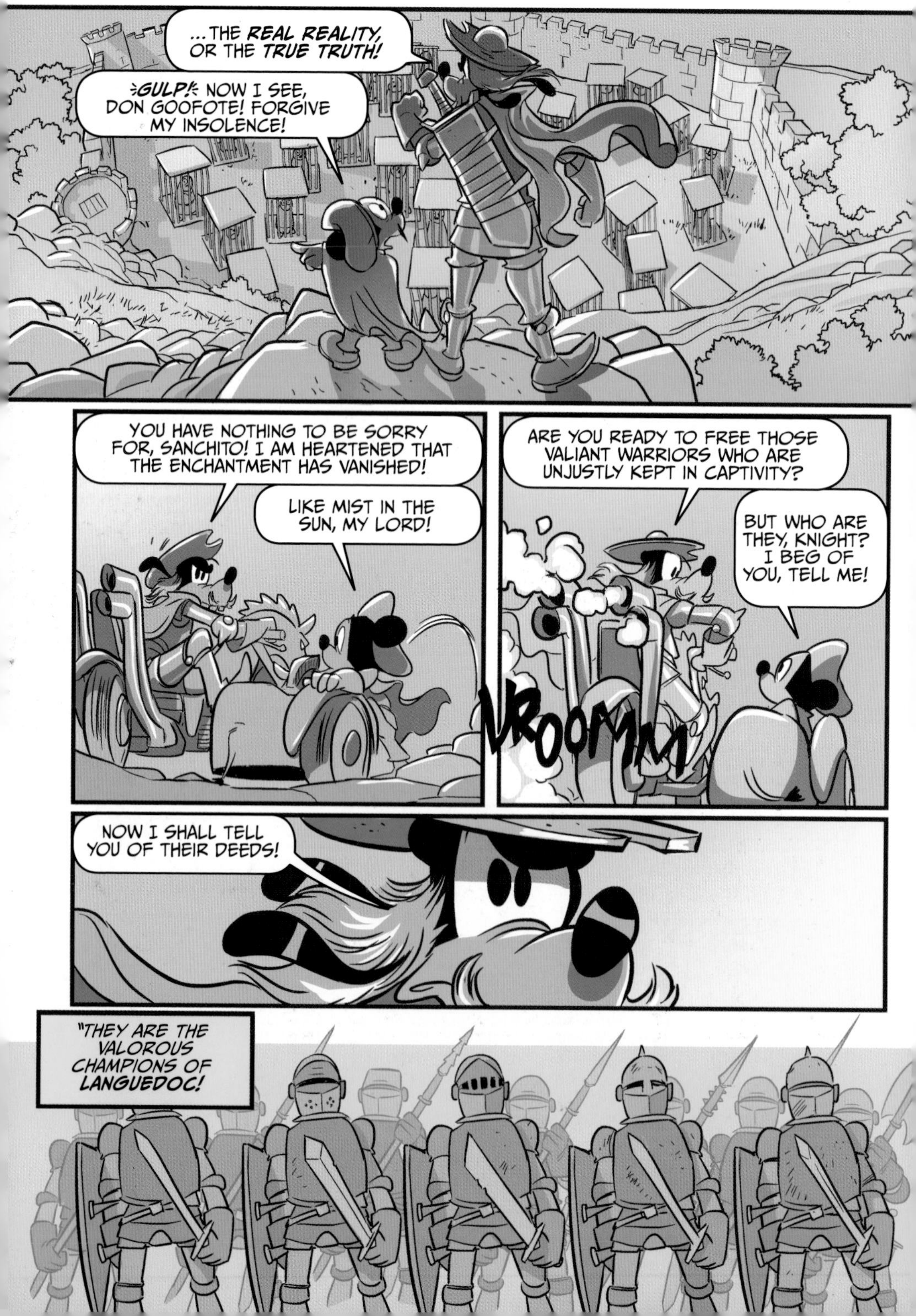
...THE REAL REALITY, OR THE TRUE TRUTH!
GULP! NOW I SEE, DON GOOFOTE! FORGIVE MY INSOLENCE!
YOU HAVE NOTHING TO BE SORRY FOR, SANCHITO! I AM HEARTENED THAT THE ENCHANTMENT HAS VANISHED!
LIKE MIST IN THE SUN, MY LORD!
ARE YOU READY TO FREE THOSE VALIANT WARRIORS WHO ARE UNJUSTLY KEPT IN CAPTIVITY?
BUT WHO ARE THEY, KNIGHT? I BEG OF YOU, TELL ME!
VROOMMM
NOW I SHALL TELL YOU OF THEIR DEEDS!
"THEY ARE THE VALOROUS CHAMPIONS OF LANGUEDOC!

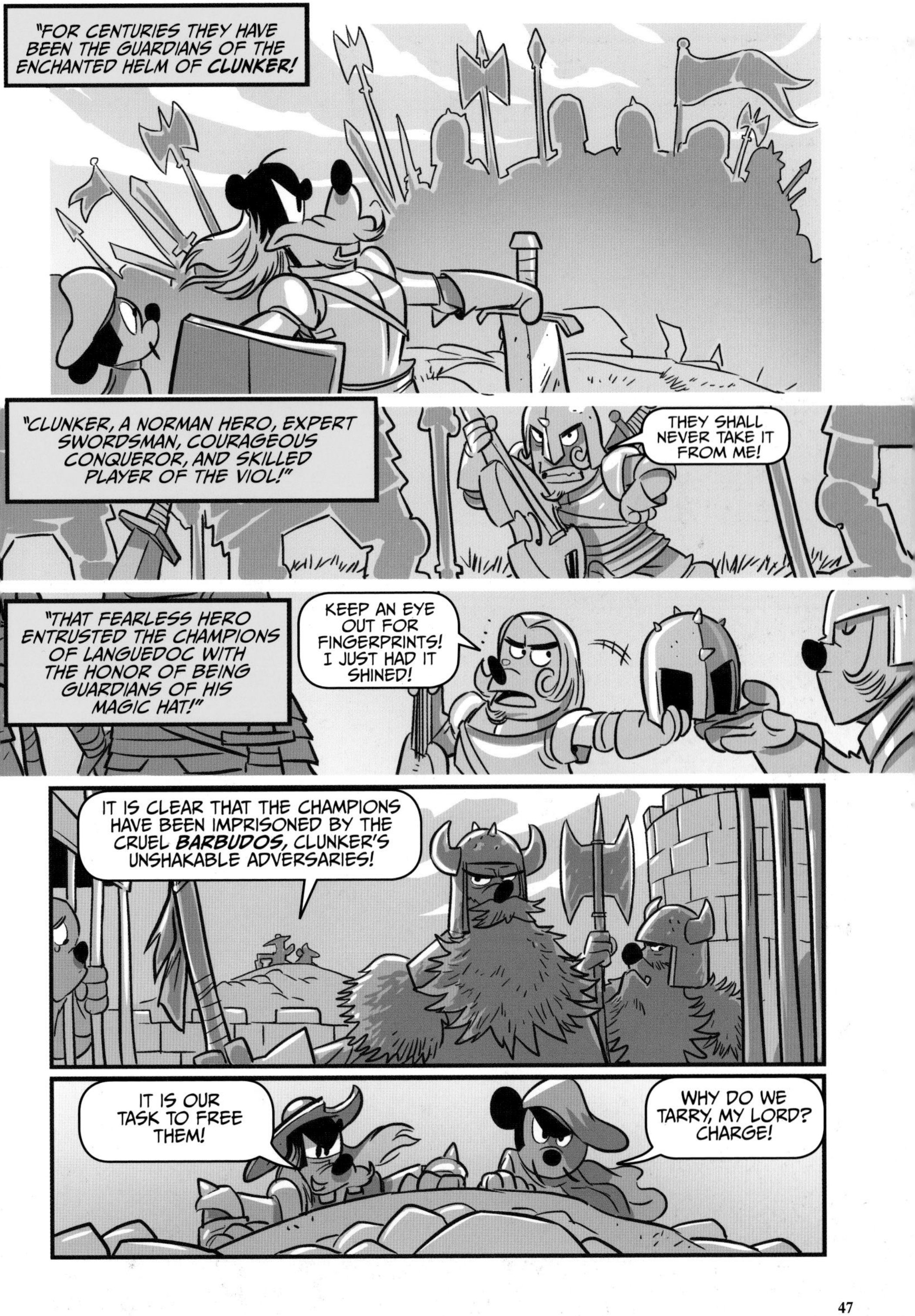
"FOR CENTURIES THEY HAVE BEEN THE GUARDIANS OF THE ENCHANTED HELM OF CLUNKER!
"CLUNKER, A NORMAN HERO, EXPERT SWORDSMAN, COURAGEOUS CONQUEROR, AND SKILLED PLAYER OF THE VIOL!"
THEY SHALL NEVER TAKE IT FROM ME!
"THAT FEARLESS HERO ENTRUSTED THE CHAMPIONS OF LANGUEDOC WITH THE HONOR OF BEING GUARDIANS OF HIS MAGIC HAT!"
KEEP AN EYE OUT FOR FINGERPRINTS! I JUST HAD IT SHINED!
IT IS CLEAR THAT THE CHAMPIONS HAVE BEEN IMPRISONED BY THE CRUEL BARBUDOS, CLUNKER'S UNSHAKABLE ADVERSARIES!
IT IS OUR TASK TO FREE THEM!
WHY DO WE TARRY, MY LORD? CHARGE!

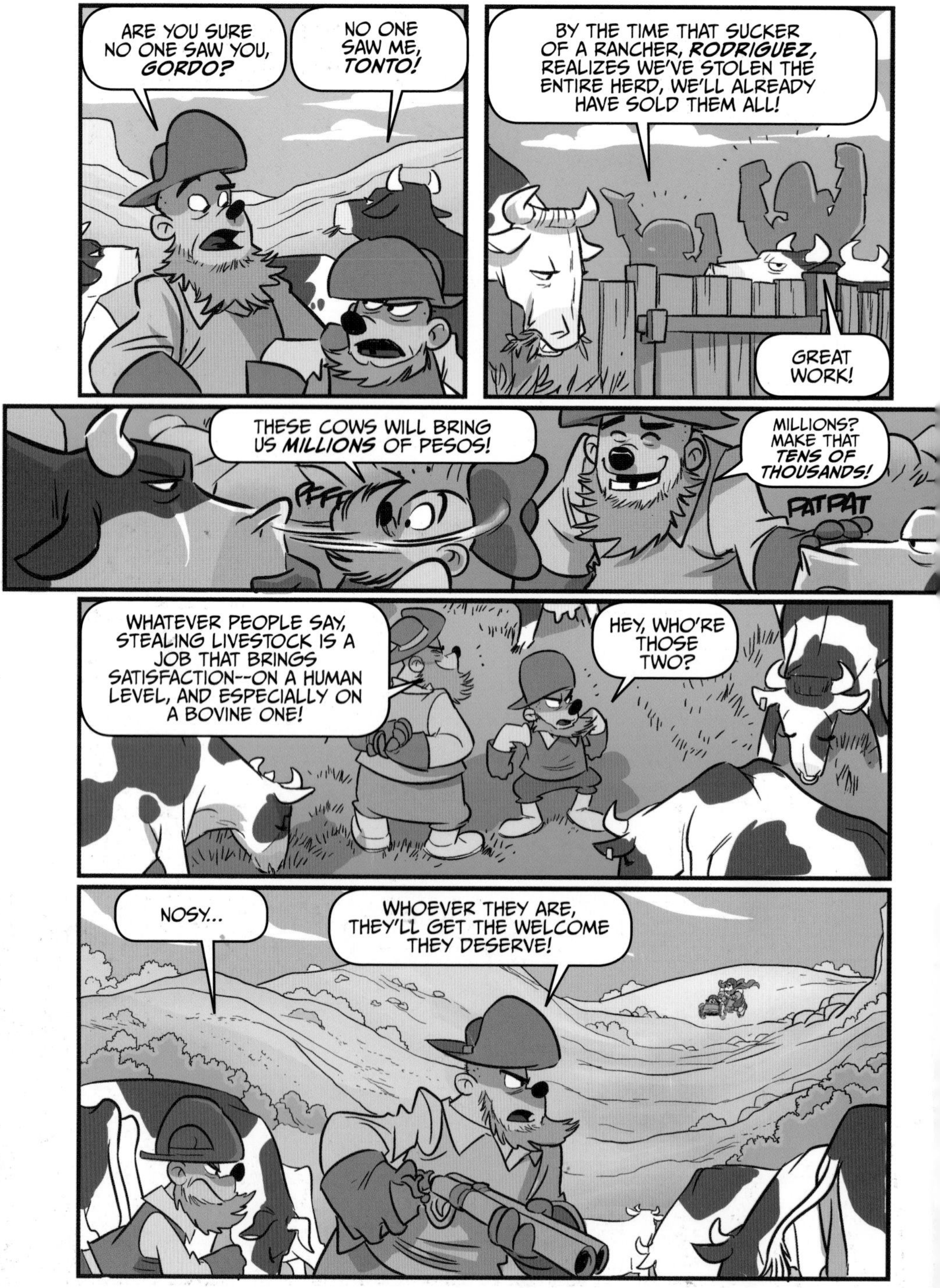

ARE YOU SURE NO ONE SAW YOU, GORDO?
NO ONE SAW ME, TONTO!
BY THE TIME THAT SUCKER OF A RANCHER, RODRIGUEZ, REALIZES WE'VE STOLEN THE ENTIRE HERD, WE'LL ALREADY HAVE SOLD THEM ALL!
GREAT WORK!
THESE COWS WILL BRING US MILLIONS OF PESOS!
PFFF
MILLIONS? MAKE THAT TENS OF THOUSANDS!
PAT PAT
WHATEVER PEOPLE SAY, STEALING LIVESTOCK IS A JOB THAT BRINGS SATISFACTION--ON A HUMAN LEVEL, AND ESPECIALLY ON A BOVINE ONE!
HEY, WHO'RE THOSE TWO?
NOSY...
WHOEVER THEY ARE, THEY'LL GET THE WELCOME THEY DESERVE!

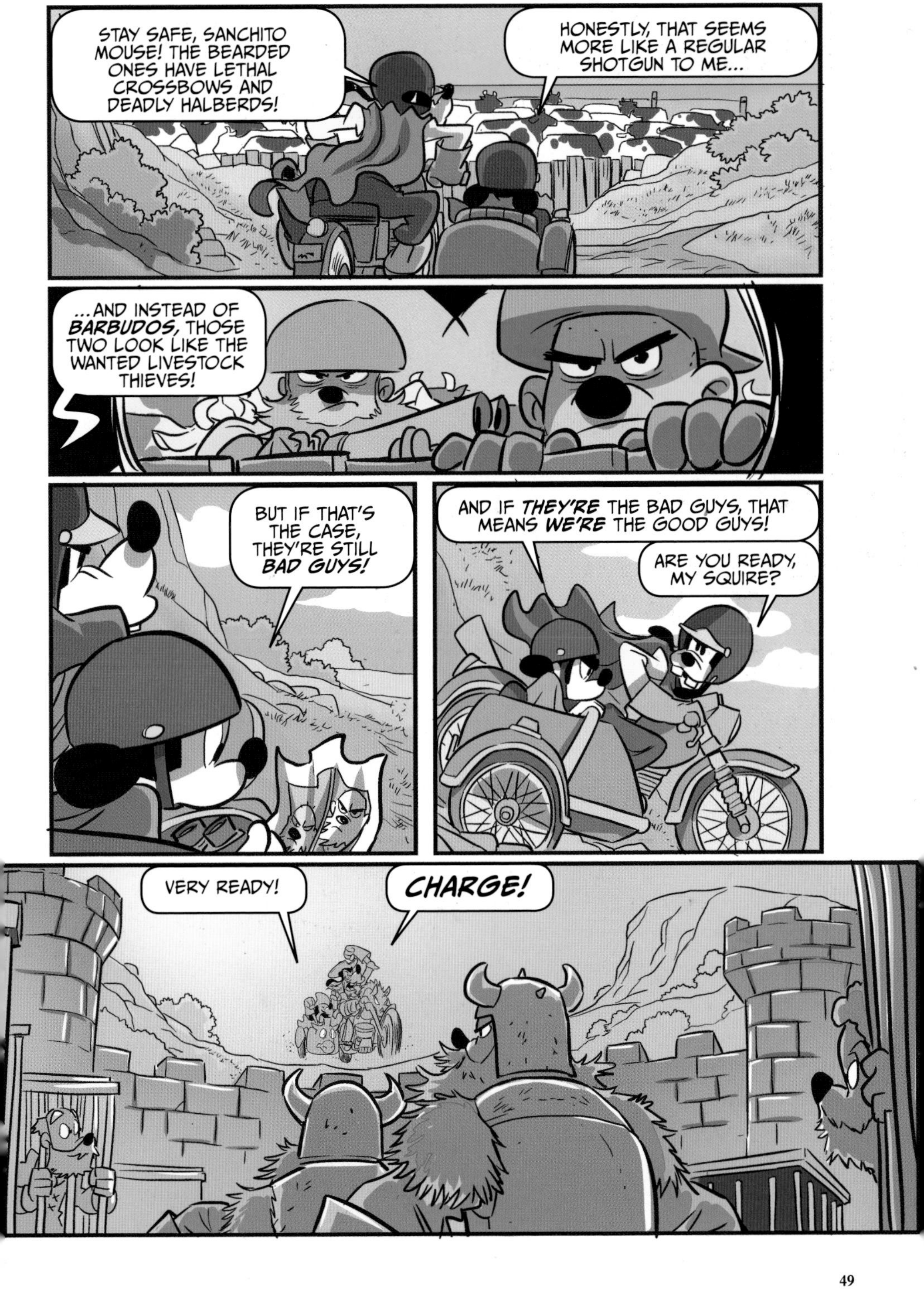
STAY SAFE, SANCHITO MOUSE! THE BEARDED ONES HAVE LETHAL CROSSBOWS AND DEADLY HALBERDS!
HONESTLY, THAT SEEMS MORE LIKE A REGULAR SHOTGUN TO ME...
...AND INSTEAD OF BARBUDOS, THOSE TWO LOOK LIKE THE WANTED LIVESTOCK THIEVES!
BUT IF THAT'S THE CASE, THEY'RE STILL BAD GUYS!
AND IF THEY'RE THE BAD GUYS, THAT MEANS WE'RE THE GOOD GUYS!
ARE YOU READY, MY SQUIRE?
VERY READY!
CHARGE!

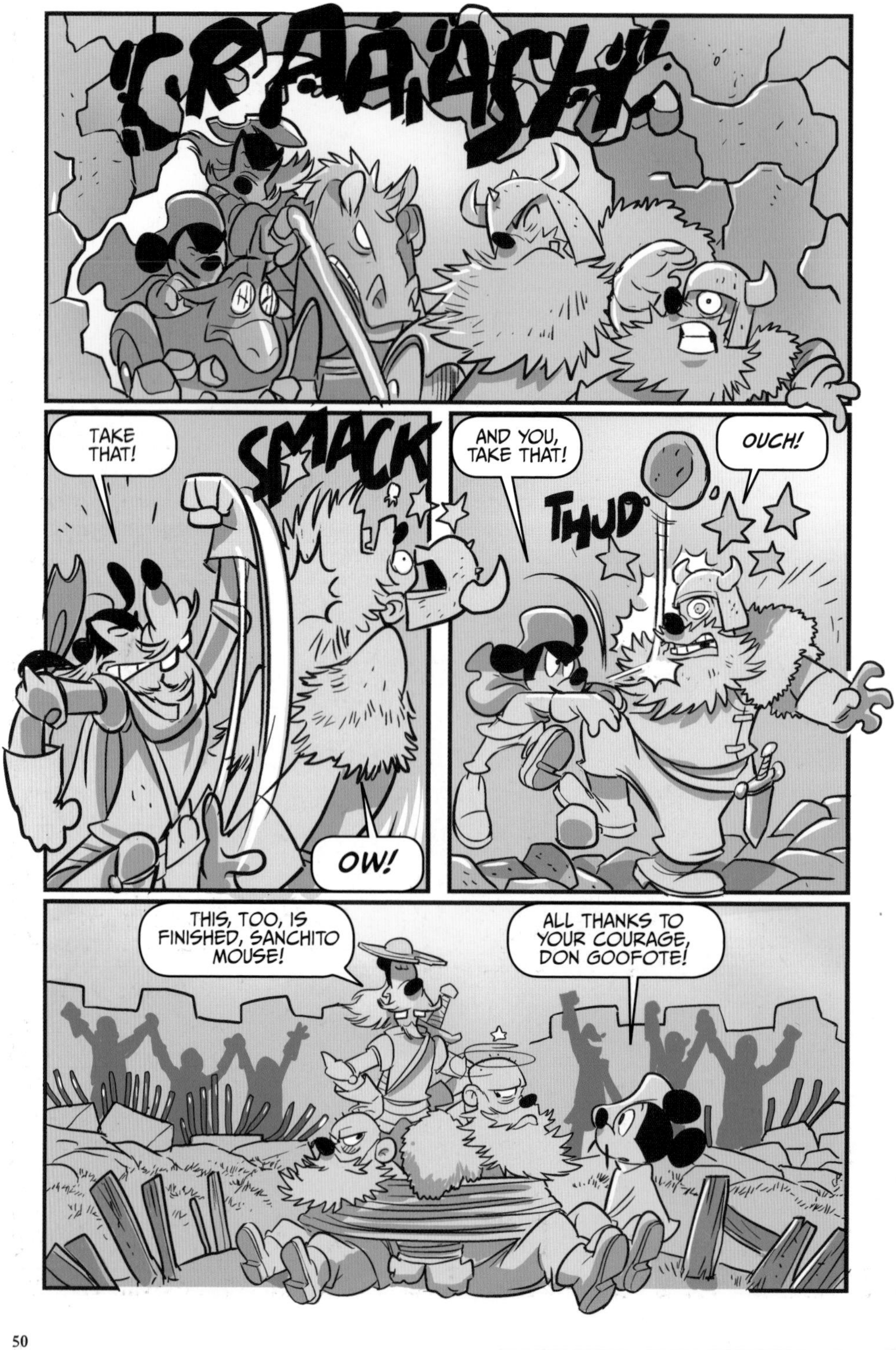
CRAAASH!
TAKE THAT!
SMACK
OW!
AND YOU, TAKE THAT!
THUD
OUCH!
THIS, TOO, IS FINISHED, SANCHITO MOUSE!
ALL THANKS TO YOUR COURAGE, DON GOOFOTE!

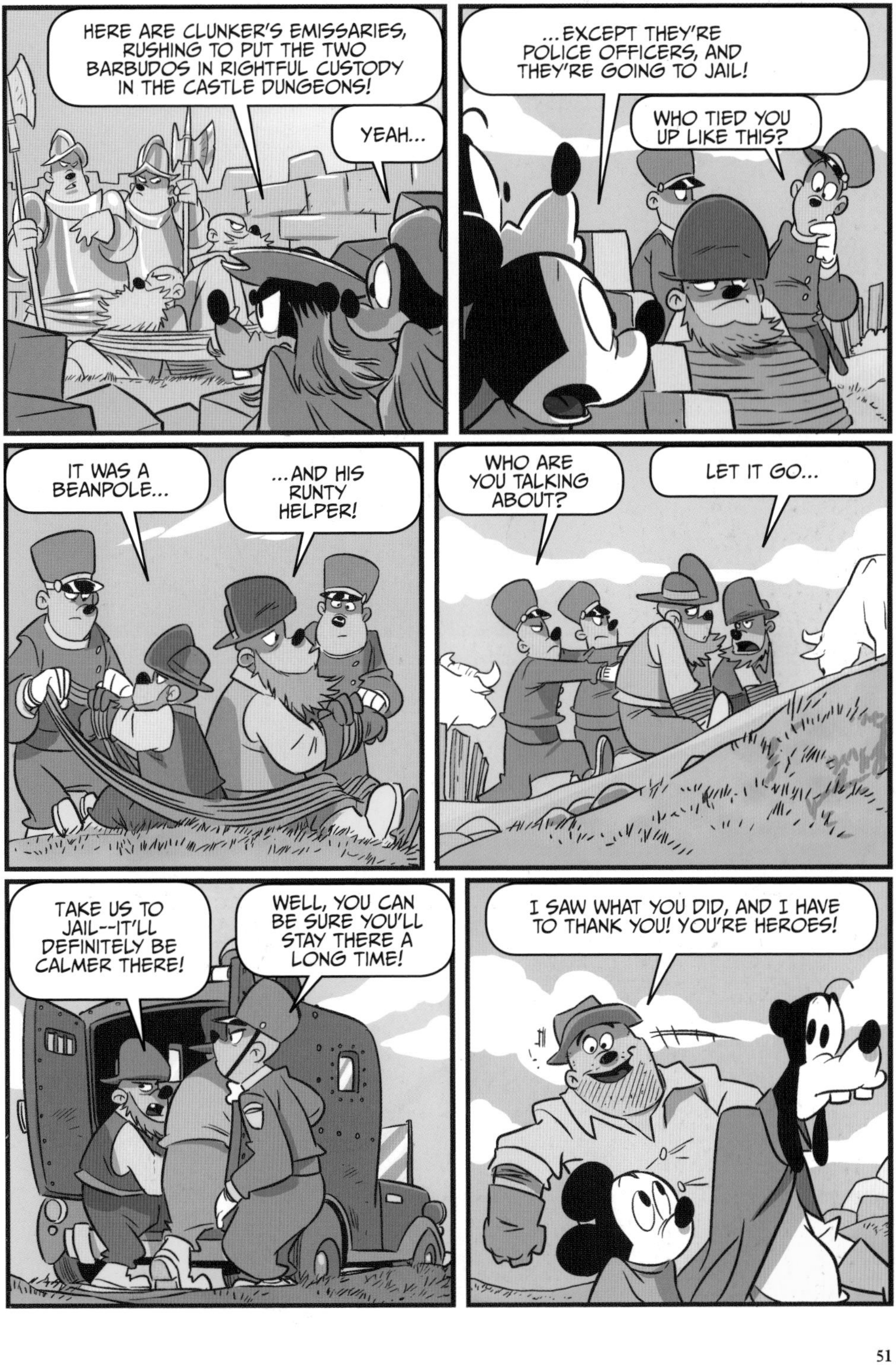
HERE ARE CLUNKER'S EMISSARIES, RUSHING TO PUT THE TWO BARBUDOS IN RIGHTFUL CUSTODY IN THE CASTLE DUNGEONS!
YEAH...
...EXCEPT THEY'RE POLICE OFFICERS, AND THEY'RE GOING TO JAIL!
WHO TIED YOU UP LIKE THIS?
IT WAS A BEANPOLE...
...AND HIS RUNTY HELPER!
WHO ARE YOU TALKING ABOUT?
LET IT GO...
TAKE US TO JAIL--IT'LL DEFINITELY BE CALMER THERE!
WELL, YOU CAN BE SURE YOU'LL STAY THERE A LONG TIME!
I SAW WHAT YOU DID, AND I HAVE TO THANK YOU! YOU'RE HEROES!

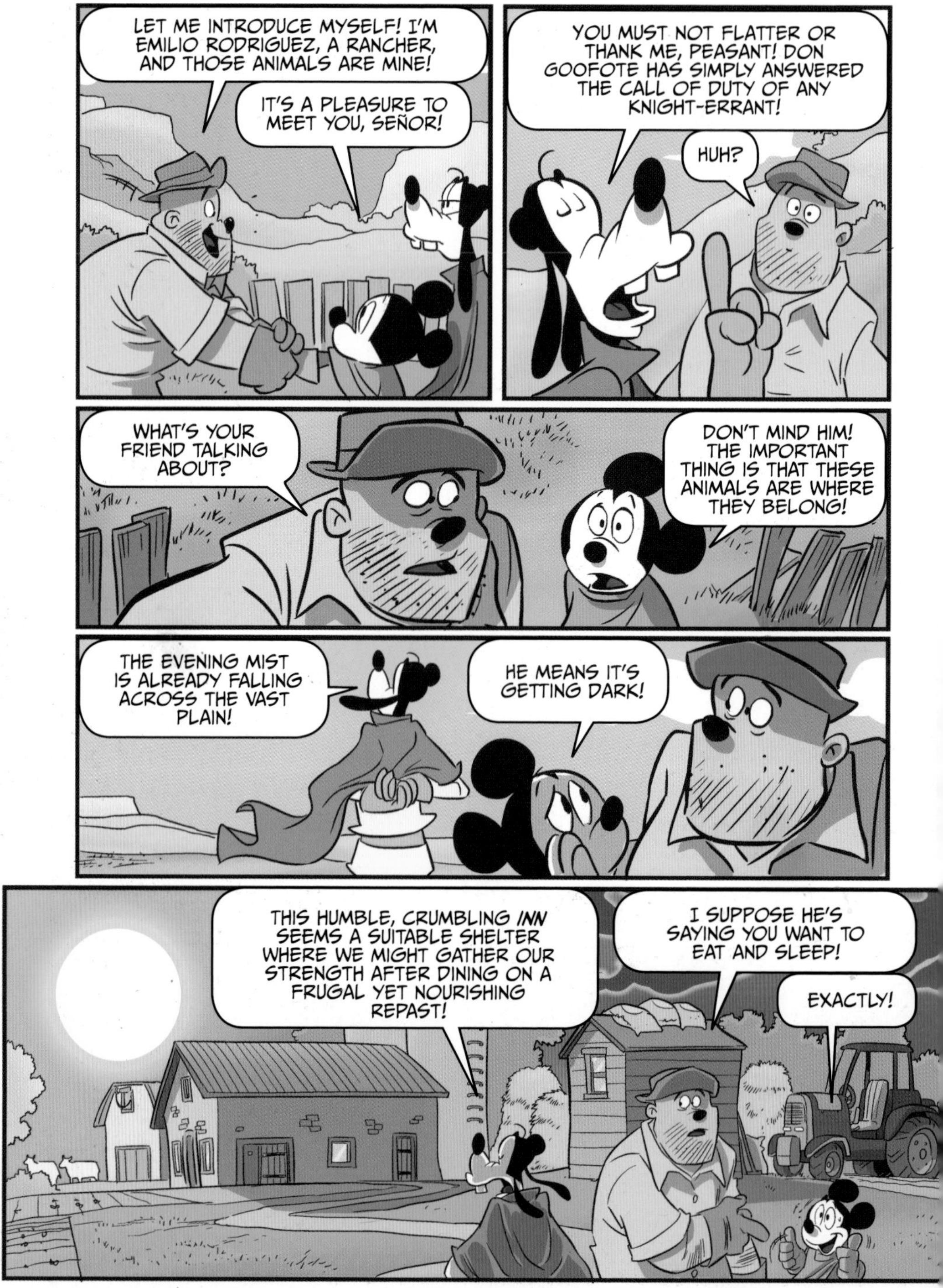
LET ME INTRODUCE MYSELF! I'M EMILIO RODRIGUEZ, A RANCHER, AND THOSE ANIMALS ARE MINE!
IT'S A PLEASURE TO MEET YOU, SEÑOR!
YOU MUST NOT FLATTER OR THANK ME, PEASANT! DON GOOFOTE HAS SIMPLY ANSWERED THE CALL OF DUTY OF ANY KNIGHT-ERRANT!
HUH?
WHAT'S YOUR FRIEND TALKING ABOUT?
DON'T MIND HIM! THE IMPORTANT THING IS THAT THESE ANIMALS ARE WHERE THEY BELONG!
THE EVENING MIST IS ALREADY FALLING ACROSS THE VAST PLAIN!
HE MEANS IT'S GETTING DARK!
THIS HUMBLE, CRUMBLING *INN* SEEMS A SUITABLE SHELTER WHERE WE MIGHT GATHER OUR STRENGTH AFTER DINING ON A FRUGAL YET NOURISHING REPAST!
I SUPPOSE HE'S SAYING YOU WANT TO EAT AND SLEEP!
EXACTLY!

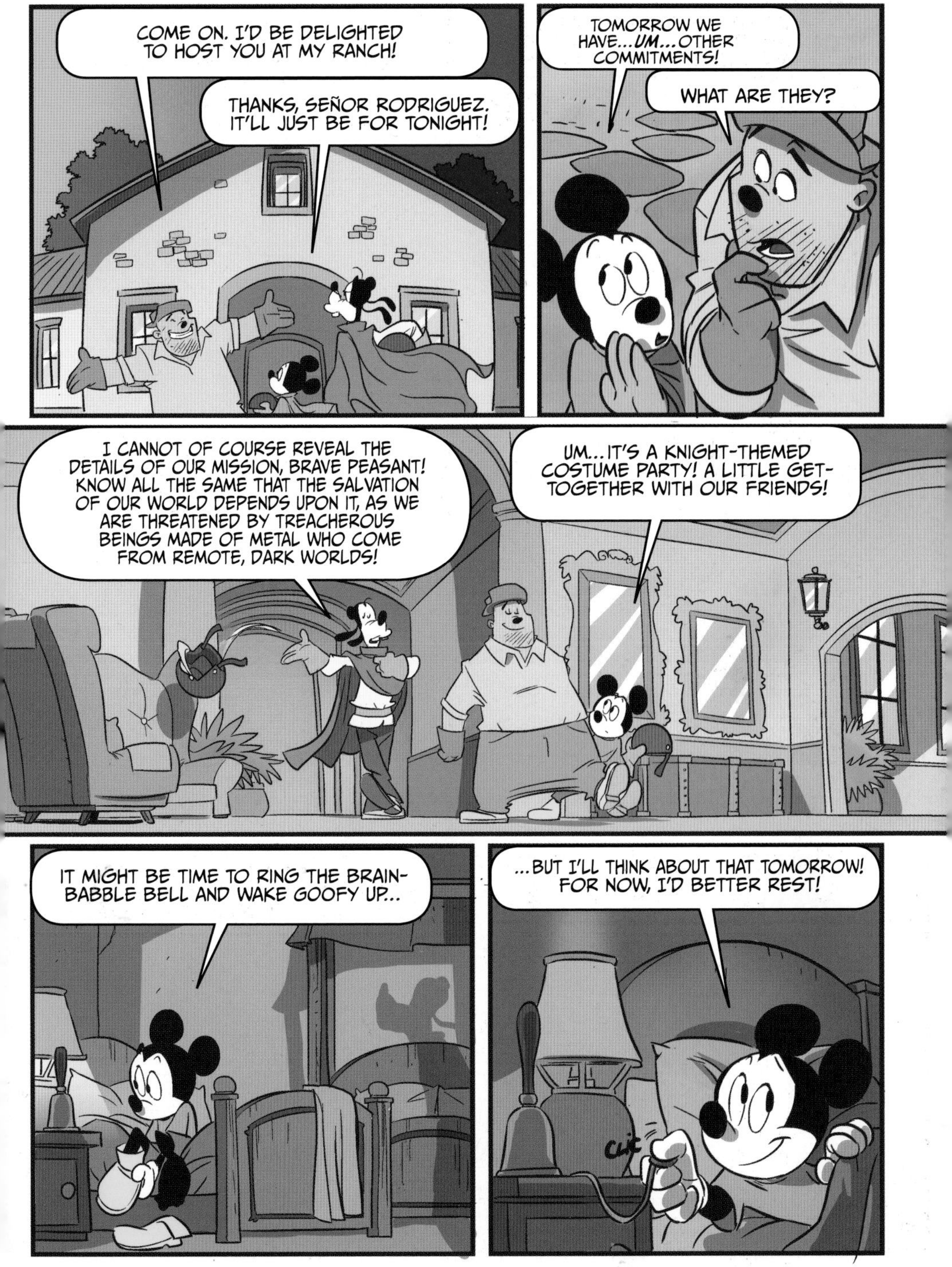
COME ON. I'D BE DELIGHTED TO HOST YOU AT MY RANCH!
THANKS, SEÑOR RODRIGUEZ. IT'LL JUST BE FOR TONIGHT!
TOMORROW WE HAVE... UM... OTHER COMMITMENTS!
WHAT ARE THEY?
I CANNOT OF COURSE REVEAL THE DETAILS OF OUR MISSION, BRAVE PEASANT! KNOW ALL THE SAME THAT THE SALVATION OF OUR WORLD DEPENDS UPON IT, AS WE ARE THREATENED BY TREACHEROUS BEINGS MADE OF METAL WHO COME FROM REMOTE, DARK WORLDS!
UM... IT'S A KNIGHT-THEMED COSTUME PARTY! A LITTLE GET-TOGETHER WITH OUR FRIENDS!
IT MIGHT BE TIME TO RING THE BRAIN-BABBLE BELL AND WAKE GOOFY UP...
...BUT I'LL THINK ABOUT THAT TOMORROW! FOR NOW, I'D BETTER REST!
CLIC

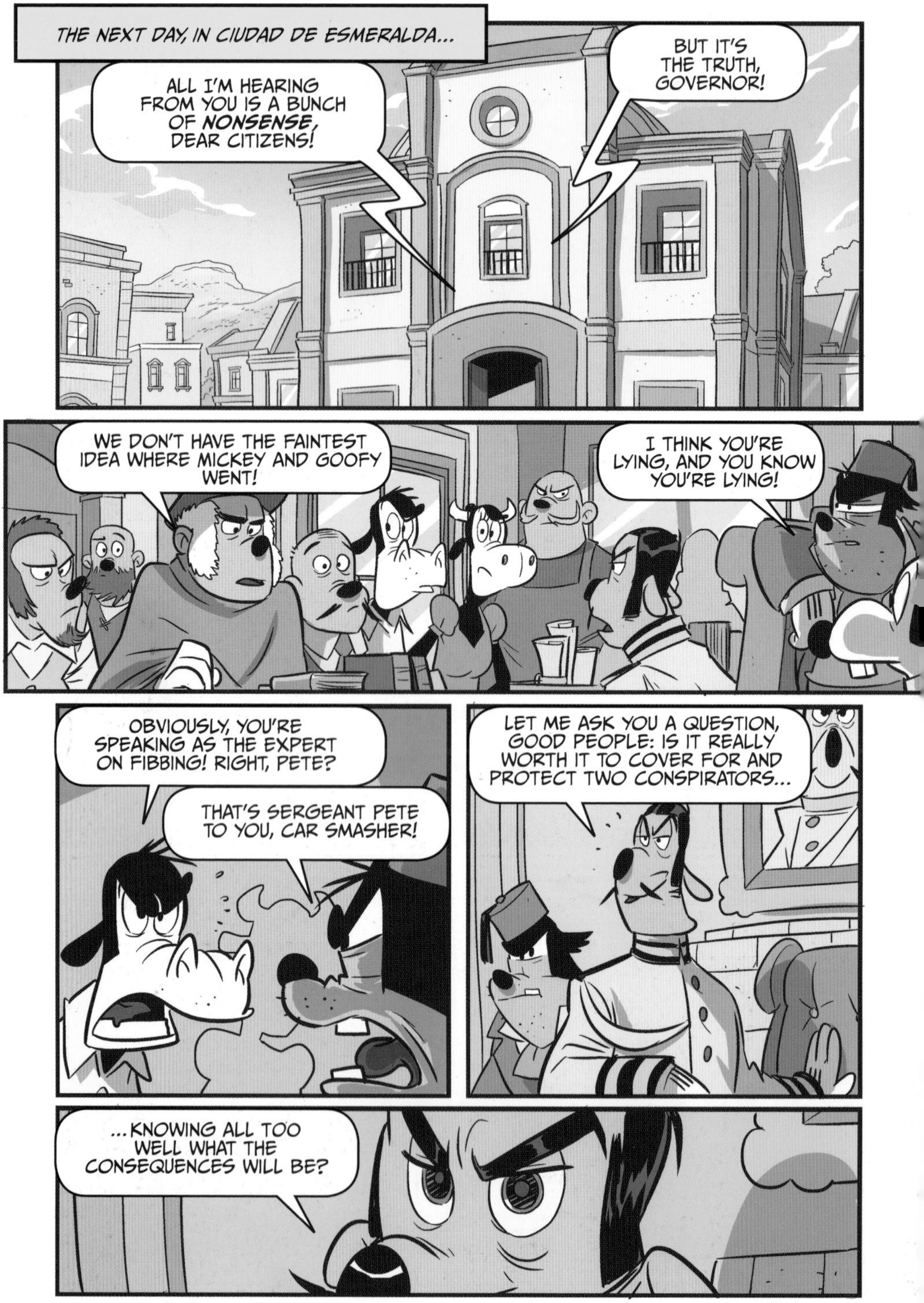
THE NEXT DAY, IN CIUDAD DE ESMERALDA...
ALL I'M HEARING FROM YOU IS A BUNCH OF NONSENSE, DEAR CITIZENS!
BUT IT'S THE TRUTH, GOVERNOR!
WE DON'T HAVE THE FAINTEST IDEA WHERE MICKEY AND GOOFY WENT!
I THINK YOU'RE LYING, AND YOU KNOW YOU'RE LYING!
OBVIOUSLY, YOU'RE SPEAKING AS THE EXPERT ON FIBBING! RIGHT, PETE?
THAT'S SERGEANT PETE TO YOU, CAR SMASHER!
LET ME ASK YOU A QUESTION, GOOD PEOPLE: IS IT REALLY WORTH IT TO COVER FOR AND PROTECT TWO CONSPIRATORS...
...KNOWING ALL TOO WELL WHAT THE CONSEQUENCES WILL BE?

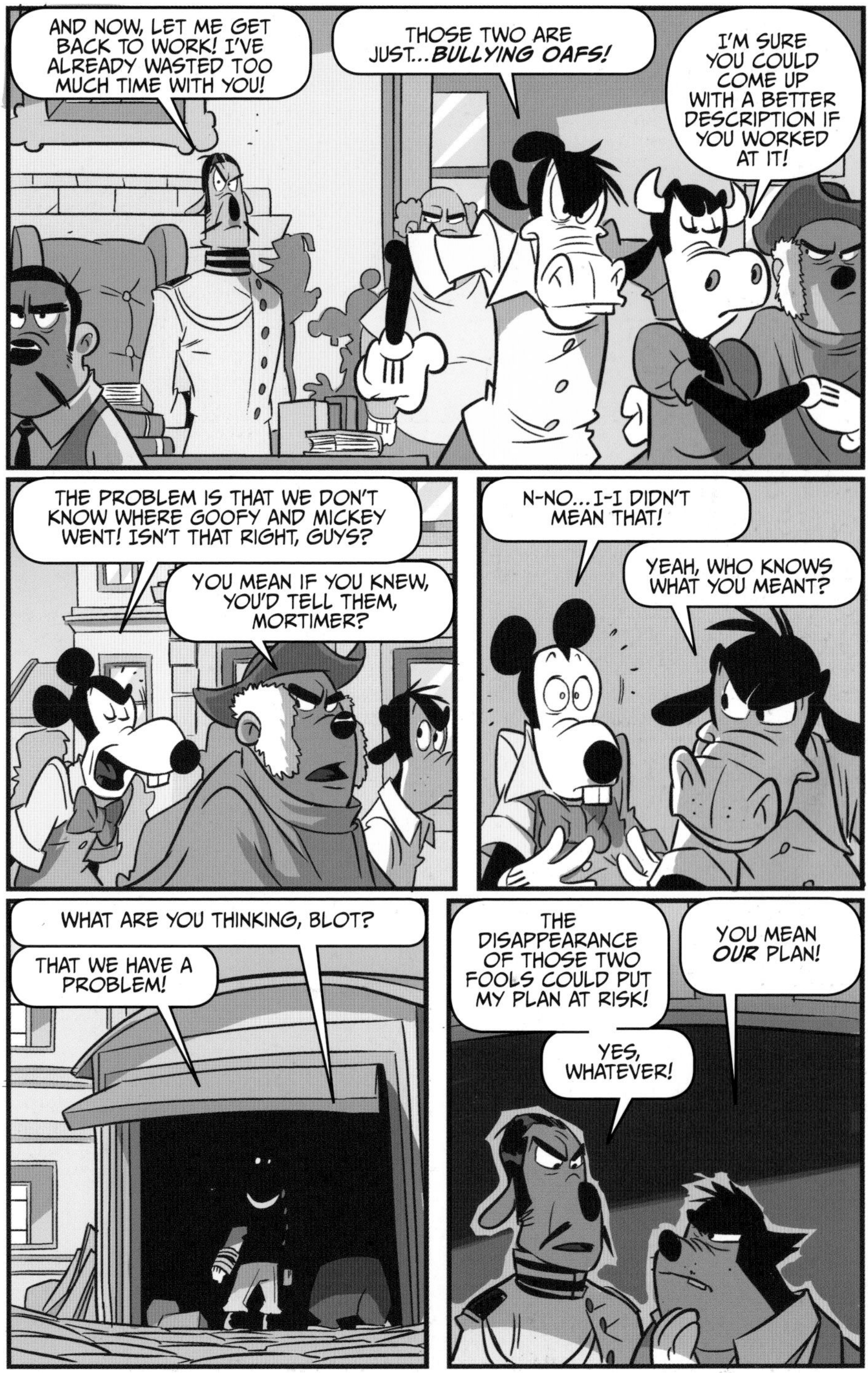

AND NOW, LET ME GET BACK TO WORK! I'VE ALREADY WASTED TOO MUCH TIME WITH YOU!
THOSE TWO ARE JUST...**BULLYING OAFS!**
I'M SURE YOU COULD COME UP WITH A BETTER DESCRIPTION IF YOU WORKED AT IT!
THE PROBLEM IS THAT WE DON'T KNOW WHERE GOOFY AND MICKEY WENT! ISN'T THAT RIGHT, GUYS?
YOU MEAN IF YOU KNEW, YOU'D TELL THEM, MORTIMER?
N-NO... I-I DIDN'T MEAN THAT!
YEAH, WHO KNOWS WHAT YOU MEANT?
WHAT ARE YOU THINKING, BLOT?
THAT WE HAVE A PROBLEM!
THE DISAPPEARANCE OF THOSE TWO FOOLS COULD PUT MY PLAN AT RISK!
YOU MEAN ***OUR*** PLAN!
YES, WHATEVER!

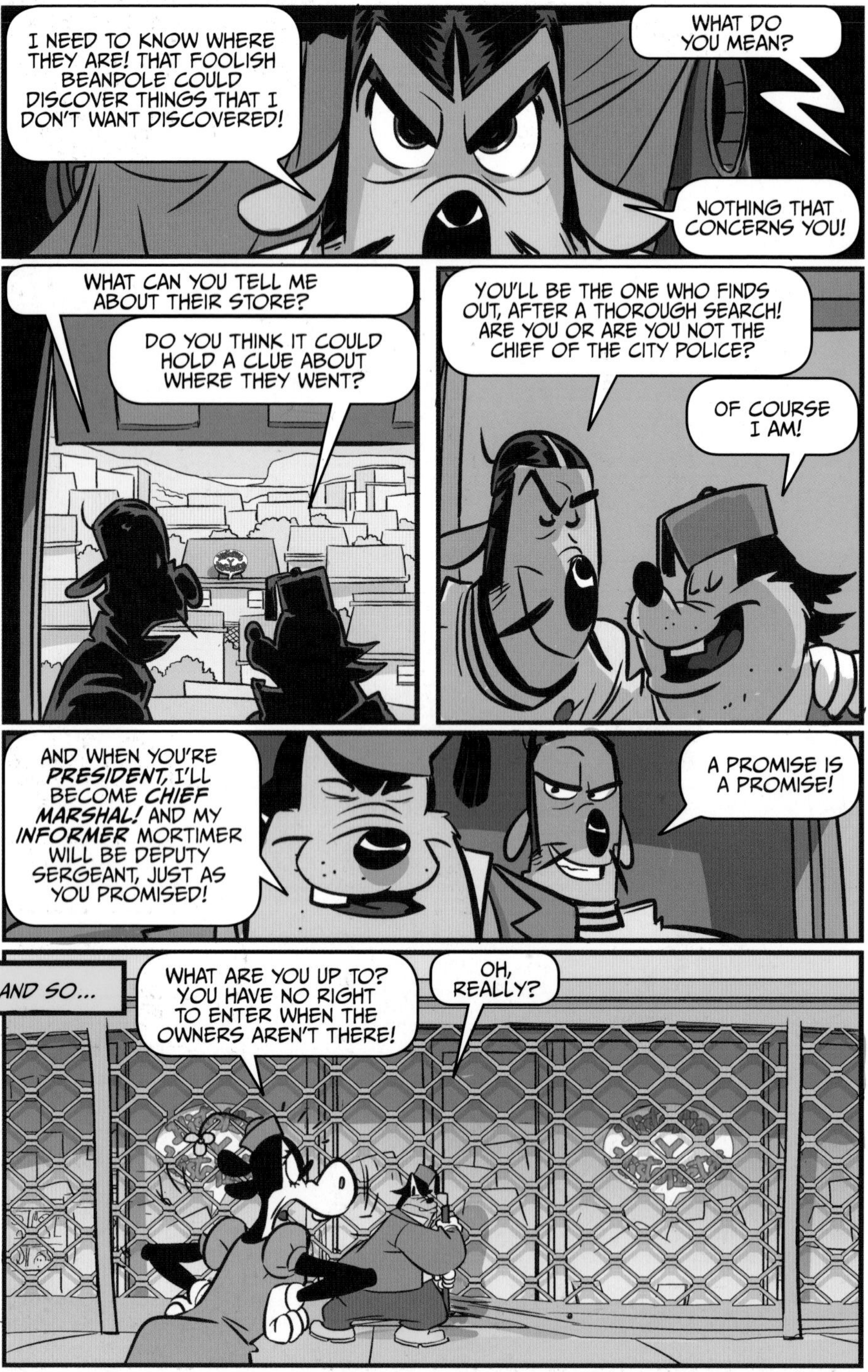
I NEED TO KNOW WHERE THEY ARE! THAT FOOLISH BEANPOLE COULD DISCOVER THINGS THAT I DON'T WANT DISCOVERED!
WHAT DO YOU MEAN?
NOTHING THAT CONCERNS YOU!
WHAT CAN YOU TELL ME ABOUT THEIR STORE?
DO YOU THINK IT COULD HOLD A CLUE ABOUT WHERE THEY WENT?
YOU'LL BE THE ONE WHO FINDS OUT, AFTER A THOROUGH SEARCH! ARE YOU OR ARE YOU NOT THE CHIEF OF THE CITY POLICE?
OF COURSE I AM!
AND WHEN YOU'RE PRESIDENT, I'LL BECOME CHIEF MARSHAL! AND MY INFORMER MORTIMER WILL BE DEPUTY SERGEANT, JUST AS YOU PROMISED!
A PROMISE IS A PROMISE!
AND SO...
WHAT ARE YOU UP TO? YOU HAVE NO RIGHT TO ENTER WHEN THE OWNERS AREN'T THERE!
OH, REALLY?

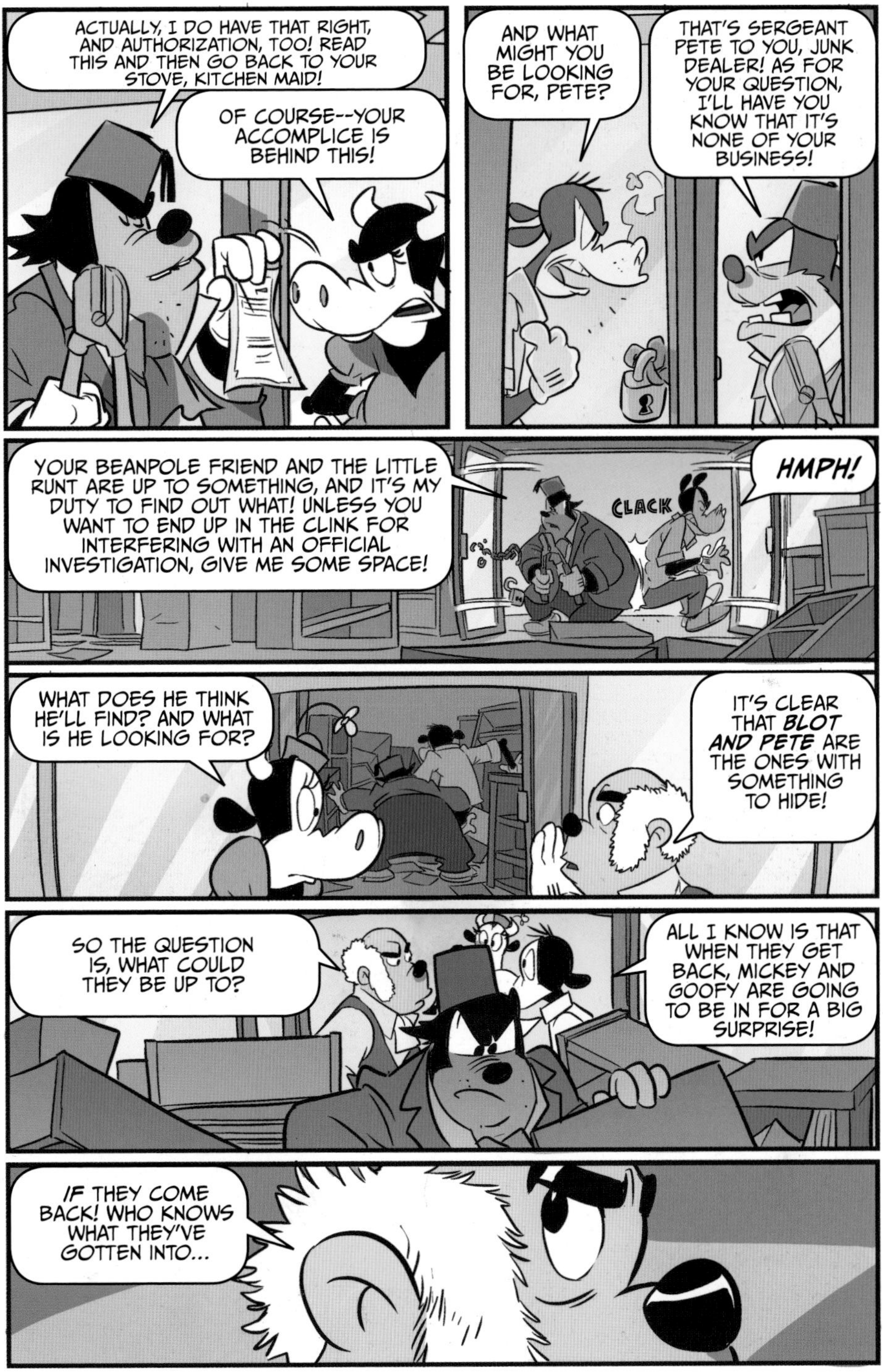
ACTUALLY, I DO HAVE THAT RIGHT, AND AUTHORIZATION, TOO! READ THIS AND THEN GO BACK TO YOUR STOVE, KITCHEN MAID!
OF COURSE--YOUR ACCOMPLICE IS BEHIND THIS!
AND WHAT MIGHT YOU BE LOOKING FOR, PETE?
THAT'S SERGEANT PETE TO YOU, JUNK DEALER! AS FOR YOUR QUESTION, I'LL HAVE YOU KNOW THAT IT'S NONE OF YOUR BUSINESS!
YOUR BEANPOLE FRIEND AND THE LITTLE RUNT ARE UP TO SOMETHING, AND IT'S MY DUTY TO FIND OUT WHAT! UNLESS YOU WANT TO END UP IN THE CLINK FOR INTERFERING WITH AN OFFICIAL INVESTIGATION, GIVE ME SOME SPACE!
CLACK
HMPH!
WHAT DOES HE THINK HE'LL FIND? AND WHAT IS HE LOOKING FOR?
IT'S CLEAR THAT BLOT AND PETE ARE THE ONES WITH SOMETHING TO HIDE!
SO THE QUESTION IS, WHAT COULD THEY BE UP TO?
ALL I KNOW IS THAT WHEN THEY GET BACK, MICKEY AND GOOFY ARE GOING TO BE IN FOR A BIG SURPRISE!
IF THEY COME BACK! WHO KNOWS WHAT THEY'VE GOTTEN INTO...

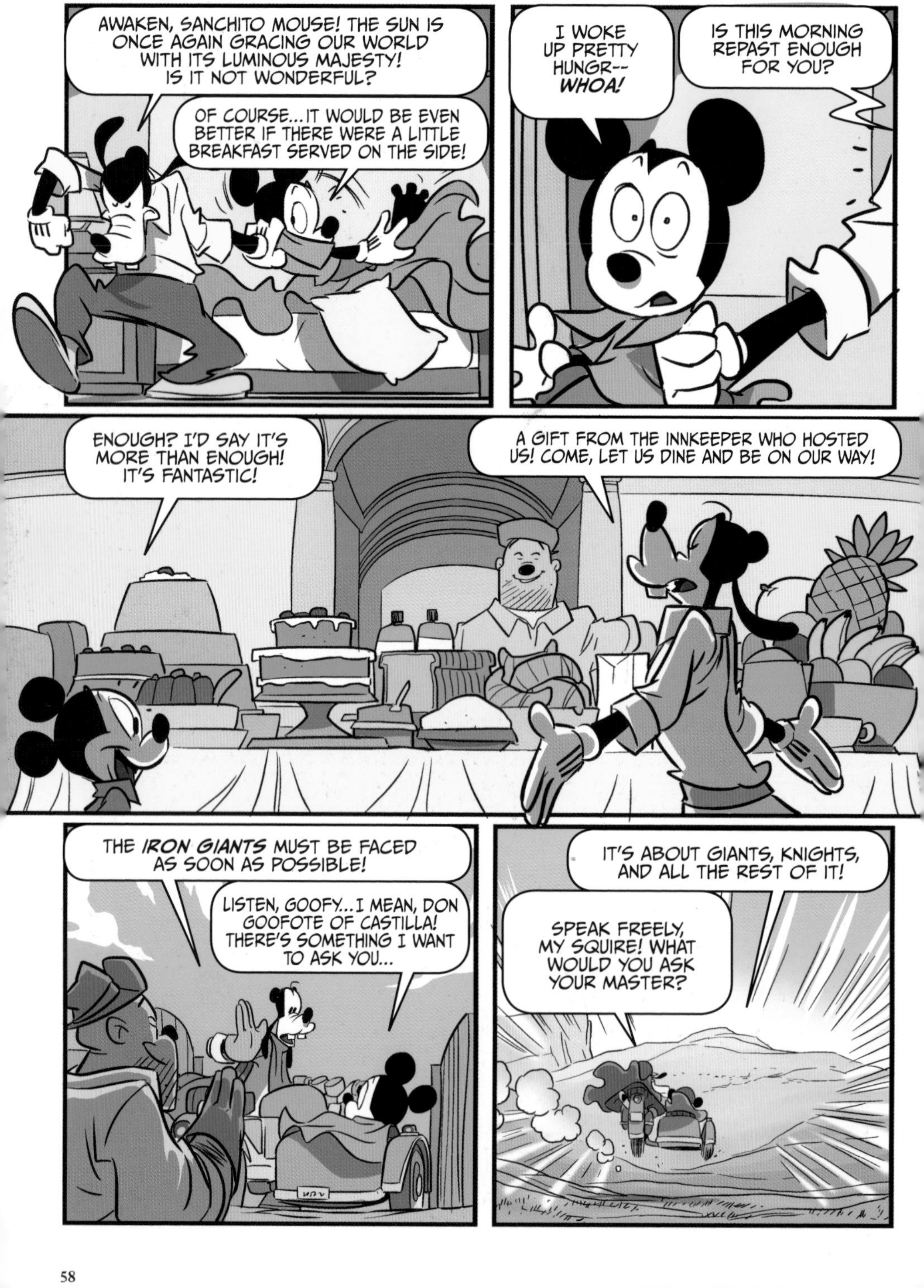
AWAKEN, SANCHITO MOUSE! THE SUN IS ONCE AGAIN GRACING OUR WORLD WITH ITS LUMINOUS MAJESTY! IS IT NOT WONDERFUL?
OF COURSE... IT WOULD BE EVEN BETTER IF THERE WERE A LITTLE BREAKFAST SERVED ON THE SIDE!
I WOKE UP PRETTY HUNGR-- WHOA!
IS THIS MORNING REPAST ENOUGH FOR YOU?
ENOUGH? I'D SAY IT'S MORE THAN ENOUGH! IT'S FANTASTIC!
A GIFT FROM THE INNKEEPER WHO HOSTED US! COME, LET US DINE AND BE ON OUR WAY!
THE IRON GIANTS MUST BE FACED AS SOON AS POSSIBLE!
LISTEN, GOOFY... I MEAN, DON GOOFOTE OF CASTILLA! THERE'S SOMETHING I WANT TO ASK YOU...
SPEAK FREELY, MY SQUIRE! WHAT WOULD YOU ASK YOUR MASTER?
IT'S ABOUT GIANTS, KNIGHTS, AND ALL THE REST OF IT!

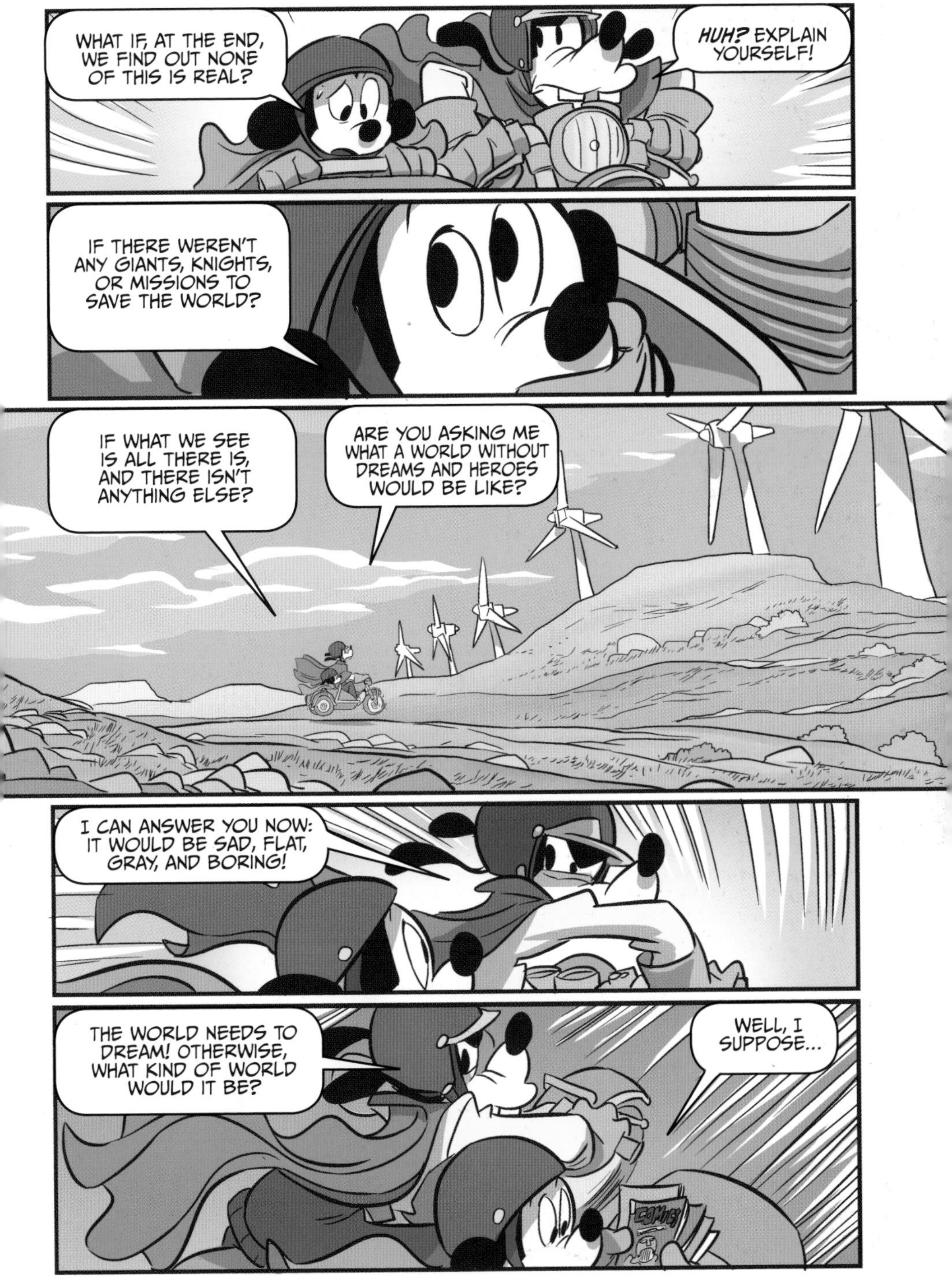
WHAT IF, AT THE END, WE FIND OUT NONE OF THIS IS REAL?
HUH? EXPLAIN YOURSELF!
IF THERE WEREN'T ANY GIANTS, KNIGHTS, OR MISSIONS TO SAVE THE WORLD?
IF WHAT WE SEE IS ALL THERE IS, AND THERE ISN'T ANYTHING ELSE?
ARE YOU ASKING ME WHAT A WORLD WITHOUT DREAMS AND HEROES WOULD BE LIKE?
I CAN ANSWER YOU NOW: IT WOULD BE SAD, FLAT, GRAY, AND BORING!
THE WORLD NEEDS TO DREAM! OTHERWISE, WHAT KIND OF WORLD WOULD IT BE?
WELL, I SUPPOSE...

FORTUNATELY, HEROES DO EXIST, AND SO DO GIANTS TO BATTLE! AND NOW, ENOUGH OF THIS IDLE CHITCHAT--IT IS TIME FOR ACTION!

WHAT KIND OF ACTION?

⸘GASP!⸘ WHAT DO I SPY WITH MY BINOCULARED EYES?

WHAT IS IT?

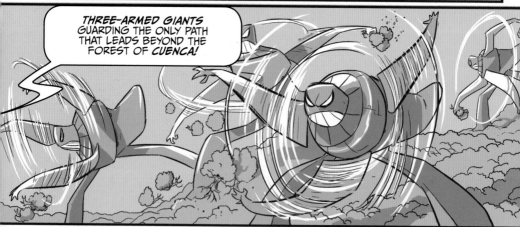

THREE-ARMED GIANTS GUARDING THE ONLY PATH THAT LEADS BEYOND THE FOREST OF CUENCA!

THOSE AREN'T THREE-ARMED GIANTS--THEY'RE WIND TURBINES! WINDMILLS THAT PRODUCE ELECTRICITY!

⸘TSK⸘ ...I DO NOT WISH YOU TO BE FURTHER BESPELLED!

THEY ARE SHAPE-SHIFTING CREATURES, CAPABLE OF TRICKING THE SENSES AND MAKING YOU SEE WHAT THEY WANT!

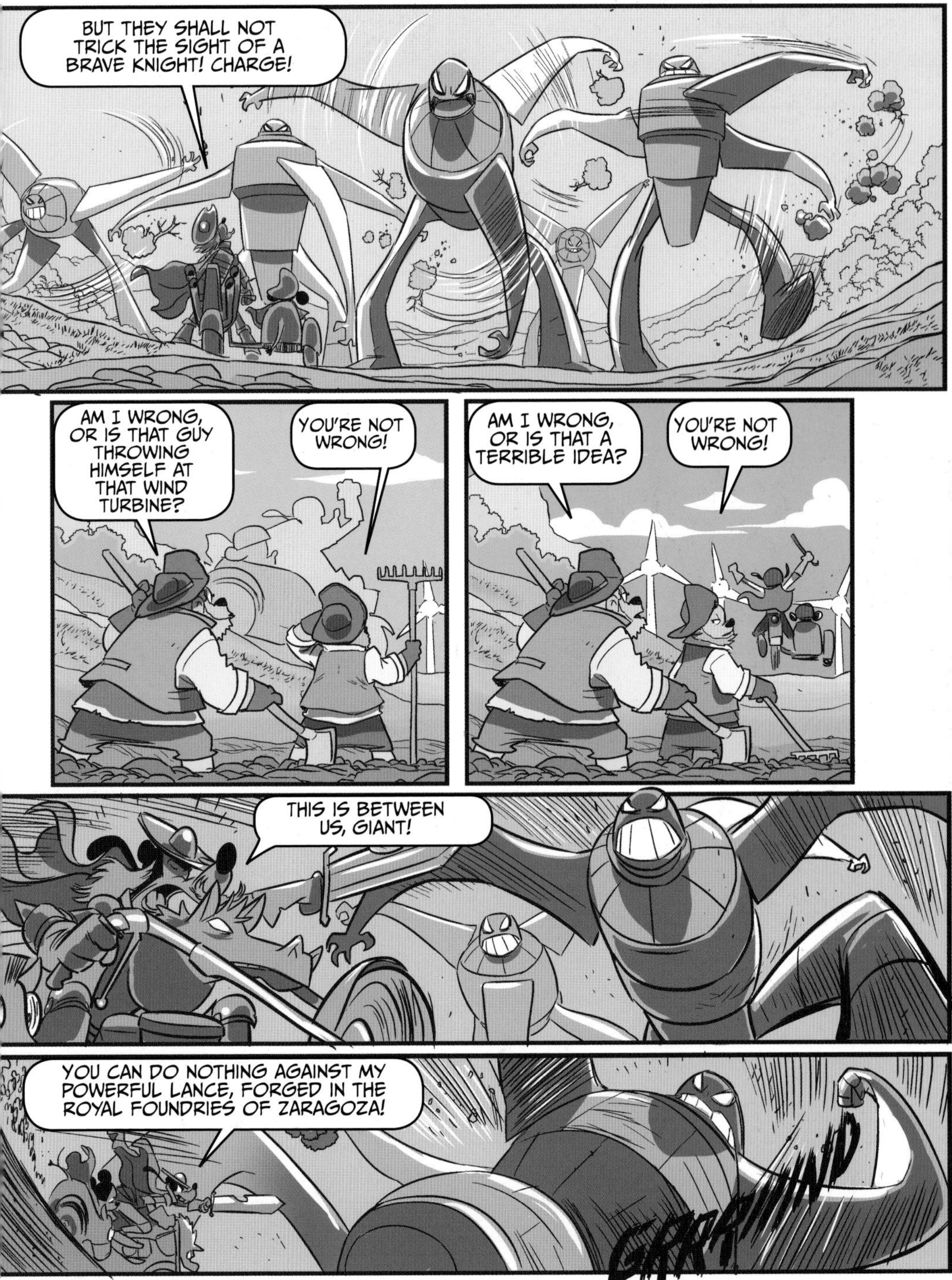

BUT THEY SHALL NOT TRICK THE SIGHT OF A BRAVE KNIGHT! CHARGE!
AM I WRONG, OR IS THAT GUY THROWING HIMSELF AT THAT WIND TURBINE?
YOU'RE NOT WRONG!
AM I WRONG, OR IS THAT A TERRIBLE IDEA?
YOU'RE NOT WRONG!
THIS IS BETWEEN US, GIANT!
YOU CAN DO NOTHING AGAINST MY POWERFUL LANCE, FORGED IN THE ROYAL FOUNDRIES OF ZARAGOZA!

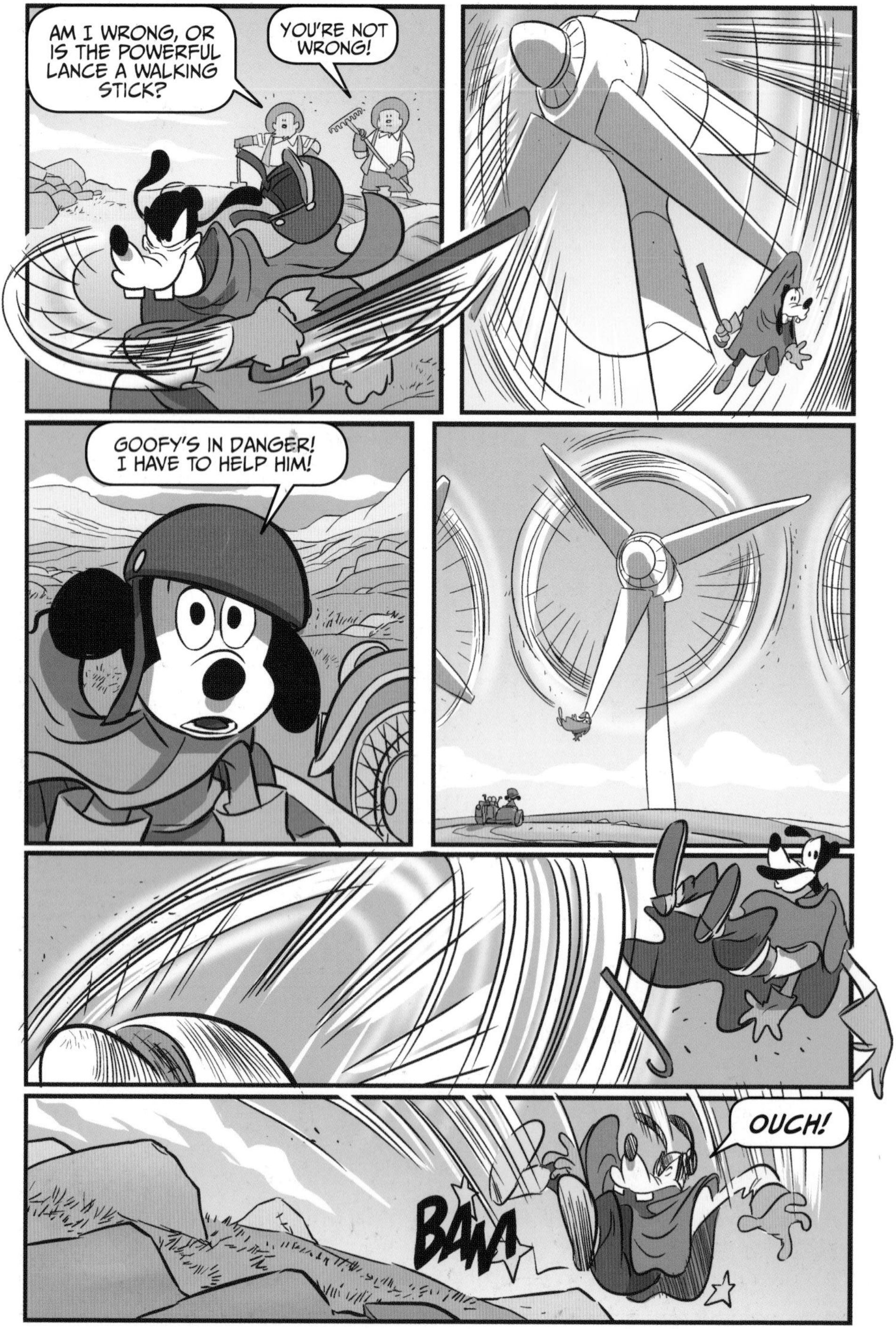
AM I WRONG, OR IS THE POWERFUL LANCE A WALKING STICK?
YOU'RE NOT WRONG!
GOOFY'S IN DANGER! I HAVE TO HELP HIM!
BAM
OUCH!

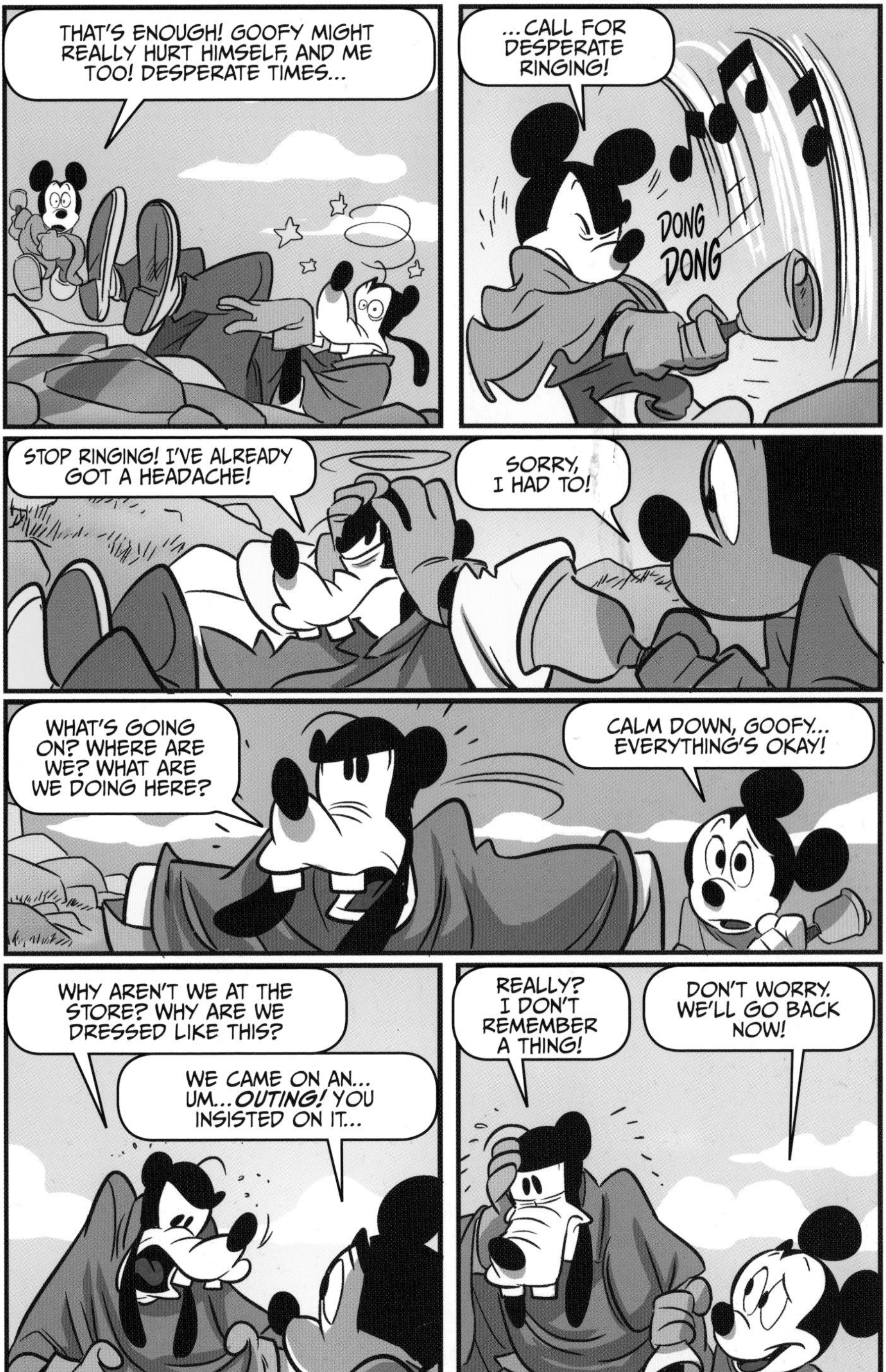
THAT'S ENOUGH! GOOFY MIGHT REALLY HURT HIMSELF, AND ME TOO! DESPERATE TIMES...
...CALL FOR DESPERATE RINGING!
DONG DONG
STOP RINGING! I'VE ALREADY GOT A HEADACHE!
SORRY, I HAD TO!
WHAT'S GOING ON? WHERE ARE WE? WHAT ARE WE DOING HERE?
CALM DOWN, GOOFY... EVERYTHING'S OKAY!
WHY AREN'T WE AT THE STORE? WHY ARE WE DRESSED LIKE THIS?
WE CAME ON AN... UM...*OUTING!* YOU INSISTED ON IT...
REALLY? I DON'T REMEMBER A THING!
DON'T WORRY. WE'LL GO BACK NOW!

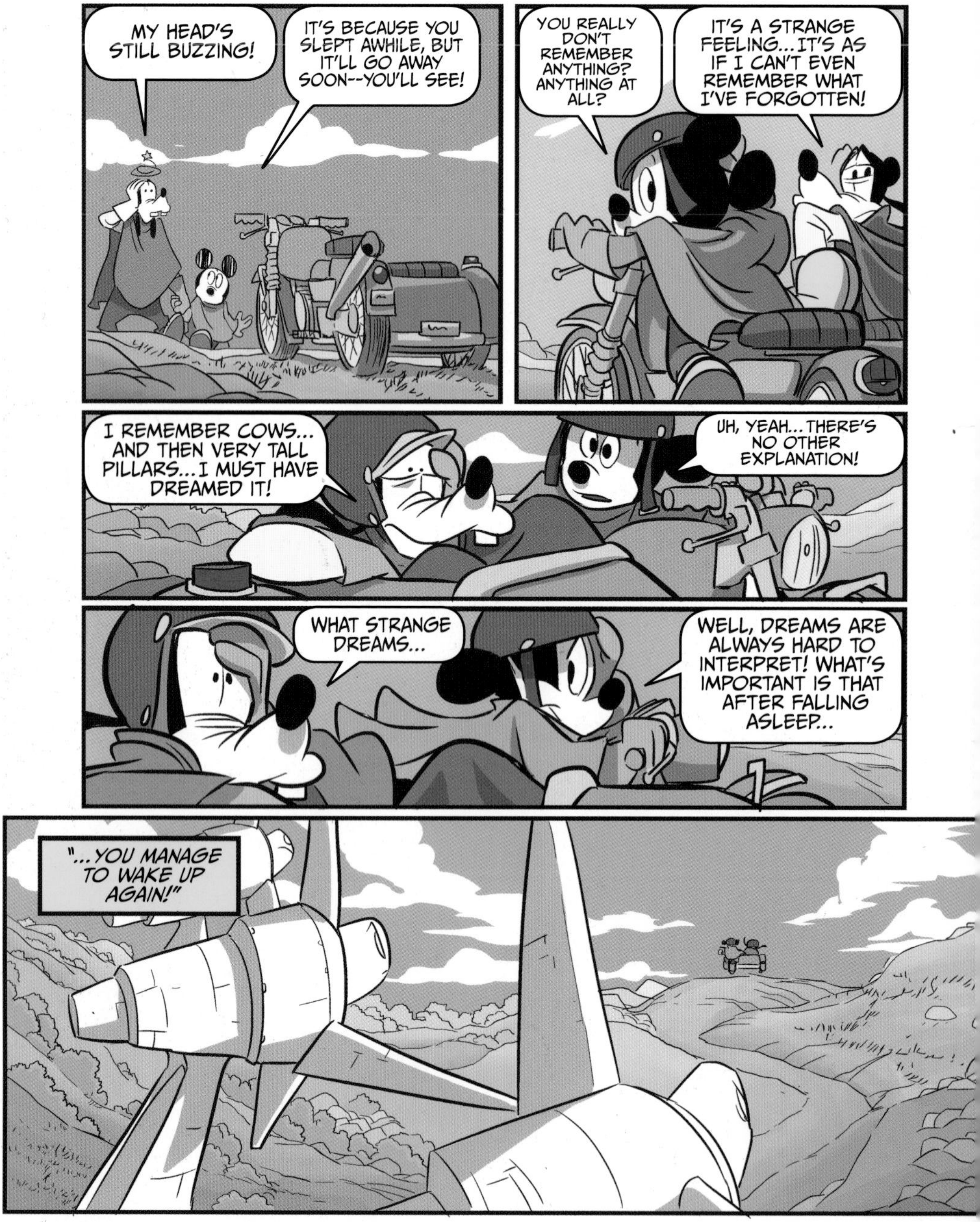
MY HEAD'S STILL BUZZING!
IT'S BECAUSE YOU SLEPT AWHILE, BUT IT'LL GO AWAY SOON--YOU'LL SEE!
YOU REALLY DON'T REMEMBER ANYTHING? ANYTHING AT ALL?
IT'S A STRANGE FEELING...IT'S AS IF I CAN'T EVEN REMEMBER WHAT I'VE FORGOTTEN!
I REMEMBER COWS... AND THEN VERY TALL PILLARS...I MUST HAVE DREAMED IT!
UH, YEAH...THERE'S NO OTHER EXPLANATION!
WHAT STRANGE DREAMS...
WELL, DREAMS ARE ALWAYS HARD TO INTERPRET! WHAT'S IMPORTANT IS THAT AFTER FALLING ASLEEP...
"...YOU MANAGE TO WAKE UP AGAIN!"

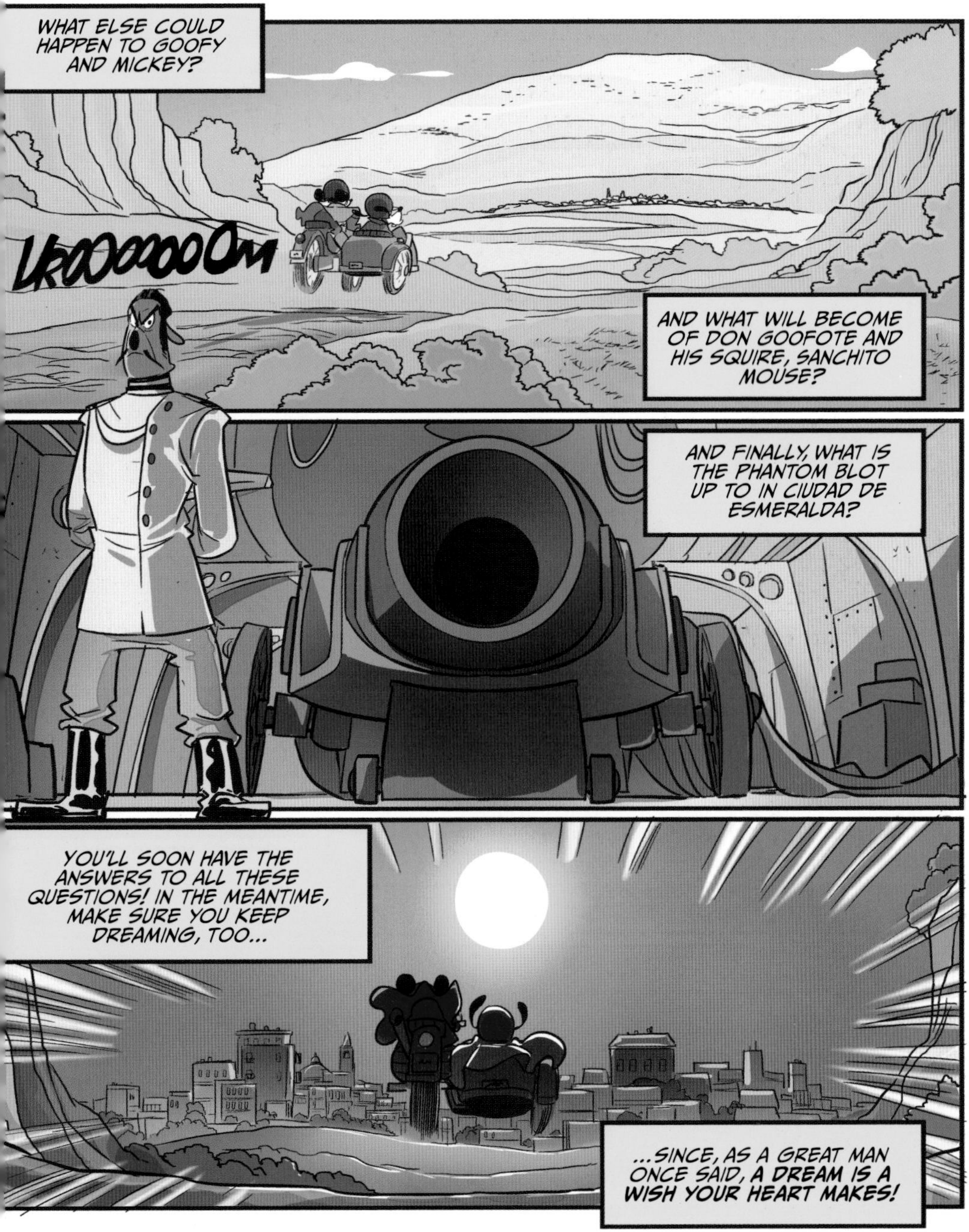
WHAT ELSE COULD HAPPEN TO GOOFY AND MICKEY?
UROOOOOOOM
AND WHAT WILL BECOME OF DON GOOFOTE AND HIS SQUIRE, SANCHITO MOUSE?
AND FINALLY, WHAT IS THE PHANTOM BLOT UP TO IN CIUDAD DE ESMERALDA?
YOU'LL SOON HAVE THE ANSWERS TO ALL THESE QUESTIONS! IN THE MEANTIME, MAKE SURE YOU KEEP DREAMING, TOO...
...SINCE, AS A GREAT MAN ONCE SAID, A DREAM IS A WISH YOUR HEART MAKES!

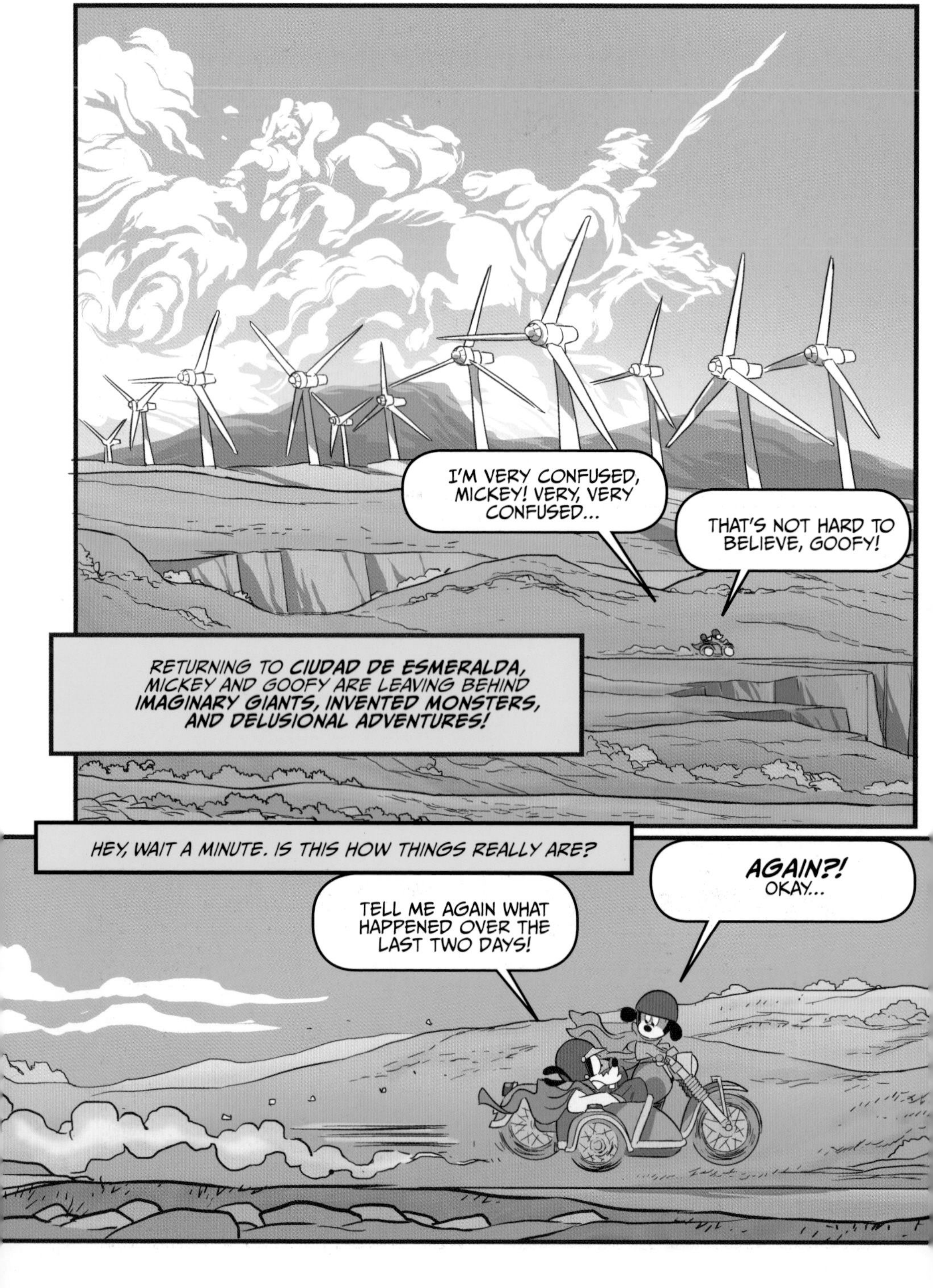
I'M VERY CONFUSED, MICKEY! VERY, VERY CONFUSED...
THAT'S NOT HARD TO BELIEVE, GOOFY!
RETURNING TO CIUDAD DE ESMERALDA, MICKEY AND GOOFY ARE LEAVING BEHIND IMAGINARY GIANTS, INVENTED MONSTERS, AND DELUSIONAL ADVENTURES!
HEY, WAIT A MINUTE. IS THIS HOW THINGS REALLY ARE?
TELL ME AGAIN WHAT HAPPENED OVER THE LAST TWO DAYS!
AGAIN?! OKAY...

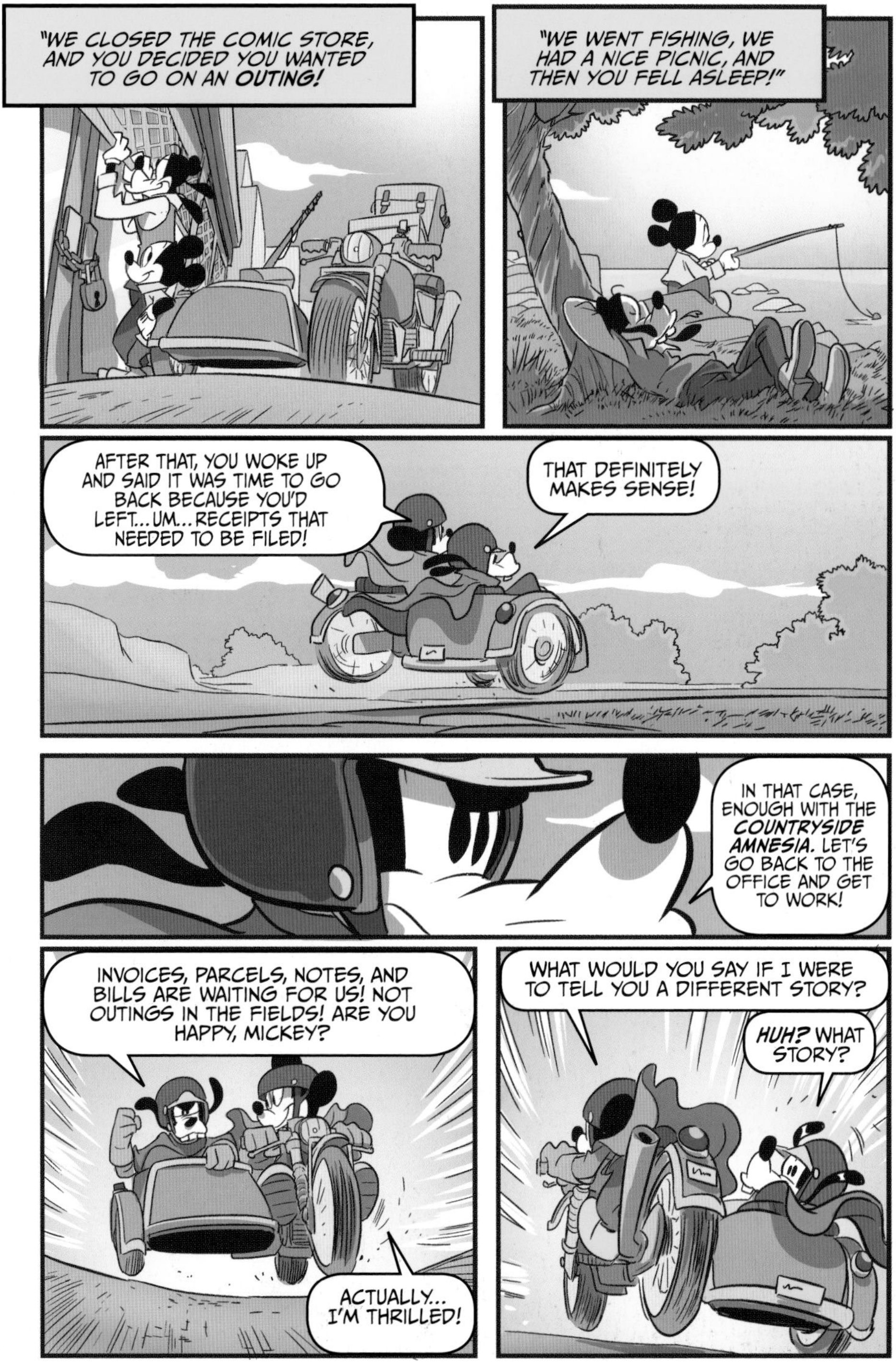
"WE CLOSED THE COMIC STORE, AND YOU DECIDED YOU WANTED TO GO ON AN **OUTING!**
"WE WENT FISHING, WE HAD A NICE PICNIC, AND THEN YOU FELL ASLEEP!"
AFTER THAT, YOU WOKE UP AND SAID IT WAS TIME TO GO BACK BECAUSE YOU'D LEFT...UM...RECEIPTS THAT NEEDED TO BE FILED!
THAT DEFINITELY MAKES SENSE!
IN THAT CASE, ENOUGH WITH THE ***COUNTRYSIDE AMNESIA.*** LET'S GO BACK TO THE OFFICE AND GET TO WORK!
INVOICES, PARCELS, NOTES, AND BILLS ARE WAITING FOR US! NOT OUTINGS IN THE FIELDS! ARE YOU HAPPY, MICKEY?
ACTUALLY... I'M THRILLED!
WHAT WOULD YOU SAY IF I WERE TO TELL YOU A DIFFERENT STORY?
HUH? WHAT STORY?

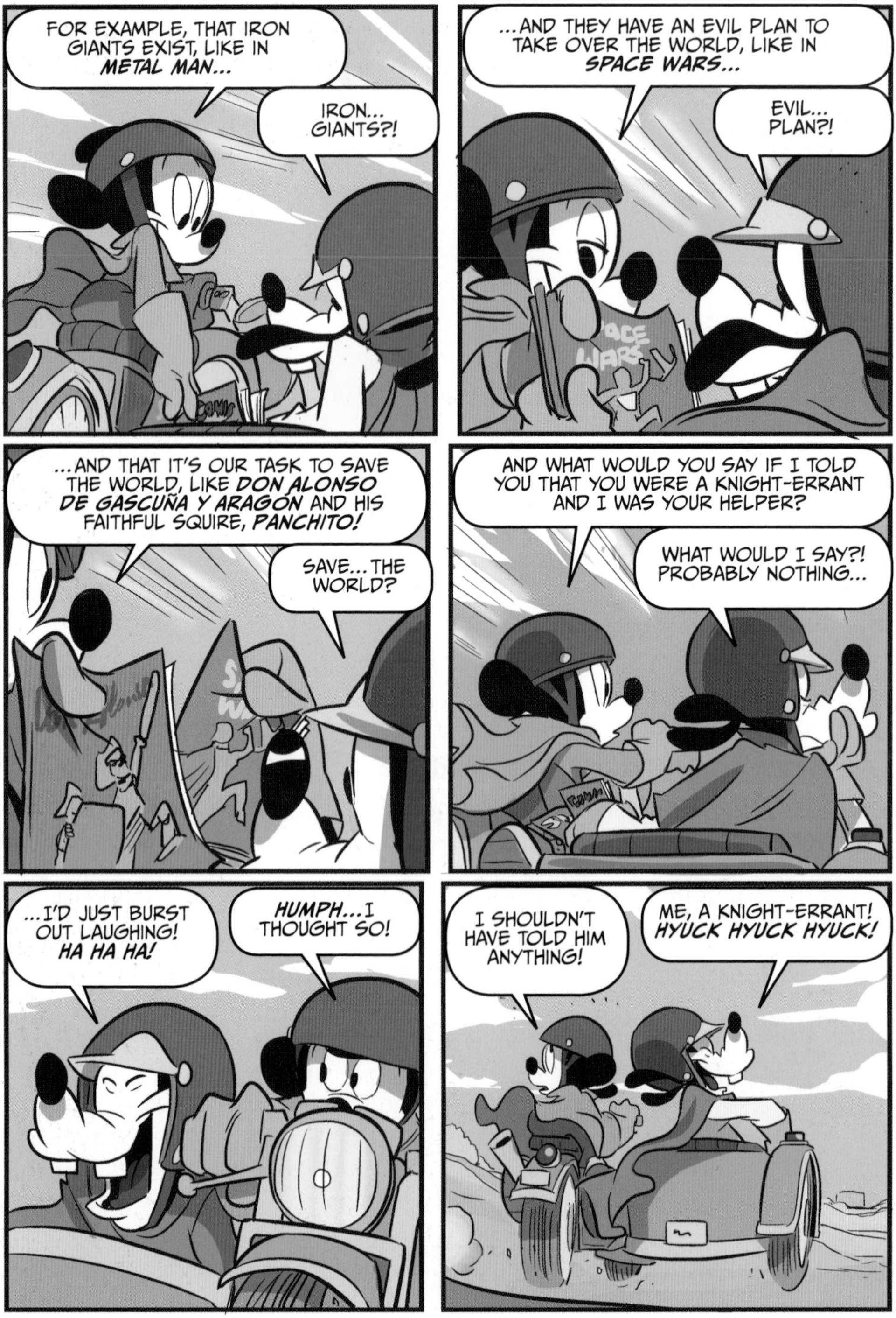
FOR EXAMPLE, THAT IRON GIANTS EXIST, LIKE IN *METAL MAN*...
IRON... GIANTS?!
...AND THEY HAVE AN EVIL PLAN TO TAKE OVER THE WORLD, LIKE IN *SPACE WARS*...
EVIL... PLAN?!
...AND THAT IT'S OUR TASK TO SAVE THE WORLD, LIKE *DON ALONSO DE GASCUÑA Y ARAGÓN* AND HIS FAITHFUL SQUIRE, *PANCHITO!*
SAVE... THE WORLD?
AND WHAT WOULD YOU SAY IF I TOLD YOU THAT YOU WERE A KNIGHT-ERRANT AND I WAS YOUR HELPER?
WHAT WOULD I SAY?! PROBABLY NOTHING...
...I'D JUST BURST OUT LAUGHING! *HA HA HA!*
HUMPH... I THOUGHT SO!
I SHOULDN'T HAVE TOLD HIM ANYTHING!
ME, A KNIGHT-ERRANT! *HYUCK HYUCK HYUCK!*

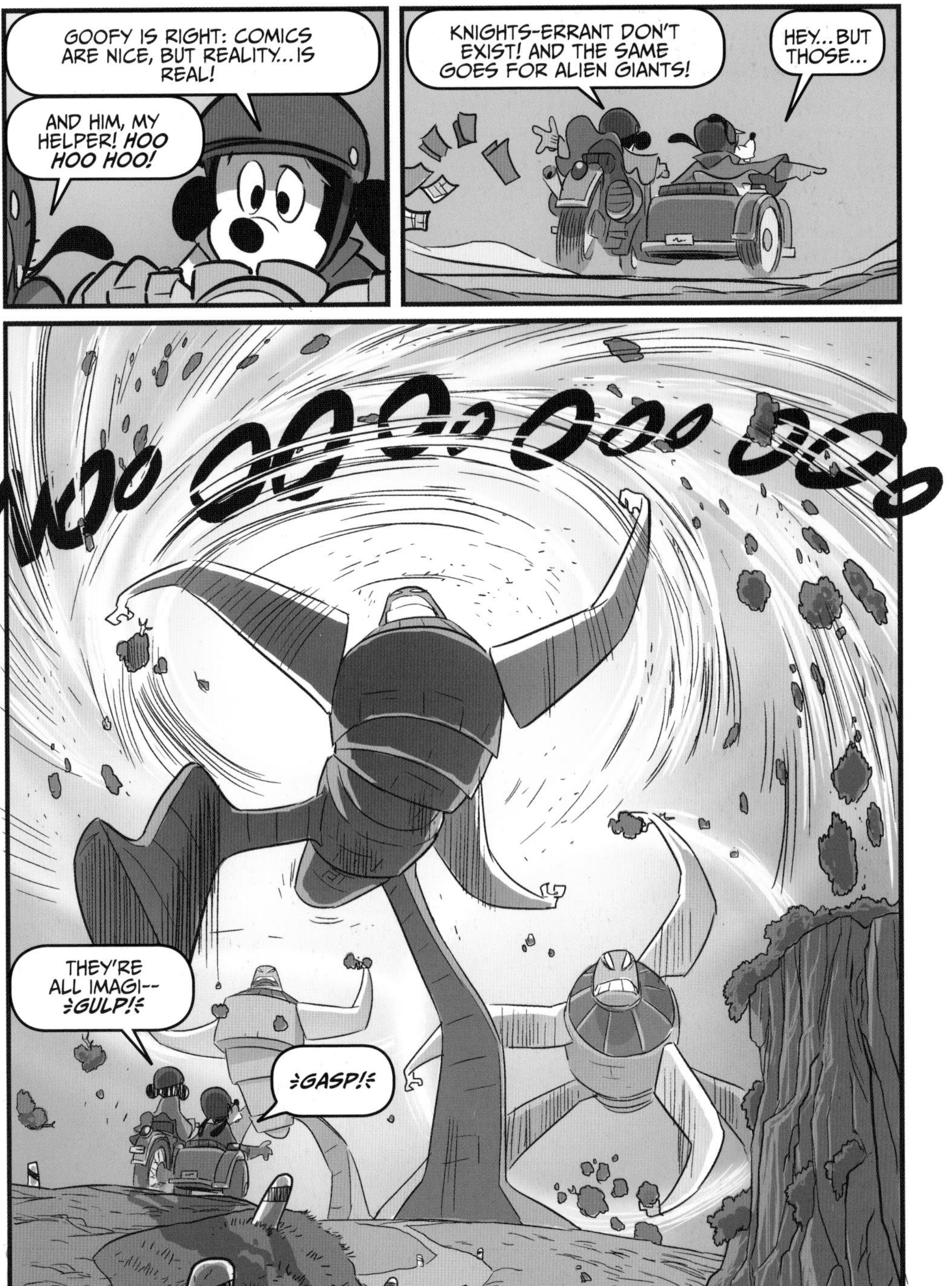
GOOFY IS RIGHT: COMICS ARE NICE, BUT REALITY... IS REAL!
AND HIM, MY HELPER! *HOO HOO HOO!*
KNIGHTS-ERRANT DON'T EXIST! AND THE SAME GOES FOR ALIEN GIANTS!
HEY... BUT THOSE...
THEY'RE ALL IMAGI-- *GULP!*
GASP!

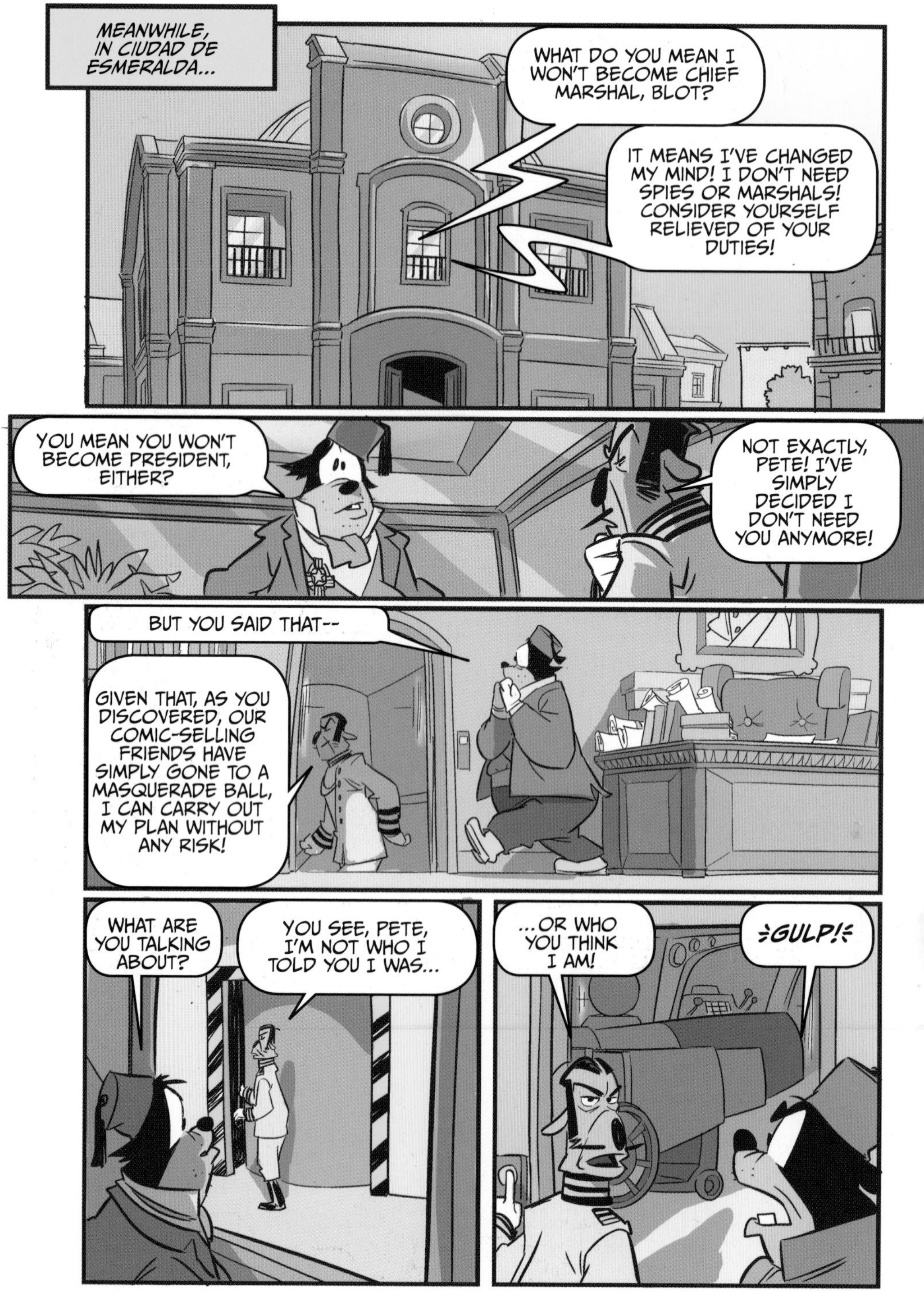
MEANWHILE, IN CIUDAD DE ESMERALDA...
WHAT DO YOU MEAN I WON'T BECOME CHIEF MARSHAL, BLOT?
IT MEANS I'VE CHANGED MY MIND! I DON'T NEED SPIES OR MARSHALS! CONSIDER YOURSELF RELIEVED OF YOUR DUTIES!
YOU MEAN YOU WON'T BECOME PRESIDENT, EITHER?
NOT EXACTLY, PETE! I'VE SIMPLY DECIDED I DON'T NEED YOU ANYMORE!
BUT YOU SAID THAT--
GIVEN THAT, AS YOU DISCOVERED, OUR COMIC-SELLING FRIENDS HAVE SIMPLY GONE TO A MASQUERADE BALL, I CAN CARRY OUT MY PLAN WITHOUT ANY RISK!
WHAT ARE YOU TALKING ABOUT?
YOU SEE, PETE, I'M NOT WHO I TOLD YOU I WAS...
...OR WHO YOU THINK I AM!
GULP!

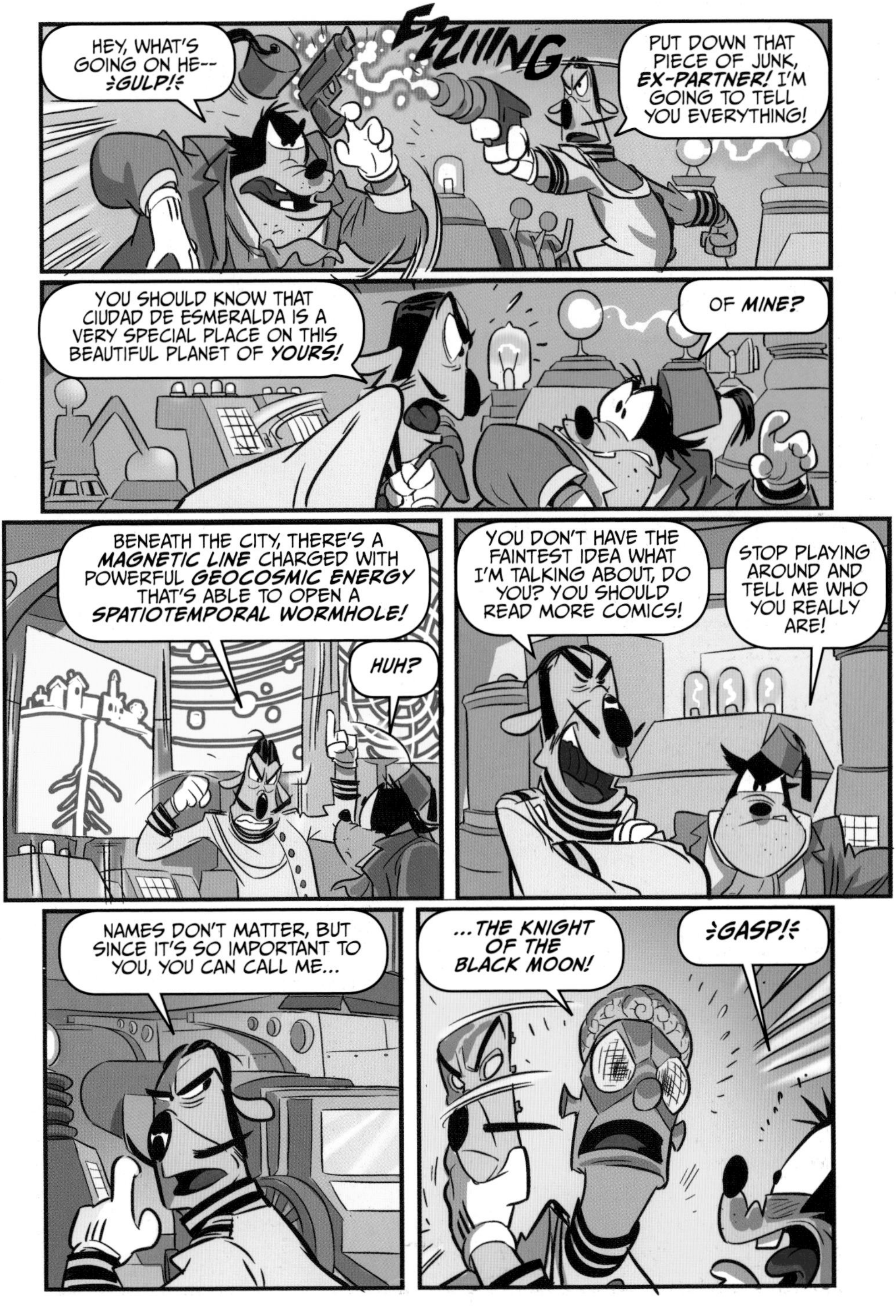
HEY, WHAT'S GOING ON HE-- ⁝GULP!⁝
FZZIIING
PUT DOWN THAT PIECE OF JUNK, EX-PARTNER! I'M GOING TO TELL YOU EVERYTHING!
YOU SHOULD KNOW THAT CIUDAD DE ESMERALDA IS A VERY SPECIAL PLACE ON THIS BEAUTIFUL PLANET OF YOURS!
OF MINE?
BENEATH THE CITY, THERE'S A MAGNETIC LINE CHARGED WITH POWERFUL GEOCOSMIC ENERGY THAT'S ABLE TO OPEN A SPATIOTEMPORAL WORMHOLE!
HUH?
YOU DON'T HAVE THE FAINTEST IDEA WHAT I'M TALKING ABOUT, DO YOU? YOU SHOULD READ MORE COMICS!
STOP PLAYING AROUND AND TELL ME WHO YOU REALLY ARE!
NAMES DON'T MATTER, BUT SINCE IT'S SO IMPORTANT TO YOU, YOU CAN CALL ME...
...THE KNIGHT OF THE BLACK MOON!
⁝GASP!⁝

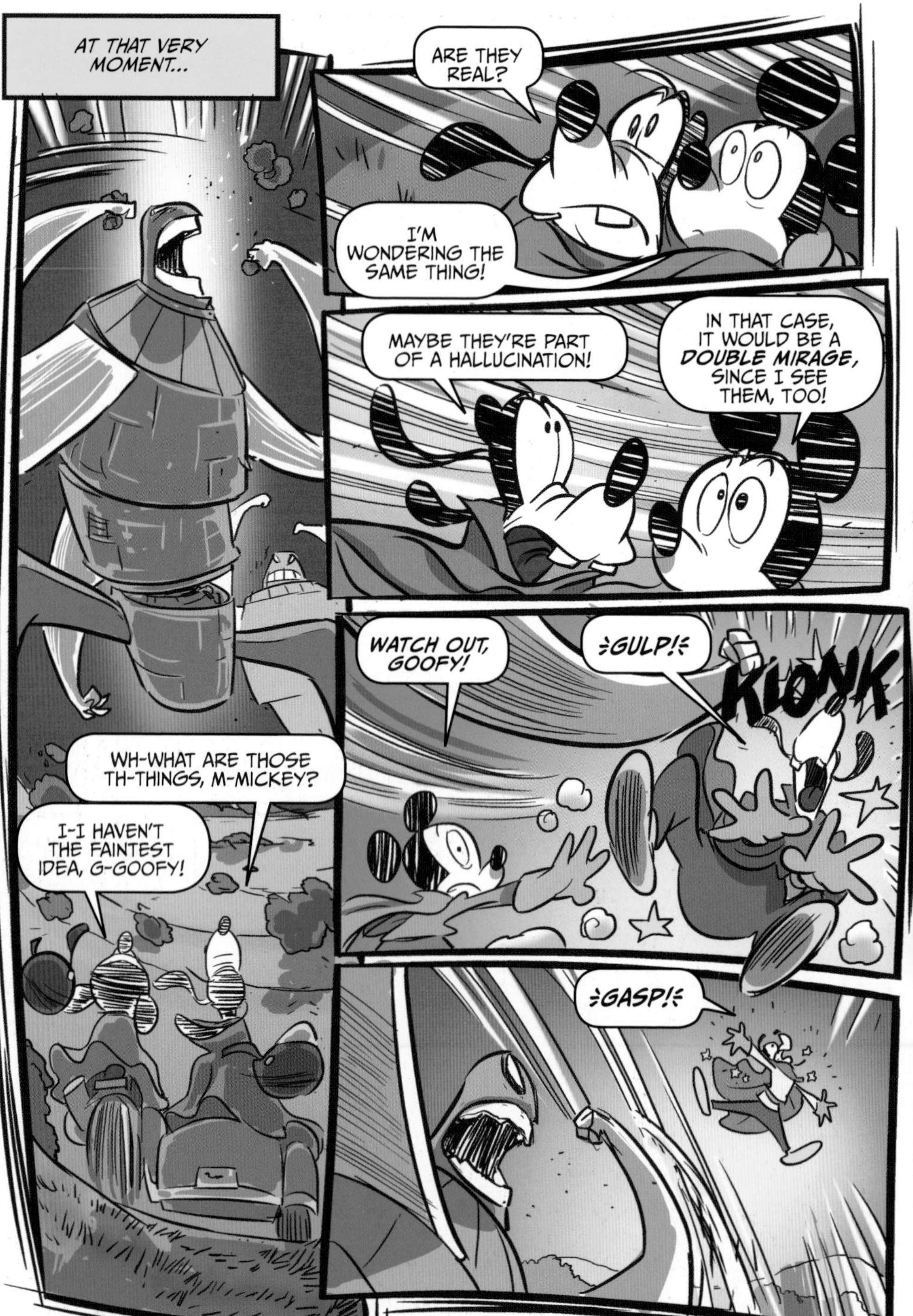

AT THAT VERY MOMENT...
ARE THEY REAL?
I'M WONDERING THE SAME THING!
MAYBE THEY'RE PART OF A HALLUCINATION!
IN THAT CASE, IT WOULD BE A *DOUBLE MIRAGE*, SINCE I SEE THEM, TOO!
WH-WHAT ARE THOSE TH-THINGS, M-MICKEY?
I-I HAVEN'T THE FAINTEST IDEA, G-GOOFY!
WATCH OUT, GOOFY!
GULP!
KLONK
GASP!

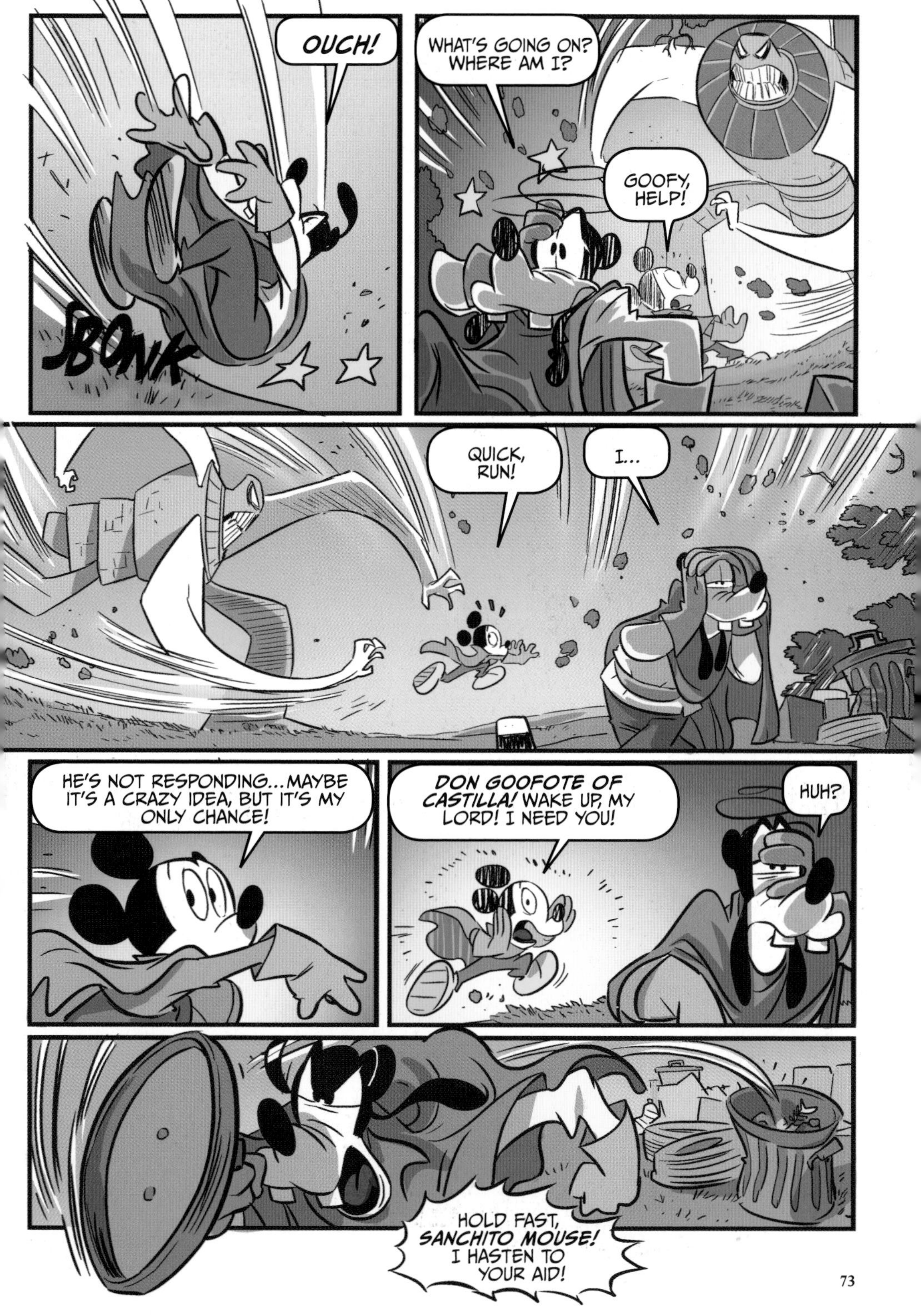
OUCH!
SBONK
WHAT'S GOING ON? WHERE AM I?
GOOFY, HELP!
QUICK, RUN!
I...
HE'S NOT RESPONDING...MAYBE IT'S A CRAZY IDEA, BUT IT'S MY ONLY CHANCE!
DON GOOFOTE OF CASTILLA! WAKE UP, MY LORD! I NEED YOU!
HUH?
HOLD FAST, SANCHITO MOUSE! I HASTEN TO YOUR AID!

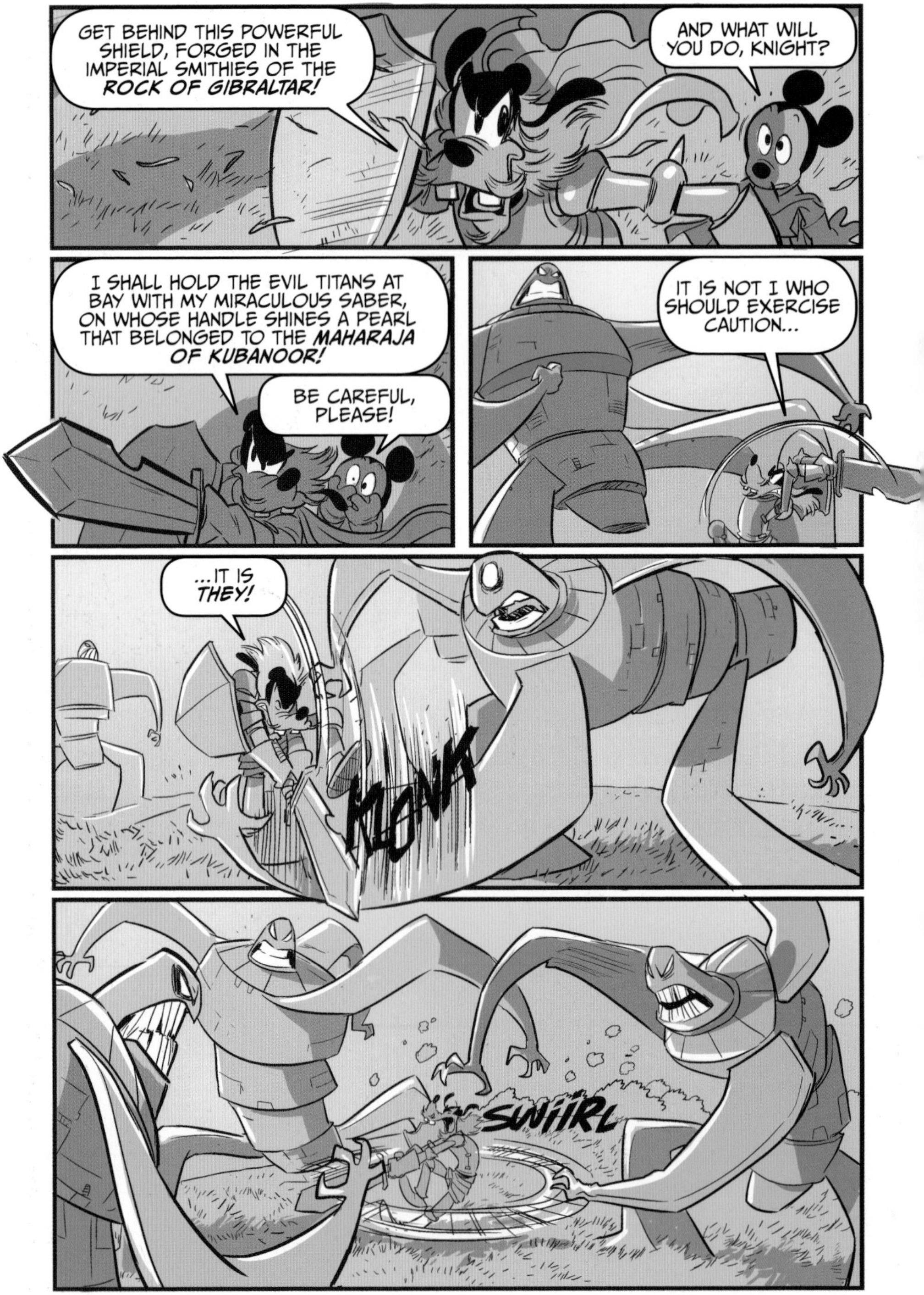

GET BEHIND THIS POWERFUL SHIELD, FORGED IN THE IMPERIAL SMITHIES OF THE ***ROCK OF GIBRALTAR!***
AND WHAT WILL YOU DO, KNIGHT?
I SHALL HOLD THE EVIL TITANS AT BAY WITH MY MIRACULOUS SABER, ON WHOSE HANDLE SHINES A PEARL THAT BELONGED TO THE ***MAHARAJA OF KUBANOOR!***
BE CAREFUL, PLEASE!
IT IS NOT I WHO SHOULD EXERCISE CAUTION...
...IT IS ***THEY!***
KLONK
SWIIRL

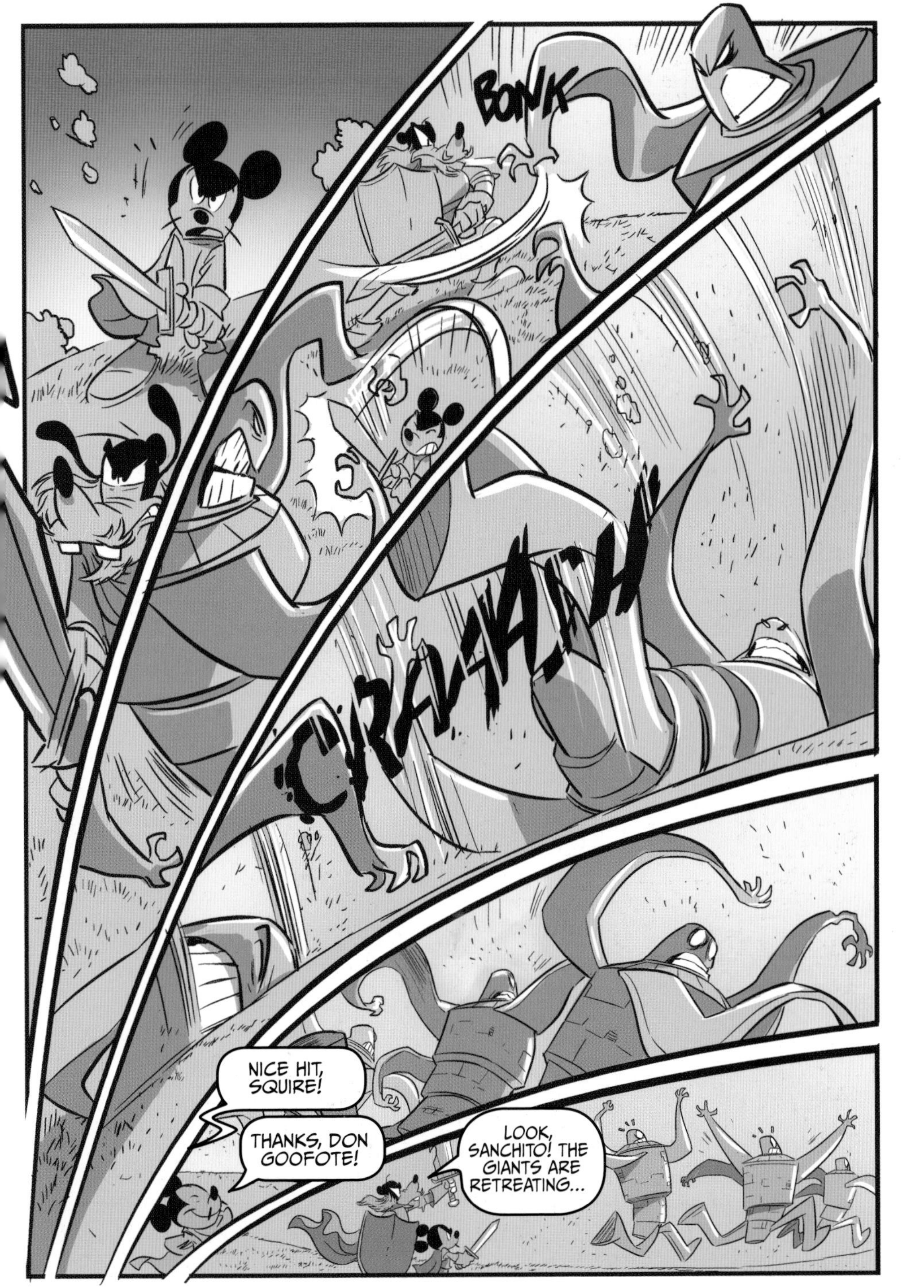
BONK
CRAAAACH
NICE HIT, SQUIRE!
THANKS, DON GOOFOTE!
LOOK, SANCHITO! THE GIANTS ARE RETREATING...

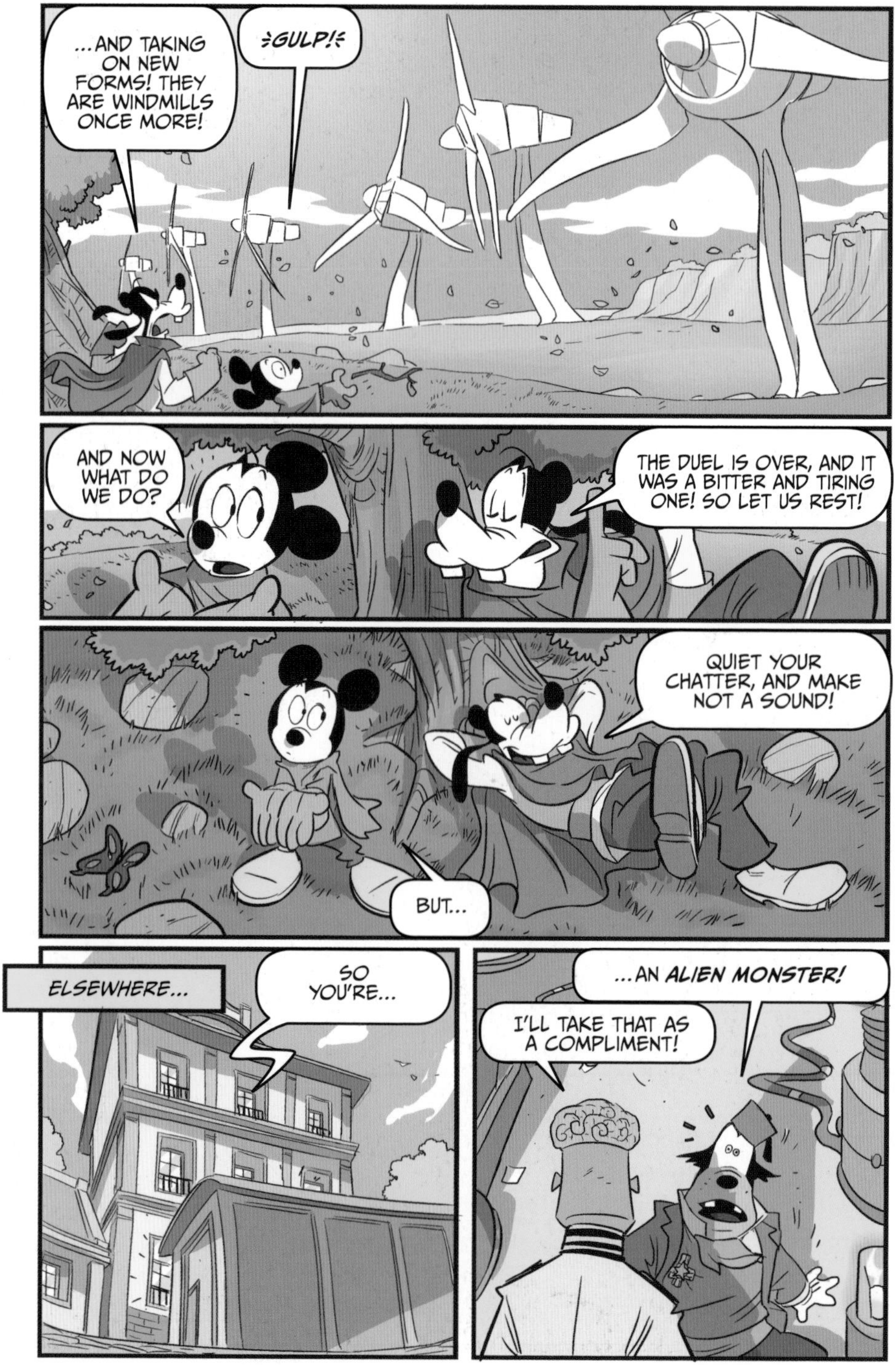
...AND TAKING ON NEW FORMS! THEY ARE WINDMILLS ONCE MORE!
GULP!
AND NOW WHAT DO WE DO?
THE DUEL IS OVER, AND IT WAS A BITTER AND TIRING ONE! SO LET US REST!
QUIET YOUR CHATTER, AND MAKE NOT A SOUND!
BUT...
ELSEWHERE...
SO YOU'RE...
...AN ALIEN MONSTER!
I'LL TAKE THAT AS A COMPLIMENT!

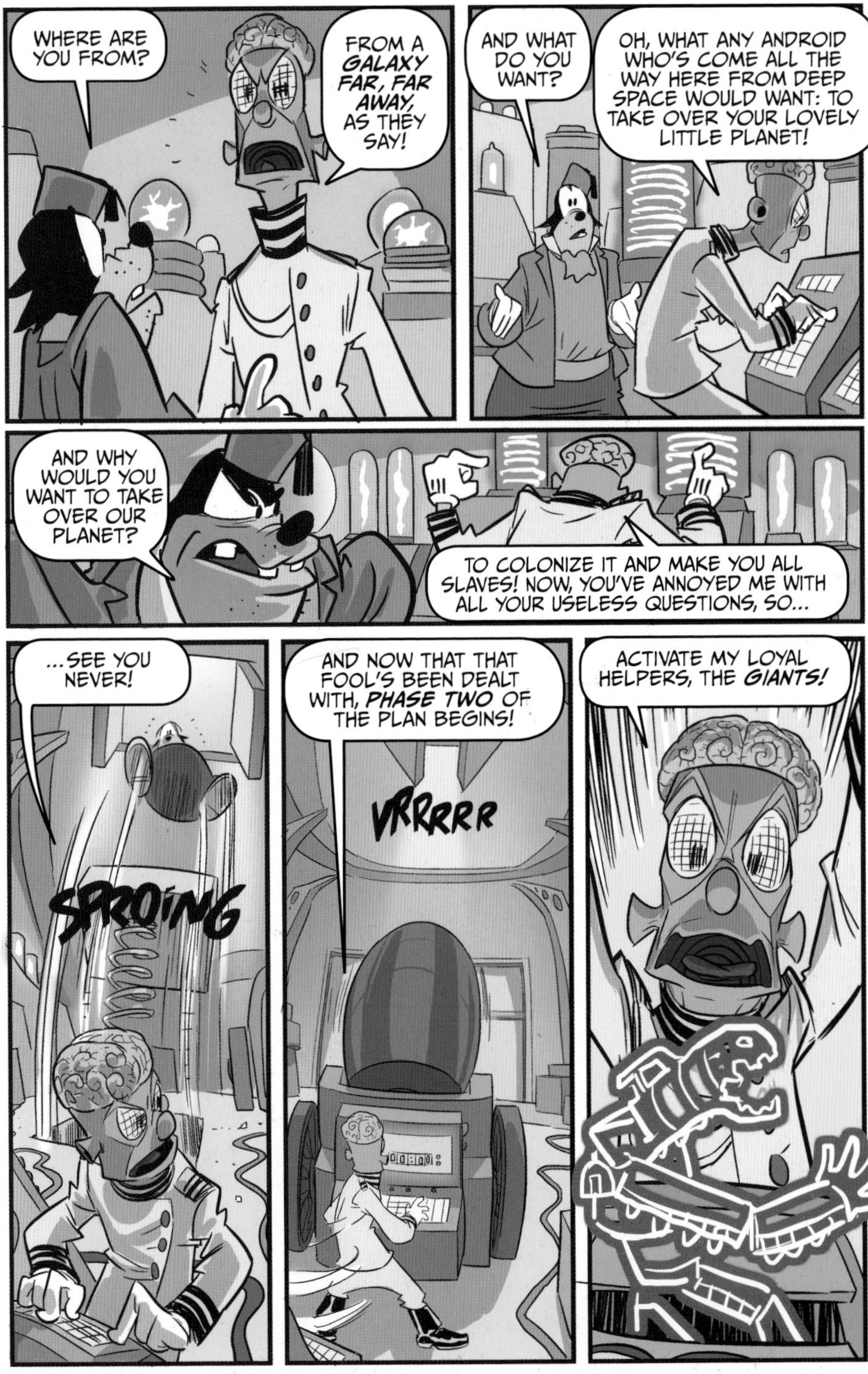
WHERE ARE YOU FROM?
FROM A GALAXY FAR, FAR AWAY, AS THEY SAY!
AND WHAT DO YOU WANT?
OH, WHAT ANY ANDROID WHO'S COME ALL THE WAY HERE FROM DEEP SPACE WOULD WANT: TO TAKE OVER YOUR LOVELY LITTLE PLANET!
AND WHY WOULD YOU WANT TO TAKE OVER OUR PLANET?
TO COLONIZE IT AND MAKE YOU ALL SLAVES! NOW, YOU'VE ANNOYED ME WITH ALL YOUR USELESS QUESTIONS, SO...
...SEE YOU NEVER!
SPROING
AND NOW THAT THAT FOOL'S BEEN DEALT WITH, PHASE TWO OF THE PLAN BEGINS!
VRRRRR
ACTIVATE MY LOYAL HELPERS, THE GIANTS!

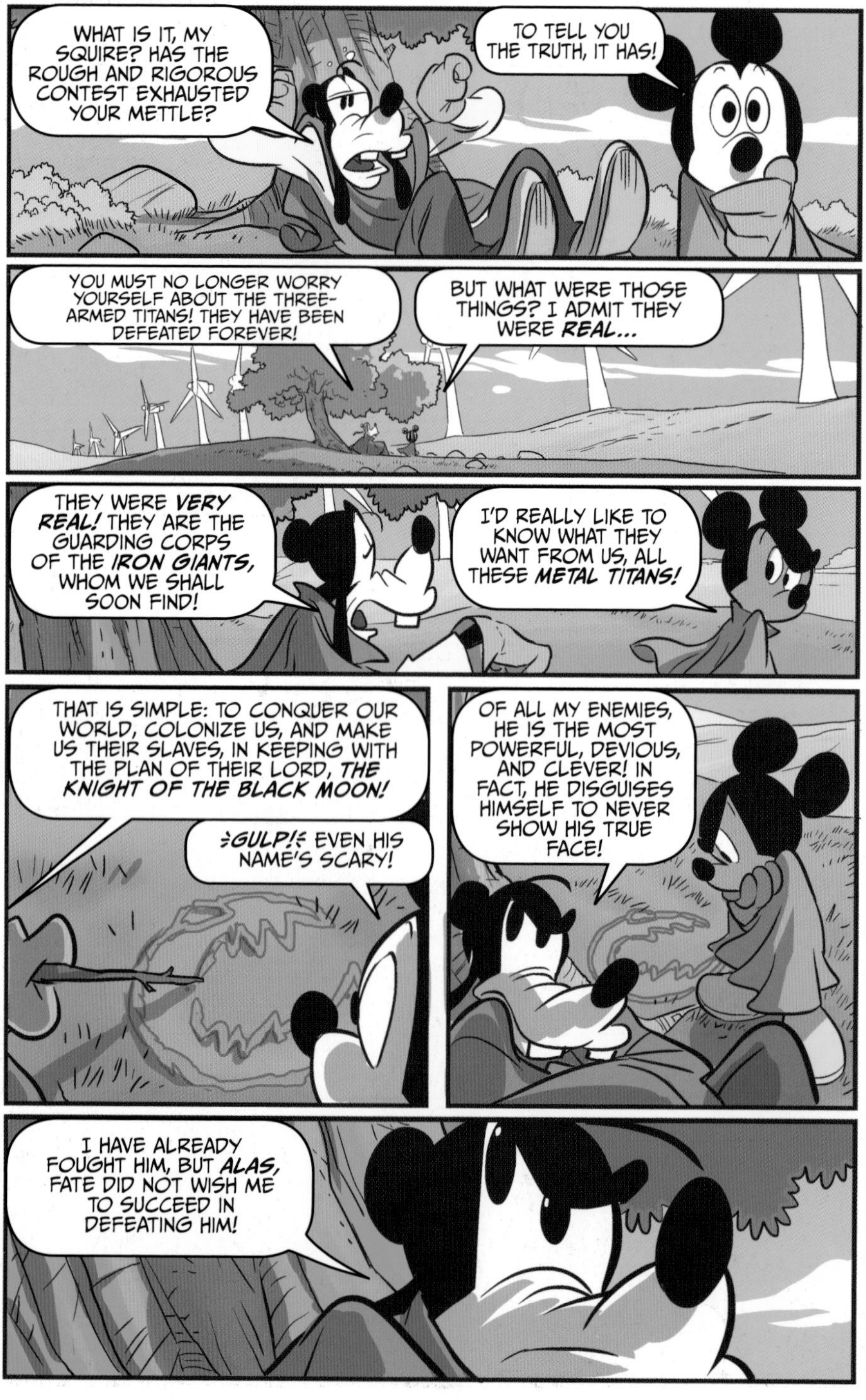
WHAT IS IT, MY SQUIRE? HAS THE ROUGH AND RIGOROUS CONTEST EXHAUSTED YOUR METTLE?
TO TELL YOU THE TRUTH, IT HAS!
YOU MUST NO LONGER WORRY YOURSELF ABOUT THE THREE-ARMED TITANS! THEY HAVE BEEN DEFEATED FOREVER!
BUT WHAT WERE THOSE THINGS? I ADMIT THEY WERE REAL...
THEY WERE VERY REAL! THEY ARE THE GUARDING CORPS OF THE IRON GIANTS, WHOM WE SHALL SOON FIND!
I'D REALLY LIKE TO KNOW WHAT THEY WANT FROM US, ALL THESE METAL TITANS!
THAT IS SIMPLE: TO CONQUER OUR WORLD, COLONIZE US, AND MAKE US THEIR SLAVES, IN KEEPING WITH THE PLAN OF THEIR LORD, THE KNIGHT OF THE BLACK MOON!
GULP! EVEN HIS NAME'S SCARY!
OF ALL MY ENEMIES, HE IS THE MOST POWERFUL, DEVIOUS, AND CLEVER! IN FACT, HE DISGUISES HIMSELF TO NEVER SHOW HIS TRUE FACE!
I HAVE ALREADY FOUGHT HIM, BUT ALAS, FATE DID NOT WISH ME TO SUCCEED IN DEFEATING HIM!

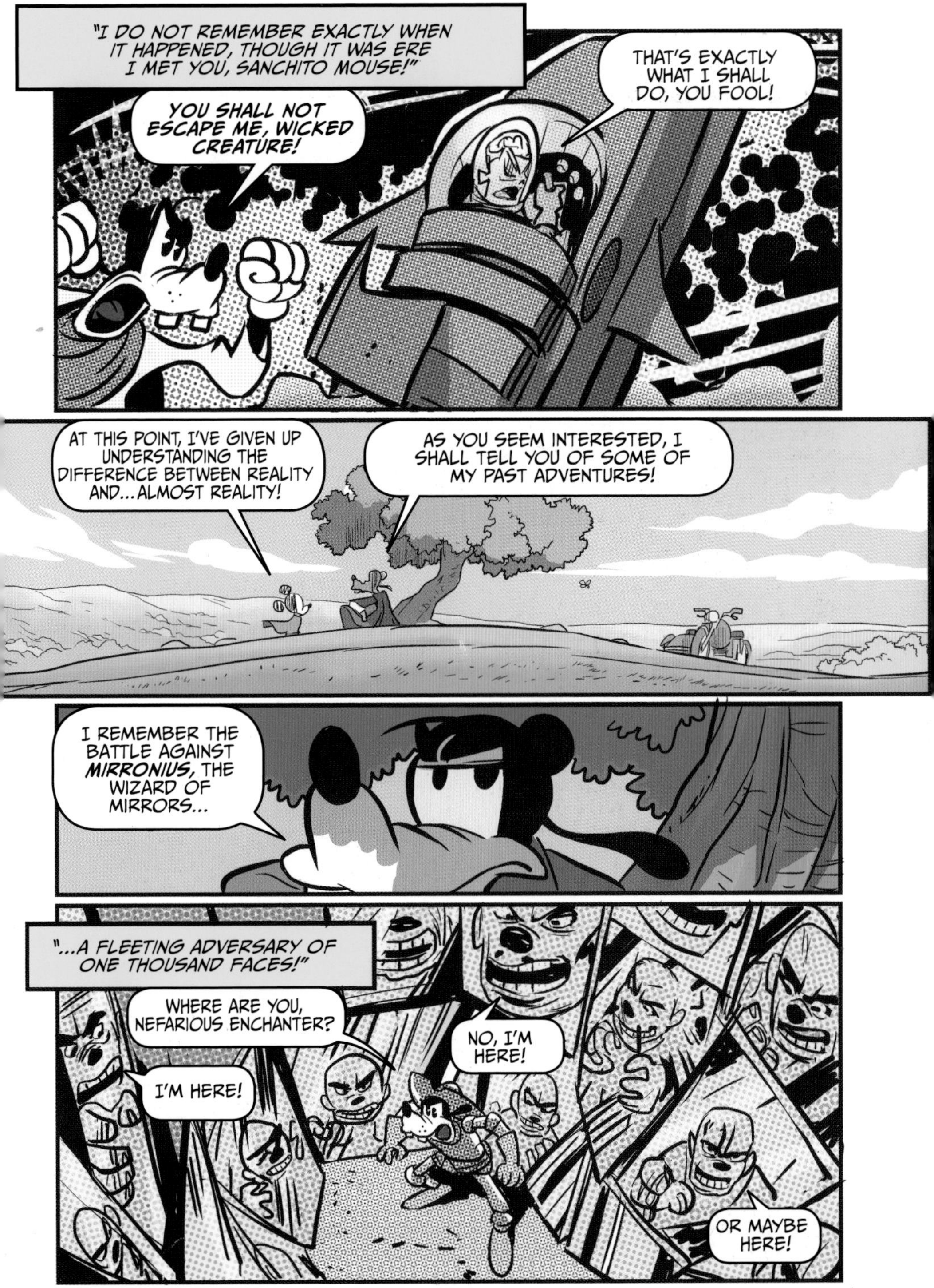
"I DO NOT REMEMBER EXACTLY WHEN IT HAPPENED, THOUGH IT WAS ERE I MET YOU, SANCHITO MOUSE!"
YOU SHALL NOT ESCAPE ME, WICKED CREATURE!
THAT'S EXACTLY WHAT I SHALL DO, YOU FOOL!
AT THIS POINT, I'VE GIVEN UP UNDERSTANDING THE DIFFERENCE BETWEEN REALITY AND...ALMOST REALITY!
AS YOU SEEM INTERESTED, I SHALL TELL YOU OF SOME OF MY PAST ADVENTURES!
I REMEMBER THE BATTLE AGAINST MIRRONIUS, THE WIZARD OF MIRRORS...
"...A FLEETING ADVERSARY OF ONE THOUSAND FACES!"
WHERE ARE YOU, NEFARIOUS ENCHANTER?
I'M HERE!
NO, I'M HERE!
OR MAYBE HERE!

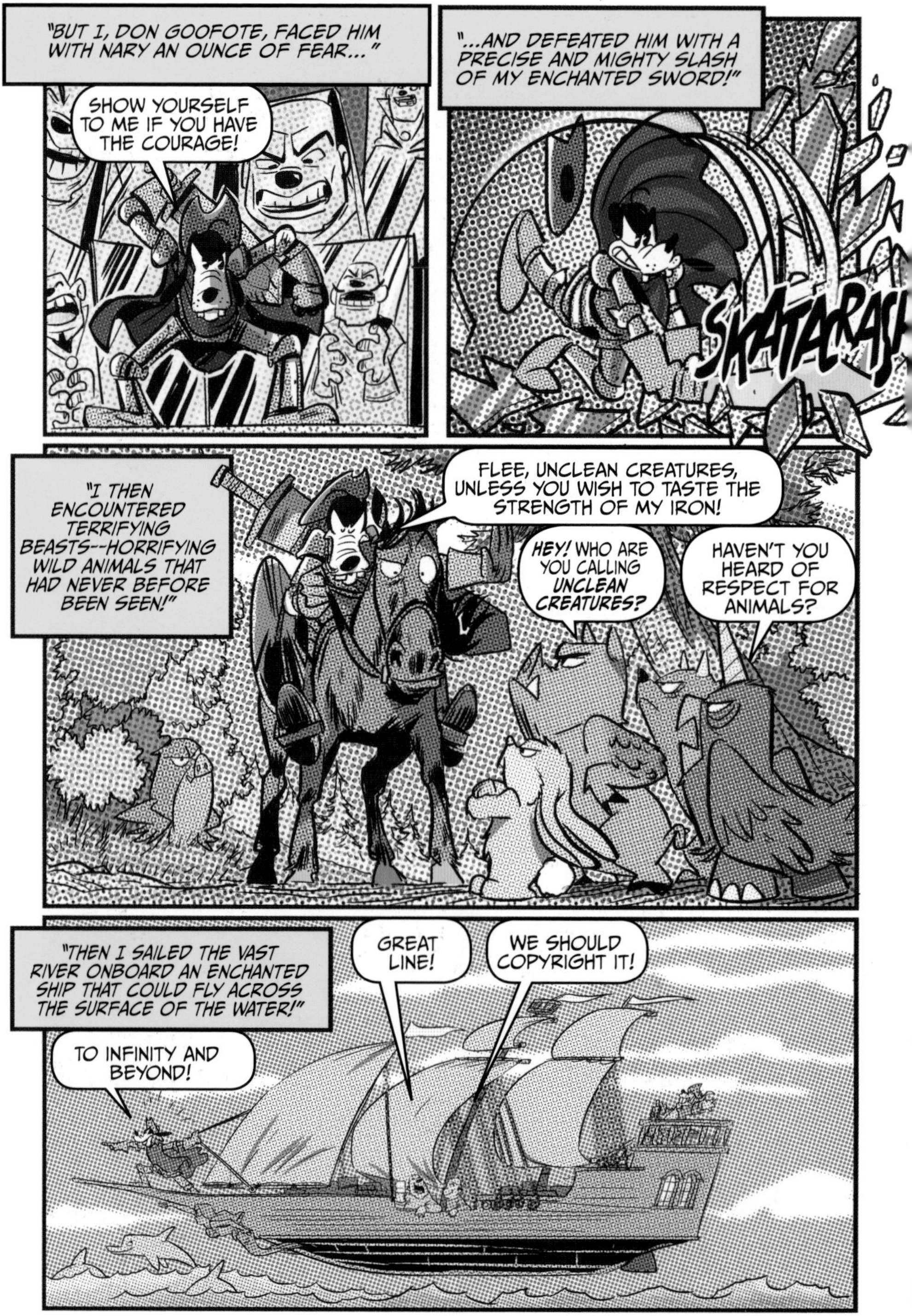
"BUT I, DON GOOFOTE, FACED HIM WITH NARY AN OUNCE OF FEAR..."
SHOW YOURSELF TO ME IF YOU HAVE THE COURAGE!
"...AND DEFEATED HIM WITH A PRECISE AND MIGHTY SLASH OF MY ENCHANTED SWORD!"
SKATACRASH
"I THEN ENCOUNTERED TERRIFYING BEASTS--HORRIFYING WILD ANIMALS THAT HAD NEVER BEFORE BEEN SEEN!"
FLEE, UNCLEAN CREATURES, UNLESS YOU WISH TO TASTE THE STRENGTH OF MY IRON!
HEY! WHO ARE YOU CALLING UNCLEAN CREATURES?
HAVEN'T YOU HEARD OF RESPECT FOR ANIMALS?
"THEN I SAILED THE VAST RIVER ONBOARD AN ENCHANTED SHIP THAT COULD FLY ACROSS THE SURFACE OF THE WATER!"
TO INFINITY AND BEYOND!
GREAT LINE!
WE SHOULD COPYRIGHT IT!

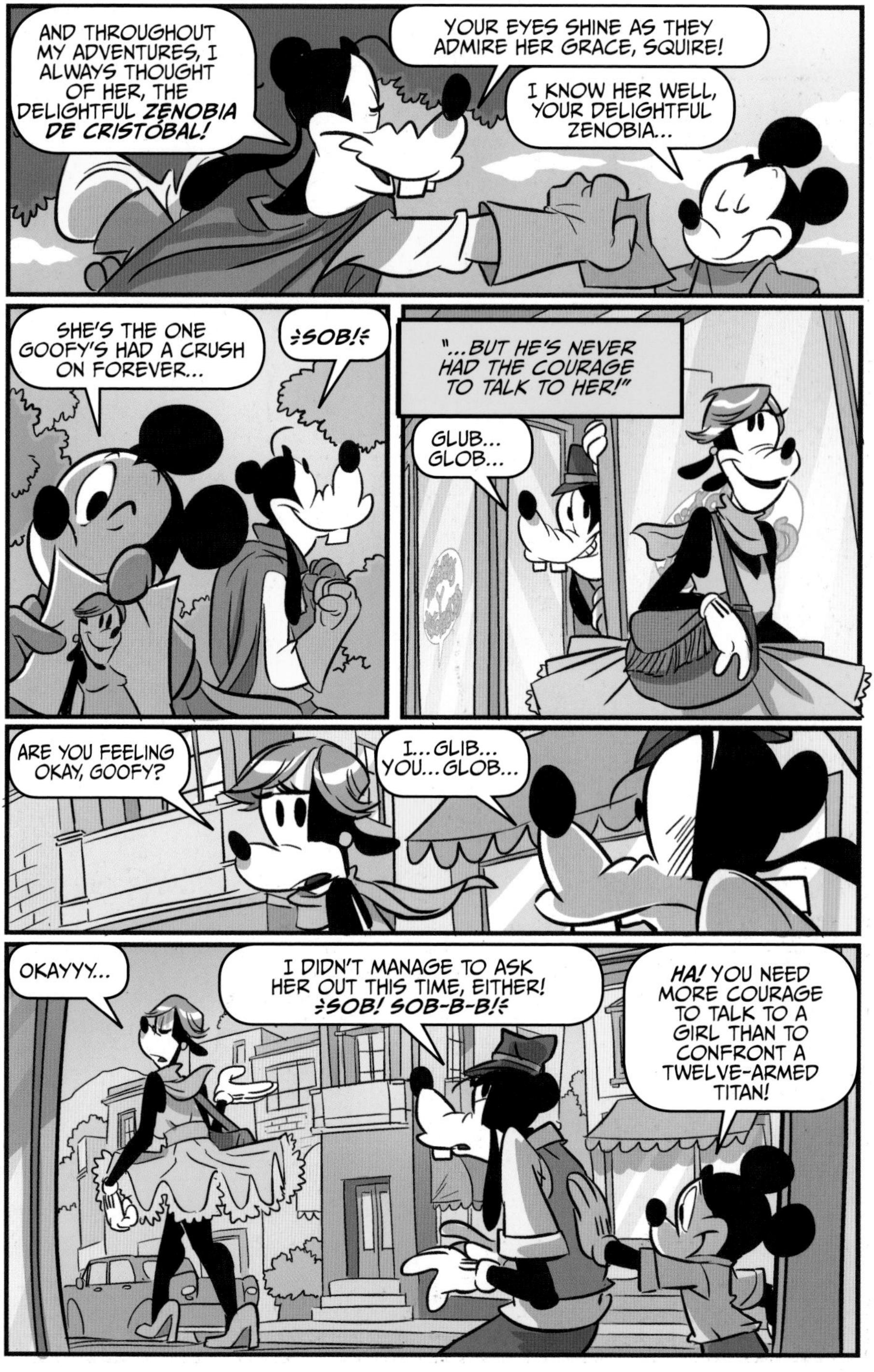

AND THROUGHOUT MY ADVENTURES, I ALWAYS THOUGHT OF HER, THE DELIGHTFUL *ZENOBIA DE CRISTÓBAL!*
YOUR EYES SHINE AS THEY ADMIRE HER GRACE, SQUIRE!
I KNOW HER WELL, YOUR DELIGHTFUL ZENOBIA...
SHE'S THE ONE GOOFY'S HAD A CRUSH ON FOREVER...
SOB!
"...BUT HE'S NEVER HAD THE COURAGE TO TALK TO HER!"
GLUB... GLOB...
ARE YOU FEELING OKAY, GOOFY?
I...GLIB... YOU...GLOB...
OKAYYY...
I DIDN'T MANAGE TO ASK HER OUT THIS TIME, EITHER! *SOB! SOB-B-B!*
HA! YOU NEED MORE COURAGE TO TALK TO A GIRL THAN TO CONFRONT A TWELVE-ARMED TITAN!

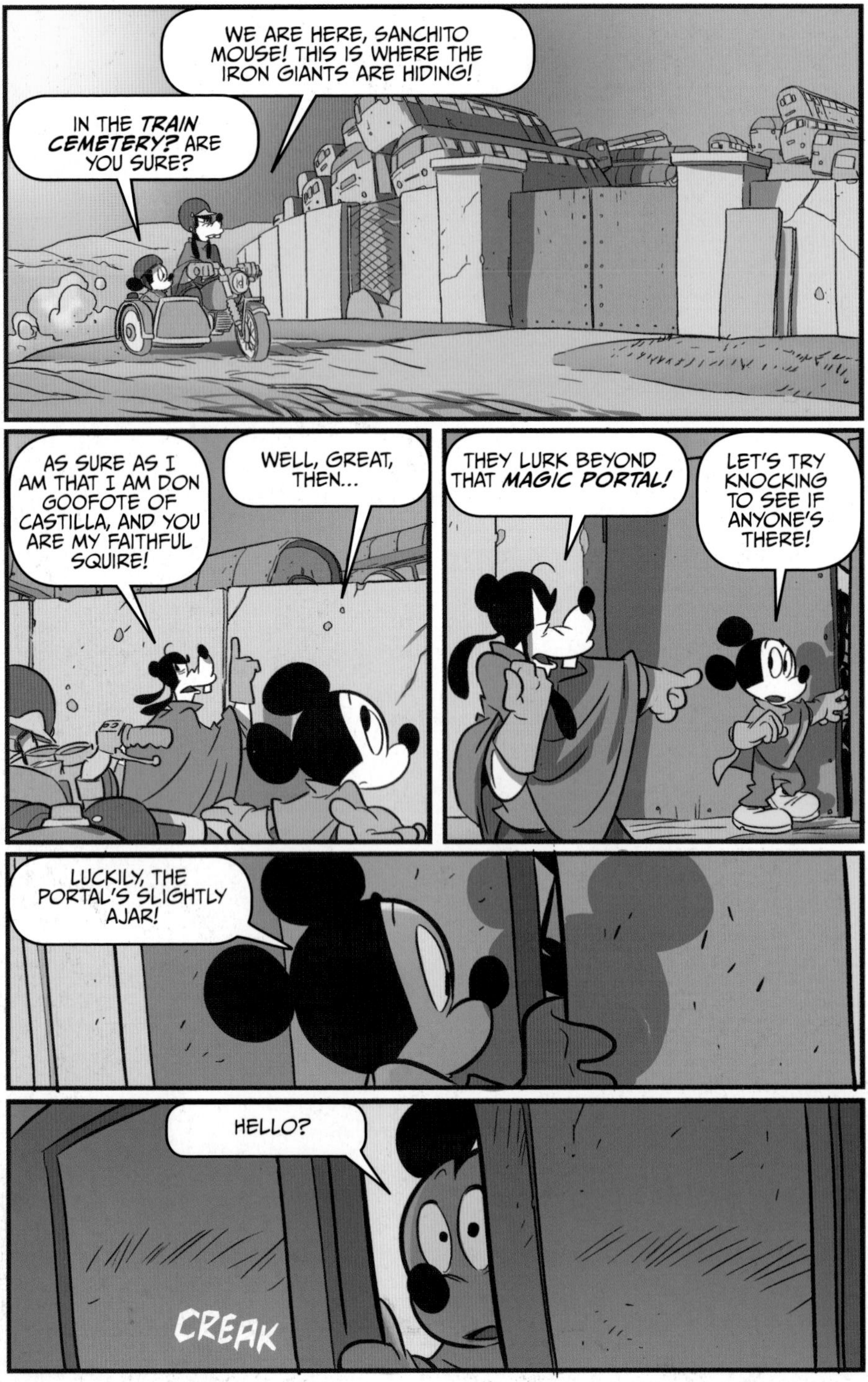
WE ARE HERE, SANCHITO MOUSE! THIS IS WHERE THE IRON GIANTS ARE HIDING!
IN THE *TRAIN CEMETERY?* ARE YOU SURE?
AS SURE AS I AM THAT I AM DON GOOFOTE OF CASTILLA, AND YOU ARE MY FAITHFUL SQUIRE!
WELL, GREAT, THEN...
THEY LURK BEYOND THAT *MAGIC PORTAL!*
LET'S TRY KNOCKING TO SEE IF ANYONE'S THERE!
LUCKILY, THE PORTAL'S SLIGHTLY AJAR!
HELLO?
CREAK

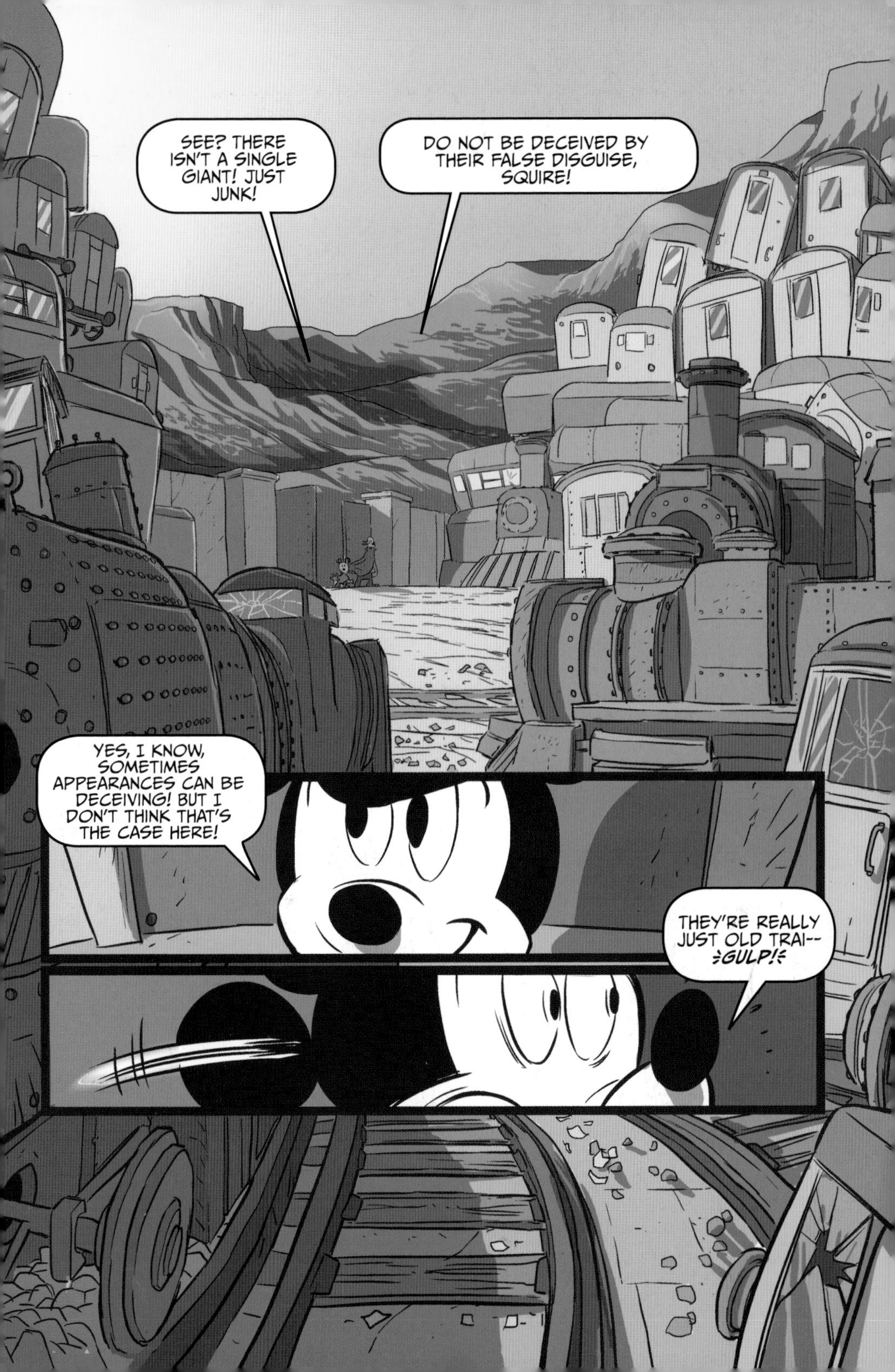
SEE? THERE ISN'T A SINGLE GIANT! JUST JUNK!
DO NOT BE DECEIVED BY THEIR FALSE DISGUISE, SQUIRE!
YES, I KNOW, SOMETIMES APPEARANCES CAN BE DECEIVING! BUT I DON'T THINK THAT'S THE CASE HERE!
THEY'RE REALLY JUST OLD TRAI-- GULP!

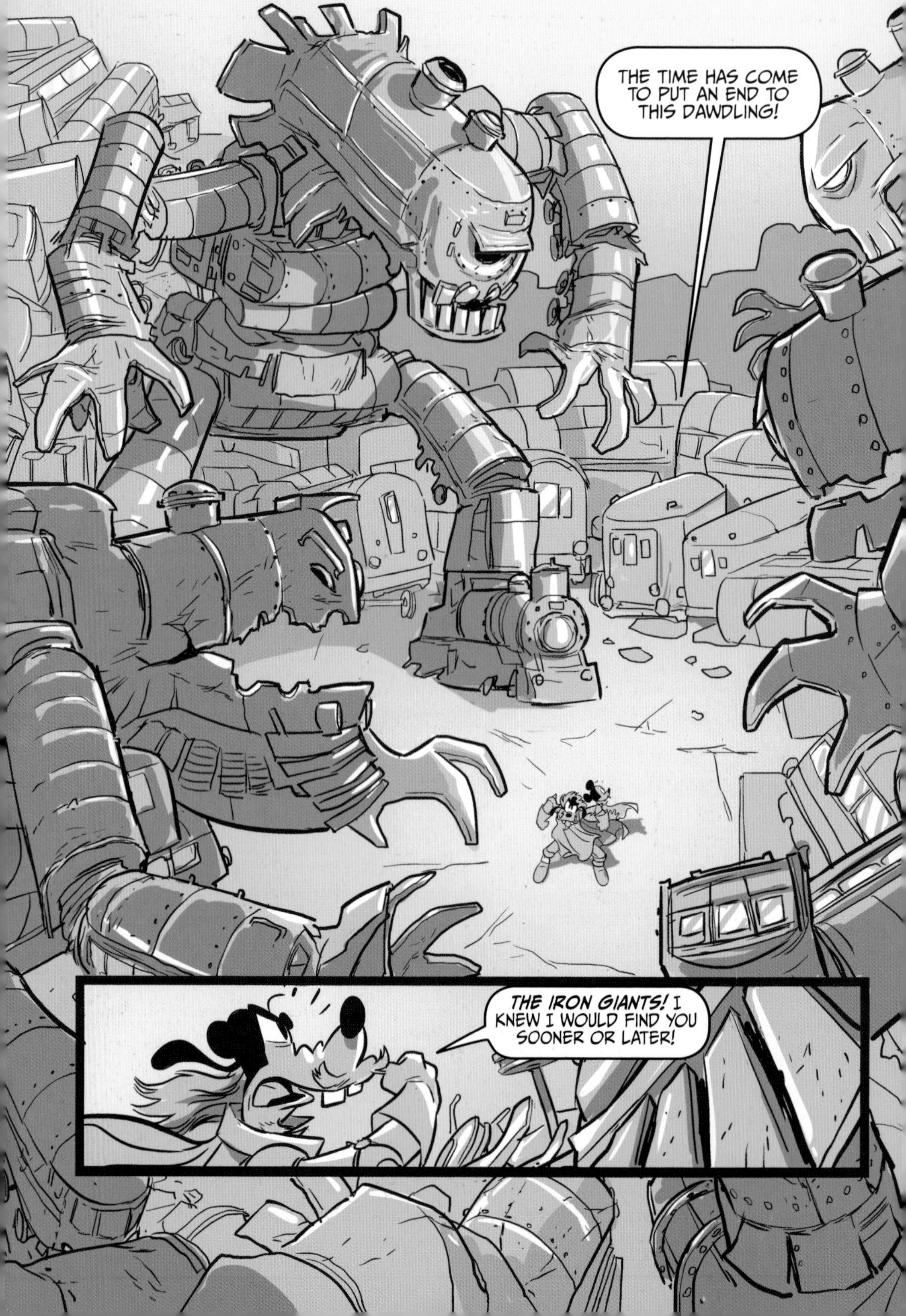
THE TIME HAS COME TO PUT AN END TO THIS DAWDLING!
THE IRON GIANTS! I KNEW I WOULD FIND YOU SOONER OR LATER!

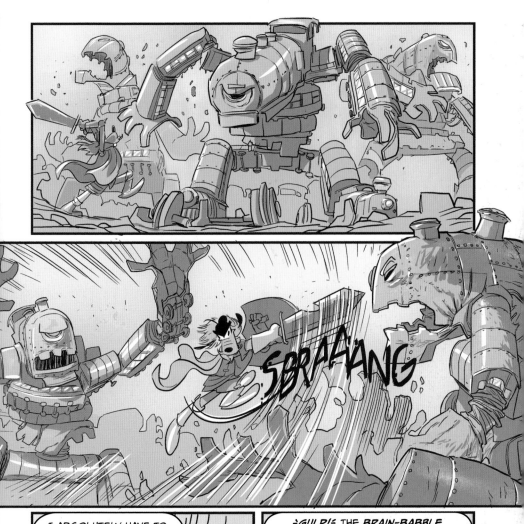

I ABSOLUTELY HAVE TO WAKE GOOFY UP! HE COULD REALLY HURT HIMSELF!

DONG DONG DONG

⹂GULP!⹂ THE *BRAIN-BABBLE BELL* ISN'T WORKING! I NEED TO DO IT MYSELF!

HALT THAT RINGING AND RUSH TO MY AID, SQUIRE!

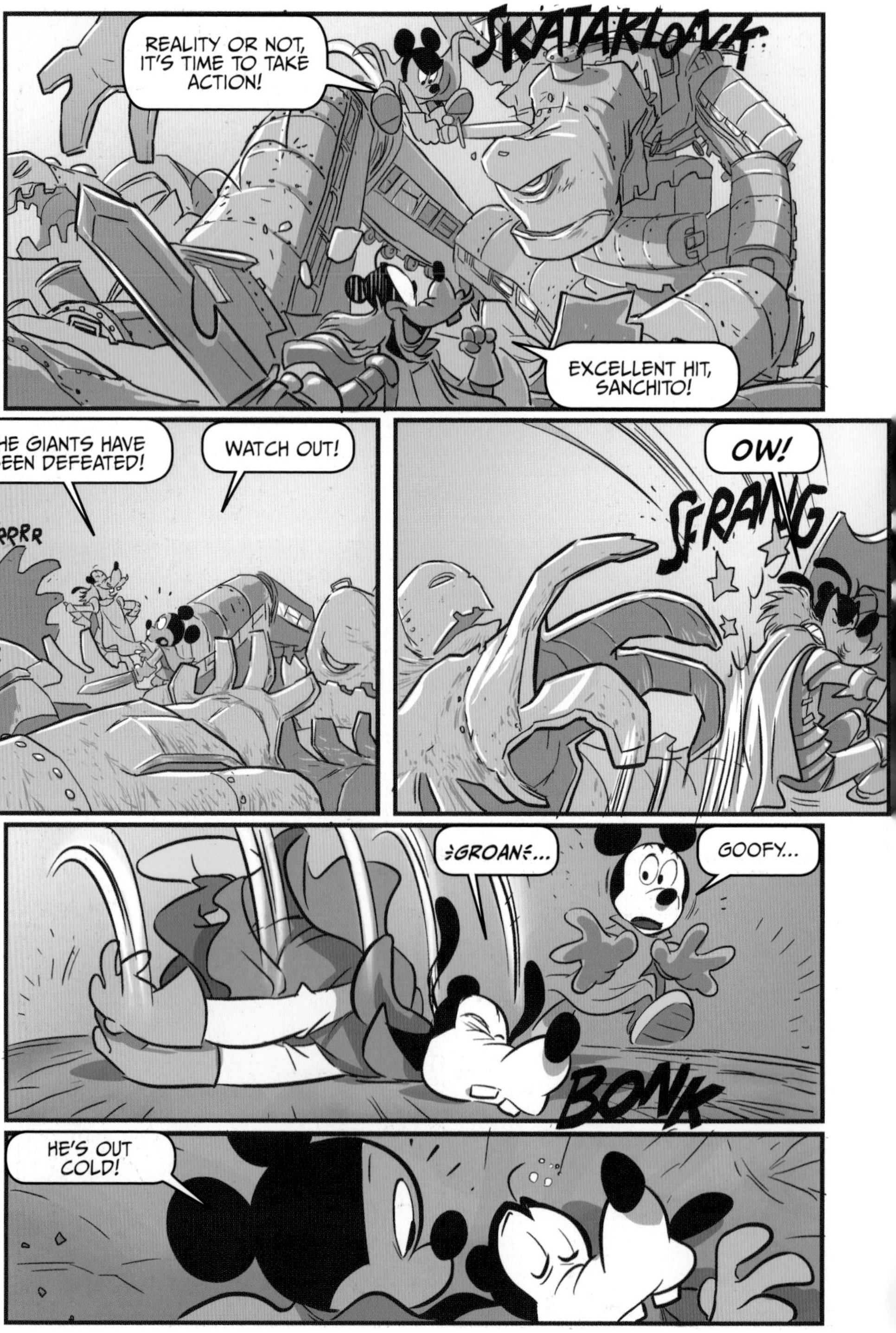
REALITY OR NOT, IT'S TIME TO TAKE ACTION!
SKATARLONK
EXCELLENT HIT, SANCHITO!
THE GIANTS HAVE BEEN DEFEATED!
WATCH OUT!
VRRRR
OW!
SCRANG
GROAN...
GOOFY...
BONK
HE'S OUT COLD!

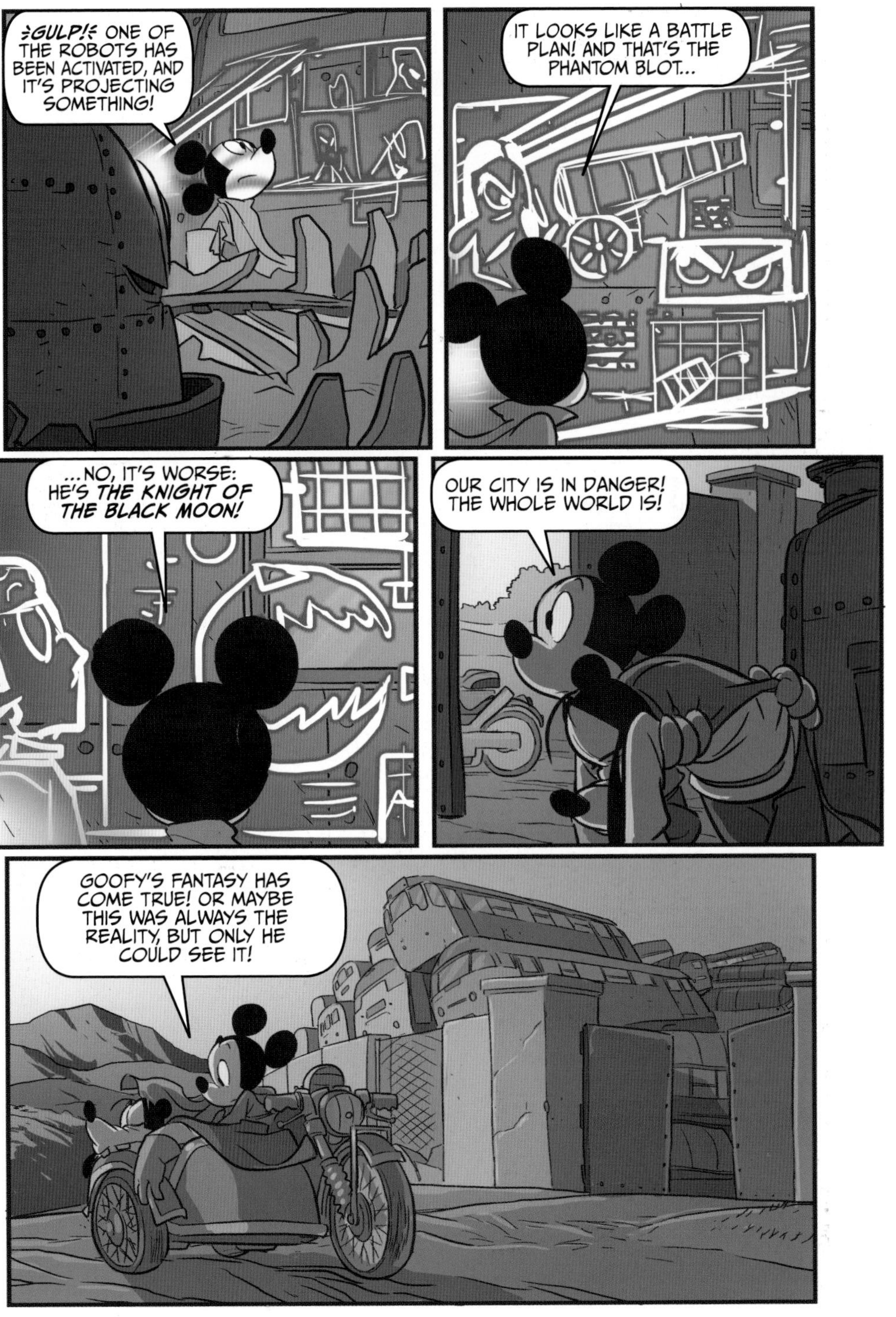

GULP! ONE OF THE ROBOTS HAS BEEN ACTIVATED, AND IT'S PROJECTING SOMETHING!
IT LOOKS LIKE A BATTLE PLAN! AND THAT'S THE PHANTOM BLOT...
...NO, IT'S WORSE: HE'S THE KNIGHT OF THE BLACK MOON!
OUR CITY IS IN DANGER! THE WHOLE WORLD IS!
GOOFY'S FANTASY HAS COME TRUE! OR MAYBE THIS WAS ALWAYS THE REALITY, BUT ONLY HE COULD SEE IT!

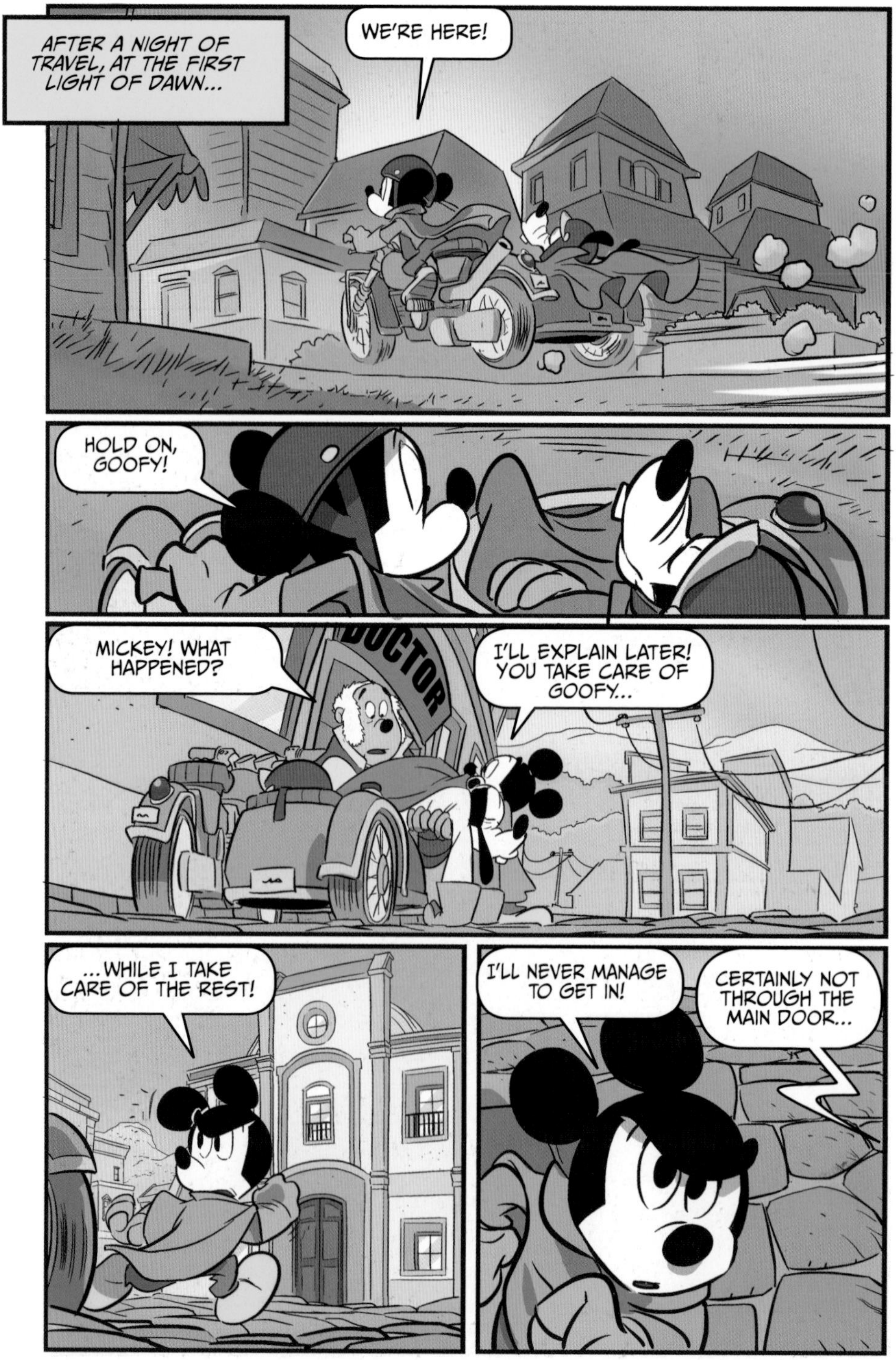

AFTER A NIGHT OF TRAVEL, AT THE FIRST LIGHT OF DAWN...
WE'RE HERE!
HOLD ON, GOOFY!
MICKEY! WHAT HAPPENED?
DOCTOR
I'LL EXPLAIN LATER! YOU TAKE CARE OF GOOFY...
...WHILE I TAKE CARE OF THE REST!
I'LL NEVER MANAGE TO GET IN!
CERTAINLY NOT THROUGH THE MAIN DOOR...

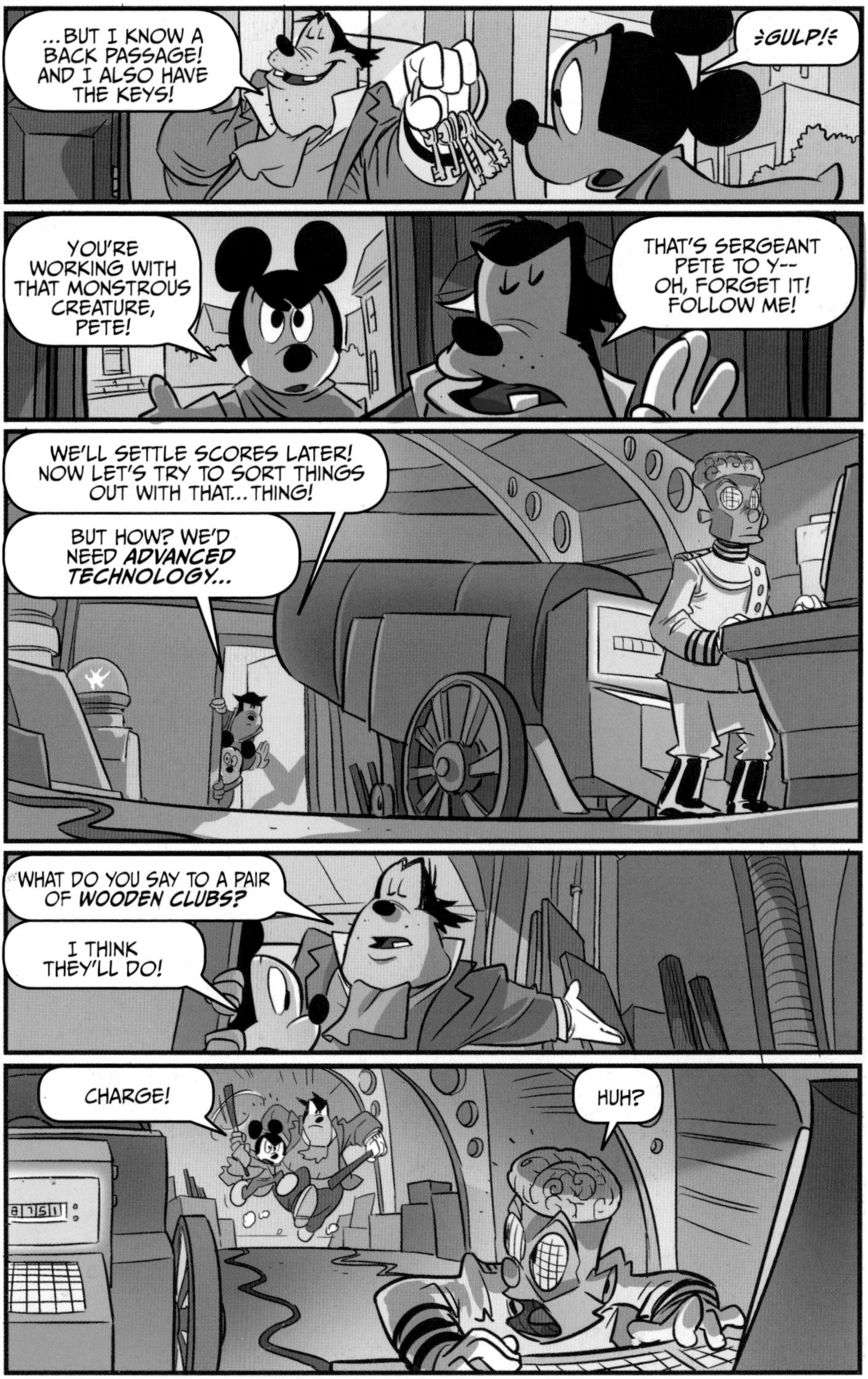
...BUT I KNOW A BACK PASSAGE! AND I ALSO HAVE THE KEYS!
GULP!
YOU'RE WORKING WITH THAT MONSTROUS CREATURE, PETE!
THAT'S SERGEANT PETE TO Y-- OH, FORGET IT! FOLLOW ME!
WE'LL SETTLE SCORES LATER! NOW LET'S TRY TO SORT THINGS OUT WITH THAT... THING!
BUT HOW? WE'D NEED ADVANCED TECHNOLOGY...
WHAT DO YOU SAY TO A PAIR OF WOODEN CLUBS?
I THINK THEY'LL DO!
CHARGE!
HUH?

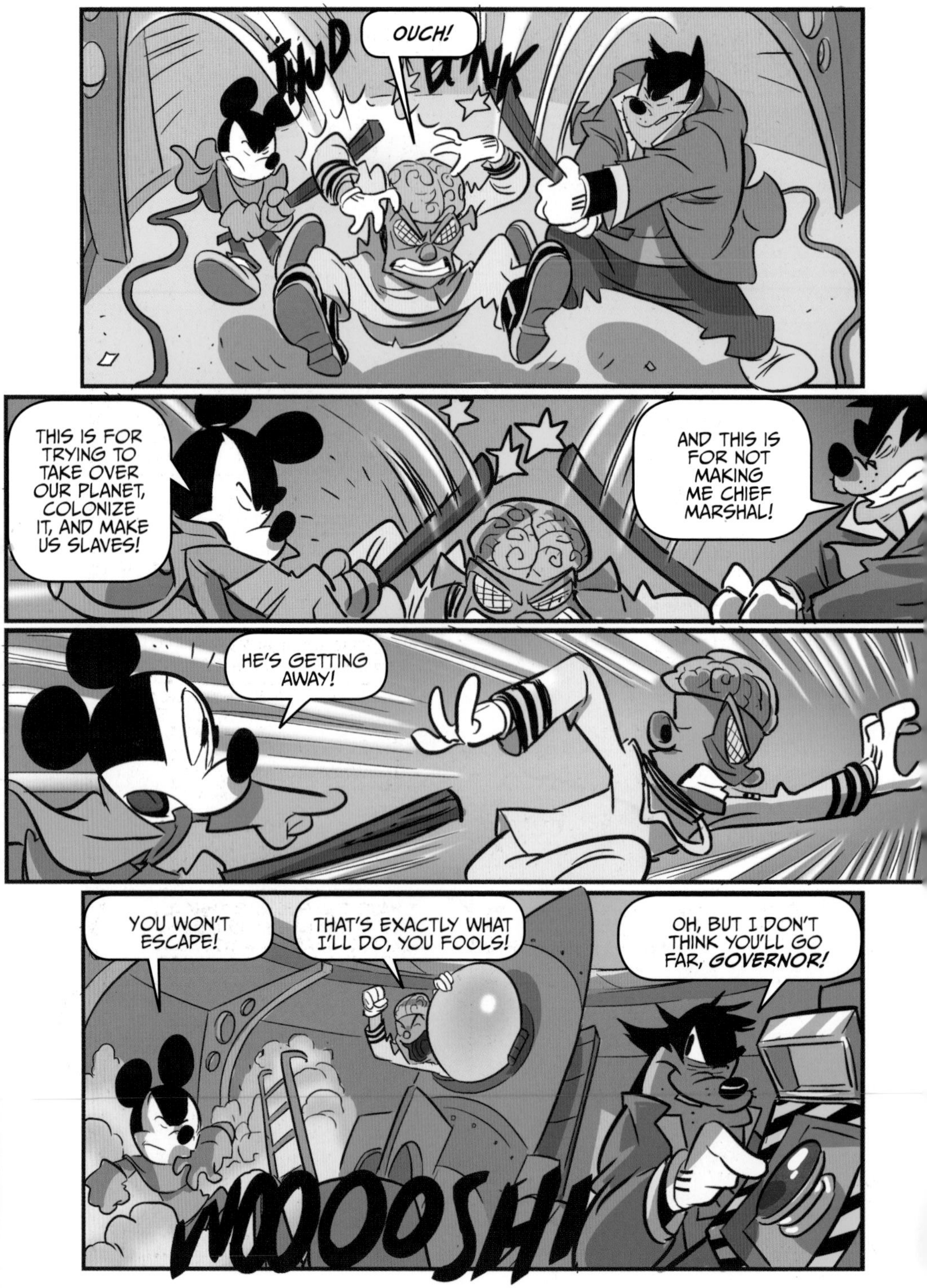
THUD
OUCH!
BONK
THIS IS FOR TRYING TO TAKE OVER OUR PLANET, COLONIZE IT, AND MAKE US SLAVES!
AND THIS IS FOR NOT MAKING ME CHIEF MARSHAL!
HE'S GETTING AWAY!
YOU WON'T ESCAPE!
THAT'S EXACTLY WHAT I'LL DO, YOU FOOLS!
OH, BUT I DON'T THINK YOU'LL GO FAR, *GOVERNOR!*
WOOOOSH!

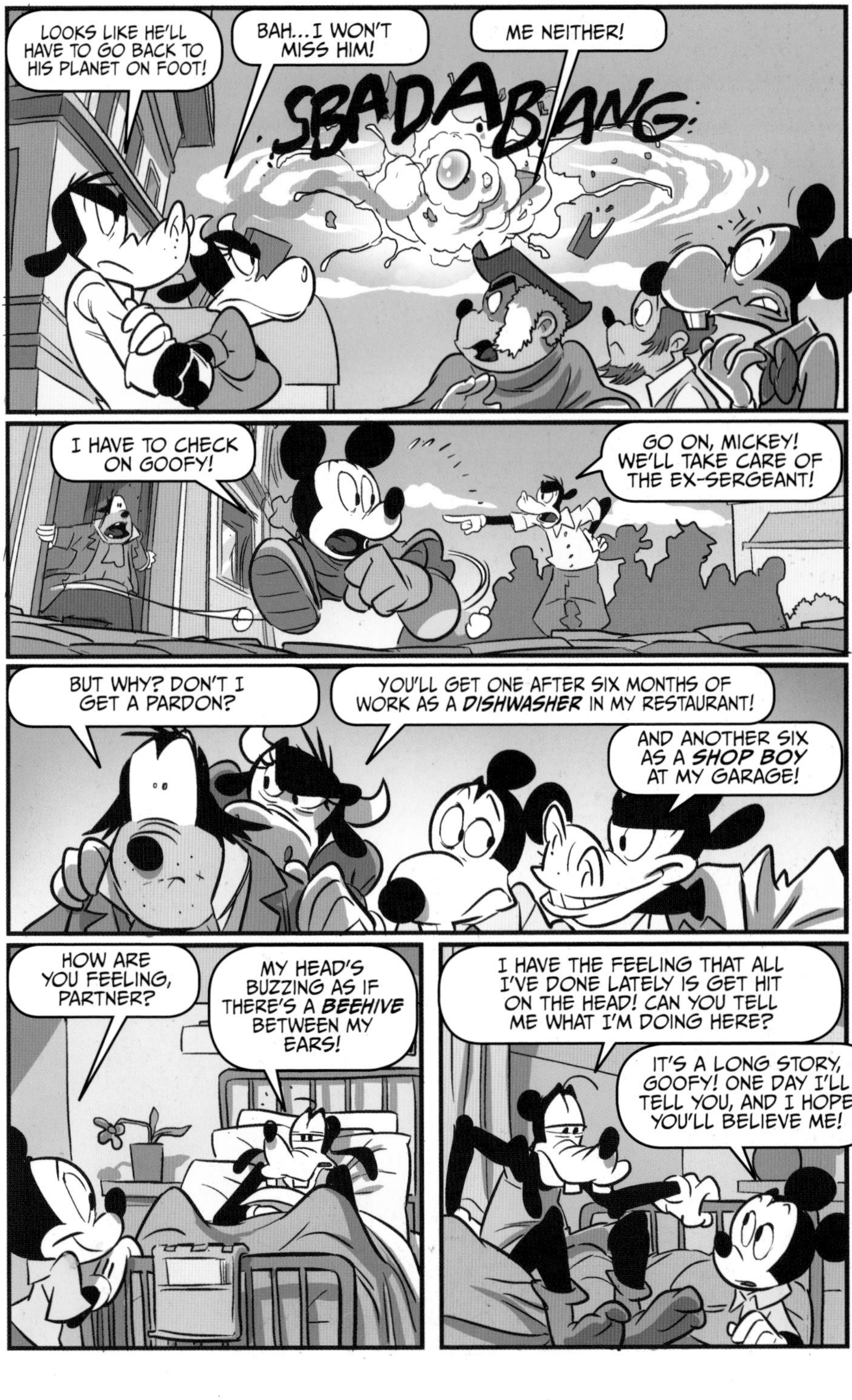

LOOKS LIKE HE'LL HAVE TO GO BACK TO HIS PLANET ON FOOT!
BAH...I WON'T MISS HIM!
ME NEITHER!
SBADABANG
I HAVE TO CHECK ON GOOFY!
GO ON, MICKEY! WE'LL TAKE CARE OF THE EX-SERGEANT!
BUT WHY? DON'T I GET A PARDON?
YOU'LL GET ONE AFTER SIX MONTHS OF WORK AS A *DISHWASHER* IN MY RESTAURANT!
AND ANOTHER SIX AS A *SHOP BOY* AT MY GARAGE!
HOW ARE YOU FEELING, PARTNER?
MY HEAD'S BUZZING AS IF THERE'S A *BEEHIVE* BETWEEN MY EARS!
I HAVE THE FEELING THAT ALL I'VE DONE LATELY IS GET HIT ON THE HEAD! CAN YOU TELL ME WHAT I'M DOING HERE?
IT'S A LONG STORY, GOOFY! ONE DAY I'LL TELL YOU, AND I HOPE YOU'LL BELIEVE ME!

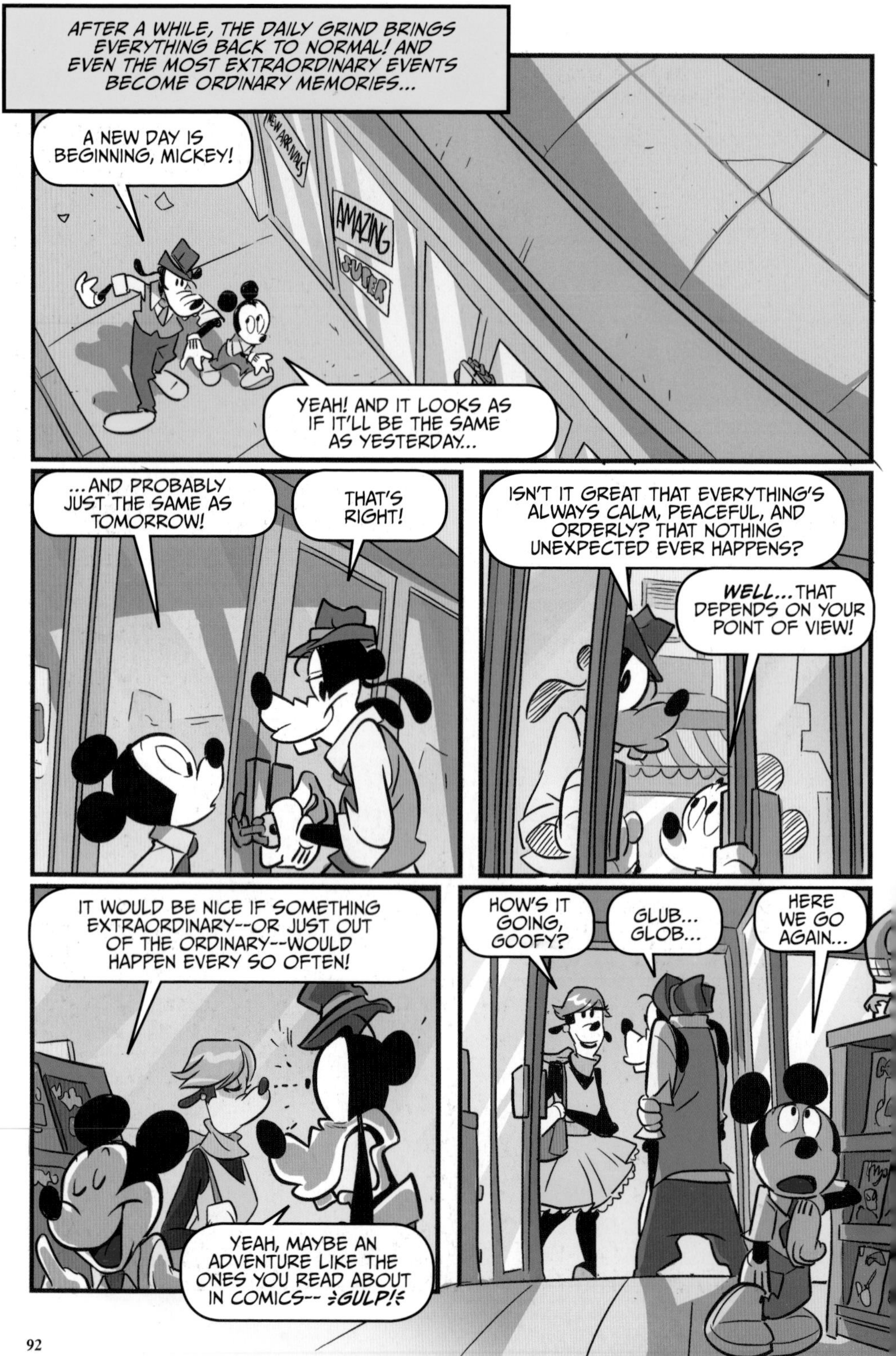
AFTER A WHILE, THE DAILY GRIND BRINGS EVERYTHING BACK TO NORMAL! AND EVEN THE MOST EXTRAORDINARY EVENTS BECOME ORDINARY MEMORIES...
A NEW DAY IS BEGINNING, MICKEY!
NEW ARRIVALS
AMAZING
SUPER
YEAH! AND IT LOOKS AS IF IT'LL BE THE SAME AS YESTERDAY...
...AND PROBABLY JUST THE SAME AS TOMORROW!
THAT'S RIGHT!
ISN'T IT GREAT THAT EVERYTHING'S ALWAYS CALM, PEACEFUL, AND ORDERLY? THAT NOTHING UNEXPECTED EVER HAPPENS?
WELL... THAT DEPENDS ON YOUR POINT OF VIEW!
IT WOULD BE NICE IF SOMETHING EXTRAORDINARY--OR JUST OUT OF THE ORDINARY--WOULD HAPPEN EVERY SO OFTEN!
YEAH, MAYBE AN ADVENTURE LIKE THE ONES YOU READ ABOUT IN COMICS-- GULP!
HOW'S IT GOING, GOOFY?
GLUB... GLOB...
HERE WE GO AGAIN...

YOU KNOW, I OFTEN GET THE FEELING THAT YOU WANT TO TELL ME SOMETHING! IS THAT TRUE?

I...GLIB... YOU...GLOB...

HEY, MICKEY, AS SOON AS YOUR PARTNER PULLS IT TOGETHER, LET ME KNOW!

GLUB... GLOB...

OF COURSE, ZENOBIA!

ANY IDEA WHEN YOU'LL DECIDE TO TALK TO HER?

ARE YOU JOKING? I'LL NEVER BE BRAVE ENOUGH!

IT'S JUST ASKING HER TO GO DANCING! YOU COULD BE LIKE A *KNIGHT IN SHINING ARMOR!*

≶TSK≶... I'M NOT A KNIGHT...

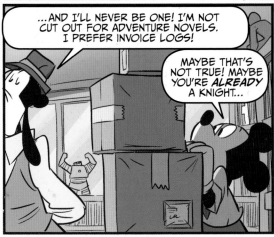

...AND I'LL NEVER BE ONE! I'M NOT CUT OUT FOR ADVENTURE NOVELS. I PREFER INVOICE LOGS!

MAYBE THAT'S NOT TRUE! MAYBE YOU'RE *ALREADY* A KNIGHT...

...BUT YOU DON'T KNOW IT!

WHAT DO YOU MEAN?

SWISH

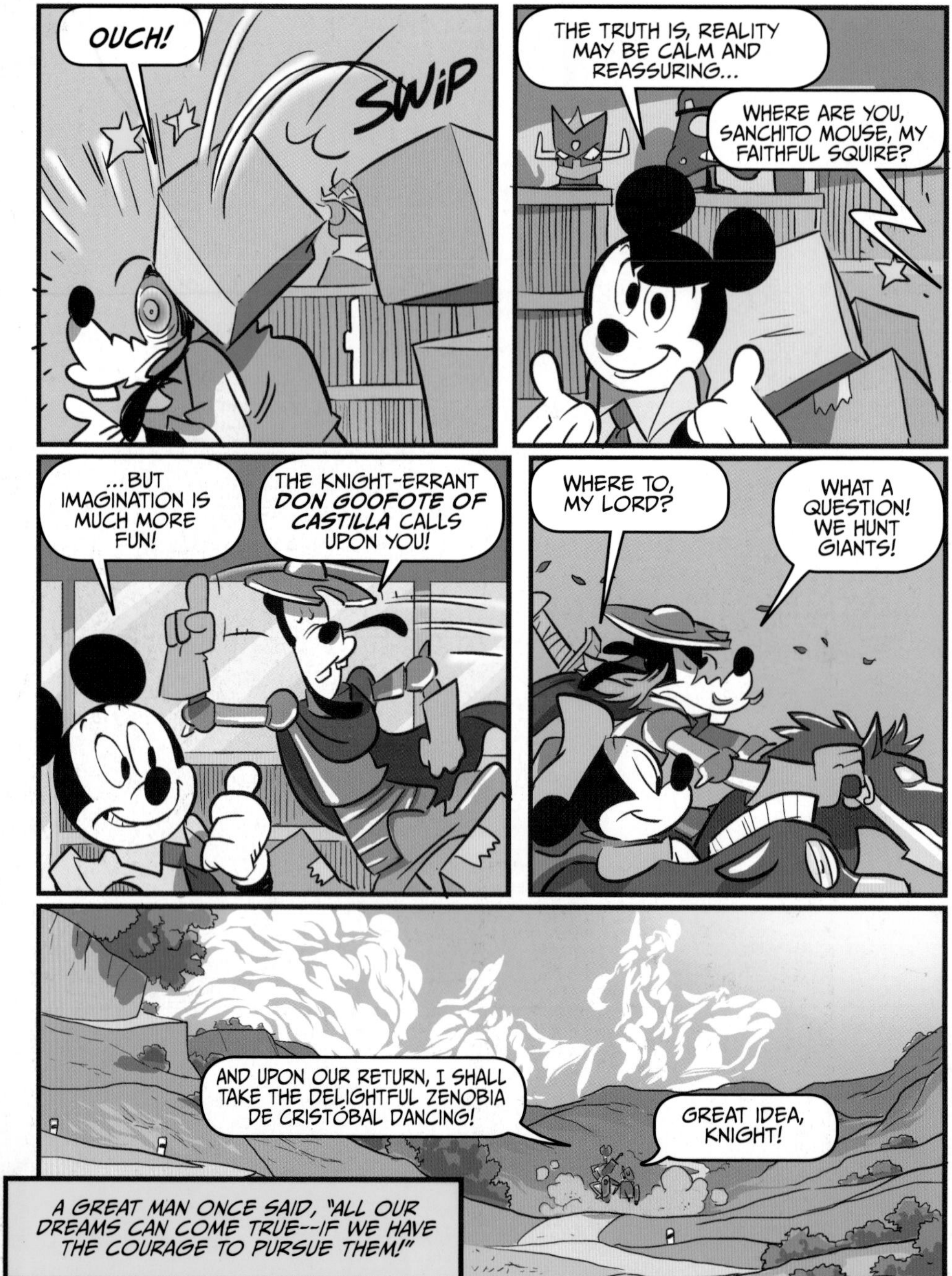
OUCH!
SWIP
THE TRUTH IS, REALITY MAY BE CALM AND REASSURING...
WHERE ARE YOU, SANCHITO MOUSE, MY FAITHFUL SQUIRE?
...BUT IMAGINATION IS MUCH MORE FUN!
THE KNIGHT-ERRANT *DON GOOFOTE OF CASTILLA* CALLS UPON YOU!
WHERE TO, MY LORD?
WHAT A QUESTION! WE HUNT GIANTS!
AND UPON OUR RETURN, I SHALL TAKE THE DELIGHTFUL ZENOBIA DE CRISTÓBAL DANCING!
GREAT IDEA, KNIGHT!
A GREAT MAN ONCE SAID, "ALL OUR DREAMS CAN COME TRUE--IF WE HAVE THE COURAGE TO PURSUE THEM!"
WE THINK THAT'S A GREAT LINE! DON'T YOU AGREE?

THE END

ABOUT THE ORIGINAL AUTHOR

MIGUEL DE CERVANTES

(1547–1616)

Miguel de Cervantes was a Spanish author in the 17th century. He is known for writing what is often considered the first modern novel, *Don Quixote*. His influence on the Spanish language is such that the language is often referred to as *la lengua de Cervantes*, meaning "the language of Cervantes."

Cervantes was born in 1547, in the city of Alcala de Henares, Spain. Not much is known about his early life as his family moved often. In his early twenties, Cervantes joined the Spanish Navy. During battle, he sustained critical injuries—one of these rendered his left arm useless for the rest of his life. He considered this wound a symbol of honor. Cervantes remained in the military until 1575 when he was taken captive by pirates. He spent five years as a prisoner and bravely made several attempts to escape with his fellow captives. He finally returned home to Spain after his family paid a ransom for his release.

Throughout the 1580s and 1590s Cervantes began writing poetry, fiction, and plays, and he worked as a civil servant—collecting goods and taxes. During these years, he fathered an illegitimate daughter, he married, and he began to experience the financial troubles that would continue throughout his life. Cervantes finally had some success with his writing in the late 1590s.

In 1605, he published "The Ingenious Hidalgo Don Quixote of La Mancha" (known as *Don Quixote*, Part I). It was a huge and immediate success in many countries, and Cervantes entered the most prolific time of his writing career. In 1615, he published *Don Quixote*, Part II, which capitalizes on the first part.

In his works, Cervantes gave readers a realistic portrayal of life and reached people from all walks of life with a common appreciation for adventure and storytelling. Among other things, his writings were accessible, relatable, and easy to read.

Mickey Mouse, Goofy, and Pegleg Pete star in Stevenson's classic pirate adventure story!

DISNEY TREASURE ISLAND
starring Mickey Mouse

Robert Louis Stevenson's classic tale of pirates, treasure, and swashbuckling adventure comes to life in this adaptation that stars Mickey, Goofy, and Pegleg Pete! When Jim Mousekins discovers a map to buried treasure, his dream of adventure is realized with a voyage on the high seas, a quest through tropical island jungles . . . and a race to evade cutthroat pirates!

ISBN 978-1-50671-158-4 × $10.99